BENDY
AND THE INK MACHINE™

DREAMS COME TO LIFE

DREAMS COME TO LIFE

BY ADRIENNE KRESS

SCHOLASTIC INC.

All rights reserved. Published by Scholastic Inc., *Publishers since 1920*. SCHOLASTIC and associated logos are trademarks and/or registered trademarks of Scholastic Inc.

The publisher does not have any control over and does not assume any responsibility for author or third-party websites or their content.

No part of this publication may be reproduced, stored in a retrieval system, or transmitted in any form or by any means, electronic, mechanical, photocopying, recording, or otherwise, without written permission of the publisher. For information regarding permission, write to Scholastic Inc., Attention: Permissions Department, 557 Broadway, New York, NY 10012.

ISBN 978-1-338-34394-6

10 9 8 7 6 5 4 3 2   19 20 21 22 23

Printed in the U.S.A.   23

First printing 2019

Book design by Betsy Peterschmidt

I see that smile everywhere. It greets me in the darkness suddenly. Around a corner. In my dreams. That big wide grin. Mouth full of teeth that look flat and even. You'd never know how sharp they are until you're sliding down his gullet.

That little devil darling.

I can't escape it.

What I'm about to tell you is going to sound unbelievable.

I'm no fool. Folks are going to read this and think, "I don't know who this Buddy guy thinks he is, but he ain't gonna grift me." But I have to write it down. I have to tell the story. Even if no one believes me. I have to while there's still time. Before . . .

Every sound, every creak, I'm looking for that smile. Anyone would say I was going loopy, but I know what's true, I know what I've seen. I know what's happened.

You've got to read carefully. Words have never really been

my thing. But I gotta use them, 'cause you can't trust drawings.

You can't *trust* the drawings.

There's a lot of other folks involved. Too many. But if I can protect just one person, just one from what they've become . . .

What we've all become . . .

If you can find this, Dot. If you can find us . . .

I guess I should begin at the beginning.

And go on.

Until the end.

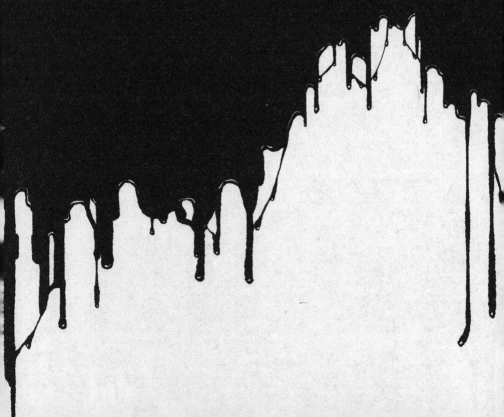

Dreams come true, Buddy, that's

what he said. Mister Drew was no liar. Problem is, yeah, dreams do come true. But so do nightmares. Package deal.

I didn't understand any of that for a long time, to be honest. Dreams came true? For who? Rich folks, sure. But my family? Dreams were quick breaks between working your hands to the bone every day.

I wish I could really capture what the Lower East Side was like the summer of 1946. I wish I could draw a picture of it: the sidewalks melting into the street and seeping into the sewer grates, steam squiggle lines rising up toward a harsh white sky, big fat juicy drops of water coming off folks' foreheads. Maybe the word "sizzle" floating in the air.

But I can't draw it. I have to tell it.

I'm trying to remember what I learned from you, Dot. How to write a good story. I have to remember what you used to say. To use all the five senses, not just sight.

Writing isn't drawing.

The five senses. What are the other four again?

Right.

Sound: kids laughing and yelling at one another, adults shouting, glass breaking and then the sound of fists on flesh. Fights always happened when it got this hot. Nothing to do, nowhere to go, and the brain doesn't work—turns to pink sloppy mush inside your skull, sloshing around and ready to pour out your ears.

Touch: Your skin was always slick with sweat and everything under your fingers felt wet because you were wet. There was no way to feel dry.

Smell: The air was always stale and still, unable to go up over the sides of the tall tenement buildings. It mostly smelled of piss. Made you want to throw up. Sometimes you did throw up. Oh! That's another one. The smell of throw-up.

Taste:

Taste:

Sorry, I can't remember the taste right now. It's too hard. All I can taste is the bitter in my mouth. That lingering taste of ink.

Okay, so you get it. It was hot. And it matters you understand that, because I would have done anything to get out of this kind of hot, out of this neighborhood. I'd been running between sweatshops for a couple of years now. Ever since Pa died. Ma had taken over sewing the precut fabrics together, and I had dropped out of school and taken over for my cousin Lenny, delivering the finished suits and jackets to the boss,

Mr. Schwartz. And then, you know, delivering the new pieces to Ma so she could do it all over again. We needed the cash. And it was the only way I could make Ma smile. I miss that.

Ma's smile. Gentle. Calm. Warm. The kind that reached all the way to her eyes.

Not like his smile. Not like his smile at all.

Anyway, I got paid, which was important.

But I was almost seventeen now, and most of the other boys were just turning twelve and it felt stupid to be so old doing this job, and so when Mr. Schwartz suggested I be his go-to delivery guy, and explained I'd get to leave the neighborhood to travel all over the city, I said yes. There was green in other parts of the city. Trees and stuff. And the fancy neighborhoods didn't smell like piss. And when I brought a finished suit to the Upper East Side, I could take a walk in the park and dip my feet in the boat lake.

More important than any of that, I could watch the artists along the mall drawing pictures for tourists. Cartoons. I could watch them closely.

This is where the problems started.

First off, evidently artists are temperamental.

"Hey, kid, what do you think you're doing?"

"Just watching, sir." Maybe this time I'd got a bit nearer to the canvas than usual.

"Get out of here with your watching!"

It was like getting to go to art school, except I bet at art school the teachers don't chase you away and tell you you're scaring off the customers because you're hovering too close.

But that wasn't the biggest thing. See, something I haven't said, because I guess you know by now, is I'm an artist. Well, now. Then I wasn't. But I wanted to be. Not sure why; maybe it had something to do with my grandfather I'd never met. Who was still back in Poland. I figured he must love art. After all, the one big thing he'd saved and sent with Ma from "the old country," as she called it, was those darn paintings. People always were super surprised to see these huge oil paintings in a small tenement apartment. She could've sold them. For a lot of money. But she didn't. And that always stayed with me.

I started by drawing sketches late at night, sleeping in and being late for class. Then I got sent to the principal's office a lot for "doodling" during the day, and, boy, I loved the funny pages. I'd run around the neighborhood, collecting discarded newspapers, hoping to read the latest Popeye or Dick Tracy. I even started drawing comics, making up adventures with Olive Oyl, Pruneface, Sparkle Plenty. Soon I was inventing my own characters. They weren't funny. I didn't show them to anyone.

But then I found the artists in Central Park. And, let's just say, I got distracted.

"You lost the suit?" Mr. Schwartz could be pretty scary for a man who was only five feet tall.

"I'm sorry, sir! I swear it'll never happen again!" I'd only put it down for a second to get a closer look at a drawing, but that was enough time for someone else to be sneaky and scoop it up.

"What about last time, when you were three hours late?

My client almost didn't make it to his appointment on time."

"I'm sorry, sir."

"You want to be my apprentice? You want to make a good, honest living?"

I did, I really did. I needed the cash. We, my ma and I, needed the cash. And no one would hire some teenager from the slums who barely had an education. To be Mr. Schwartz's right-hand man, that was more than I could have hoped for. Boy, I felt stupid. And ashamed.

"One more chance, Buddy, one more and then that's it."

One more chance.

This was my one last chance.

Then I met *him*.

When I first went to his studio to deliver him his suit, the clothing bag slung over my right shoulder, there had been a blackout 'cause of the heat. Not just in the studio's tall brick building, but also in the rest of the neighborhood. The flashing lights on the theater marquees were still, and as I passed by the dark sign for *St. Louis Woman*, two stagehands were staring up at the building, hands on hips, toothpicks dangling out of their mouths.

"Now what, Steve?"

"Show must go on."

"That's what they say, alright."

It hadn't really clicked in my mind there'd been a blackout until a few blocks later west when I passed a theater off Broadway and finally arrived at the studio next door. I'd been super focused getting there, but I was already late. This time it wasn't my fault. It was the subway, I swear. But Mr. Schwartz wouldn't know the difference. I had to make up the time, so I was walking fast and not really noticing much of the world around me. But when I stepped into the muddy dark it jarred me back to reality. And I stopped and just stood there. It was so black you couldn't really tell which way was up.

Then, suddenly, it was super bright, like someone was shining a light right at me. I held up my hand and the light flew off my face and I watched as the beam scanned the room until it found a gray-haired older woman sitting behind a huge desk. I jumped, surprised to see her just appear like that.

"Gosh dangit, Norman," she said, squeezing her eyes shut behind the lenses of her oversized glasses.

"Projector's gone out," said Norman in a gruff voice.

"In case you hadn't noticed, the power is out everywhere. Get that flashlight out of my eyes!" There was a pause. And then everything went black again with a click.

Blacker, I should say. Blacker. After the glare from the direct light it was like not just the flashlight was turned off, but my eyes too. Gave me shivers up my spine.

I didn't know what to do. I had to deliver this suit already. I thought I could remember where the desk was, so maybe I could just stumble toward it?

"Who's the kid?" asked Norman from somewhere.

"I don't know, Norman." There was the sound of a match scratching a surface and then that *womph* of a flame coming alive.

The old woman's face was distorted grotesquely with long, drawn-out shadows drooping down as she lit a lantern in her hand.

And then there was light.

It flickered and danced off the walls. There were framed posters hanging on them. They looked like movie posters. But cartoons. And of one character in particular. He was real smiley. I wanted to take a closer look. Where was I? What was this place? Why did the character kind of look familiar?

"Okay, kid, I see you now. What do you want?" asked the woman sitting down so low behind the desk only her glasses and top of her head were visible.

"I, uh . . ." It wasn't complicated, but I'd forgotten who I was delivering to and looked down, fumbling with the black clothing bag in my arms to find the name.

"Come closer, can't hear a dang word you're saying," said the woman. Her hand appeared over the top of the desk and gave me a sharp wave to come over.

I did while still searching for the name tag.

"I have a suit," I said, trying to buy time.

"Uh-huh," said the woman.

Finally I found the tag.

This was the first time his name ever made any kind of impression on me. The first time it *meant something.* All that had mattered up until then was to get it to the studio on time. To not get fired. That was the important part. So I knew the address, I knew it was on Broadway, but the name of the guy hadn't been anything I saw in my mind's eye. Hadn't pictured it.

"Come on, kid, I haven't got all day."

"Joey Drew," I said. "I'm looking for a Mister Joey Drew."

"Who's lookin' for him?" asked Norman, his voice filled with suspicion.

"Mr. Schwartz," I blurted out. It wasn't exactly the best answer but the dark and this guy's attitude made me nervous for some reason. And somehow the flickering light over that smiling cartoon character thing didn't help either.

"Who?" asked the woman.

"The tailor, who made his suit. I've got Mister Drew's suit. I'm the delivery guy. With . . . his . . . suit."

"He's dead," said Norman.

I turned to the man. He was standing so far away from the lantern light he wasn't more than an outline. "He . . . is?" My heart thudded in my chest. That didn't make sense and also scared me in a strange way I couldn't quite understand.

"Nah," replied Norman with a laugh. "Nah, he ain't."

"I . . . don't understand," I said, turning back to the old woman.

She just shrugged and said, "Norman's jokes aren't really something anyone understands."

"It was a joke?" I looked back at the outline of the man. Norman was still laughing, but it didn't seem like a happy laugh, didn't make me feel better, that's for sure. "Come with me," he said. "His girl's out for the afternoon. You can take it to him personally."

I glanced at the woman and she nodded, so I figured that

was permission to follow the guy. Even though, I'll be honest, I really didn't want to. I'd decided Norman and I were likely never going to really get on, you know?

The man clicked on his flashlight and led the way down a narrow hall. His beam was more direct than the glow from the lantern, and all I could really see was his silhouette and the far end where there was an elevator grate. Every once in a while, though, you'd catch a flash of another poster, with more cartoon characters and such. They seemed so happy, even in the darkness, but they made me feel the same way as that smiling character from the foyer did. Weird.

"Can't use the elevator," said Norman. His face was still in shadow, and I nodded because obviously with the power out and all . . . So he pushed through the door next to it. The light flashed on the word "stairs," though, I mean, I could have guessed.

We started to climb together, Norman's light leading the way. Every once in a while I'd look back into the pool of blackness. It almost felt like everything behind me was being erased, like I had to hurry up or I'd be erased too.

I'm just saying, it was really hot out and my brain was making up all kinds of stories.

They say that life is stranger than fiction. But I never thought anything could top the strange stuff in my mind.

I was wrong.

Norman stopped when we reached the third floor. I was sweating, I tell you. My shirt and undershirt were soaked through, hair matted to my head. There was this drip from the base of my neck, sneaking down under my collar.

"Here, kid," said Norman, handing me the flashlight.

"What's this for?"

"I know my way back to the booth, you don't know nothin'. Keep going. Good luck."

I took the flashlight, and as Norman slipped deep into the shadows, I called out, "Keep going where?"

"Up, kid, right up to the damn top." He laughed in the darkness. Man, I didn't like that laugh.

So here I was, Mister Drew's suit in one hand, a flashlight in the other, and a trickle of sweat that was working its way down my back to a not-so-happy location. And who knew how many stairs were ahead of me. I shone the light straight up to try to guess, but the old wooden stairs seemed like they went on forever. Straight up to heaven. I flashed the light down, saw the stairs beneath me. Going on into the dark. Straight down to . . . well, you get where I'm going with this.

So I made my way up those stairs as fast as I could, and it was exhausting and hot, and I wasn't sure I was going to make it, and maybe it was because of the stairs that any of this happened. Because I'll tell you, when I got to the top and came out of the doors, and the air was even thicker all the way up here, the way the heat rises and all, I just collapsed. Fell right onto the floor. Didn't pass out, just fell, hard and with this loud boom, and I guess Mister Drew heard it because he came out of his office.

"Hey, what's with the racket?" Even in my woozy state his voice impressed me. It was so sure of itself, and friendly. I can't tell you what makes a voice sound friendly exactly, but I don't think I'm the only one out there who would describe it like that. I think that's what made people like him.

Trust him.

"I'm sorry," I said from the floor. "I have a delivery for Mister Joey Drew."

"I'm Mister Joey Drew," he said, and a hand materialized in front of me. I was supposed to grab it. So I did. He helped me up. "You okay?"

I nodded.

"Good." He didn't let go of my hand right away, looked at it for a moment almost like he was examining it. I wasn't really sure what he was doing, but it seemed a bit odd. Finally he released it and said, "Come into my office, kid."

There were windows up here, so I could see without the flashlight.

"Sit, drink this." Mister Drew passed me a cup of warm water as I sat opposite him and his large wooden desk. I drank it and it was like it came from a fresh mountain spring. "So," he asked, leaning back in his chair, "who are you and what are you doing here?"

I took another big swig of water and then answered his questions. "I'm a delivery guy for Mr. Schwartz, and I brought you your suit."

"Ah!" said Mister Drew, slamming his hand hard on his

desk and making me jump. I didn't know then how much he did that, though I never got used to it, I'll be honest. "That's the suit! Fantastic! Pass it over."

So I did and Mister Drew unbuttoned the bag and nodded. He had this way about him, this over-the-top way like he was performing on a stage so everyone could see even the tiniest of actions. When he approved of something, like he did of the suit, it was the best feeling in the world. "This is swell, this is just swell. Look at that, that's a craftsman right there."

Maybe because I was tired and hot, I don't know, but I said, "Actually, that's my ma's work."

Mister Drew looked at me, and I felt the blood drain from my face. Why'd I say that? I swore inwardly.

"Well. She's got skills." He put the suit down on the desk and leaned forward, looking at me closely, like he was trying to look through my eyes and into my brain or something. "You got skills, kid?"

"What?"

"Your fingers, you're a writer?" he asked.

I looked at my fingers. They had ink stains on them. Especially on my thumb and forefinger. I was so used to them being like that, I hadn't remembered that wasn't normal.

"I draw sometimes," I said.

"You draw sometimes." He smiled when I said that. "I draw sometimes too."

It was then I actually looked around his office. I was feeling a bit more myself now and was able to take it all in. The shelves of books and papers. The inkwells everywhere. A drafting table in the corner. And more posters. But not just posters: sketches, unfinished drawings with unreadable words next to them, arrows, cross-throughs—it was like wallpaper, there was so much of it all over everything.

And the big desk that took up almost the whole back wall. Covered in more paper. And books. And one tall glass award for something. And a framed picture of some cartoon characters signed with the name Henry Stein.

"Wow," I said. Couldn't help myself.

"I get feelings about people, kid. I get feelings . . . I just know, sometimes." He handed me a piece of paper with a sketch of the smiling cartoon from downstairs. "What do you see?"

I looked closer at it. The character didn't seem human. His body was basically an oval with spindly legs and arms coming out of it. But he wore black boots and white gloves. Had a bow tie and everything. His face was round, and he had two big black eyes, but no nose. And that grin. That wide toothy grin. "I see a mischief maker. Someone who has a lot of fun and gets in a lot of trouble. But that's okay."

I glanced up at Mister Drew. He was smiling almost like the drawing. "Yes!" he said, pointing a finger at me. "Exactly. You know how many people just say 'a cartoon'? But you get it."

I nodded. *Sure*, I thought. *I guess*. I looked down again. It was then I noticed that the head wasn't entirely a circle. The top kind of looked like when you take a bite out of a cookie. But smooth. No teeth marks. Wait. I got it! His head had horns, those were little horns at the top. "He's a devil."

I heard Mister Drew push his chair back, scraping it along the wood floor. I looked up and watched as he walked around his desk and leaned against it, still smiling. "Kid, how would you like to come work for me? I need a delivery boy of sorts, but just within the building. A gofer, delivering stuff between departments. Whatever Schwartz is paying you, I'll double it. I'll make sure you work out of the Art Department, kind of like an apprentice. Give you a chance to prove yourself. And you might learn a few things along the way."

At first I didn't fully process what he was saying, and when I did I still didn't believe it. Here I was worried that Mr. Schwartz was going to fire me from my delivery gig, and now I was getting my dream job. Finally I was able to give the man a smile and shake his hand.

"Good," he said. "Excellent. Well, I'm Joey Drew and this is my studio. You can call me Mister Drew."

"Okay, Mister Drew."

"And you are?"

"Oh, I'm Daniel, sir, but everyone just calls me Buddy or Bud or whatever. Really I don't care."

"Nice to meet you, Buddy." He reached out and took the drawing of the character from my hand. He turned it around so it was facing me. Side by side, they mirrored each other with their big smiles. "And this," he said, tapping his finger on the picture, "this is Bendy."

"This is Bendy."

At the time, the introduction to a two-dimensional draw-ing had been kind of, well, I guess, cute. Though "cute" wasn't exactly a word I used too much in my day-to-day existence. But yeah, sure, cute. Nice to meet you, fictional character. But now, trying to explain to you what I understand about that moment . . . What I know now compared to what I knew then . . .

I didn't know, for example, that when Mister Drew smiled, you had to look close at his eyes, to look for a small crinkle in the corner. Every artist knows that crinkle, it makes for a more authentic-looking smile. But I wasn't really an artist yet. Not then. I didn't know what was missing.

I didn't know, either, that an introduction could have so much meaning—that at a party the way someone shook your hand or said their name or even the way Mister Drew intro-duced me to people—I didn't know then that it was all a kind of code. Something to decipher. I wish I'd known right then that Mister Drew had been waiting for a realization from me. Something to click inside and all come together.

Watching me carefully.

"Hi there, Bendy," I'd said, playing along. Mister Drew laughed and put the picture down.

"So you really don't know him, do you?" he asked.

I shook my head no. Because I didn't.

"That's unfortunate," said Mister Drew, but more to himself than to me. That much I recognized, so I didn't say anything.

The thing is, Mister Drew thought I should know who Bendy was. And I bet a lot of folks would ask themselves the same thing: Why didn't I know? After all, he was in those little short movies before the feature-length movie, there he was on soup cans. The little devil sold war bonds, for cryin' out loud. I know, I know.

And it's not like I hadn't seen him before. Like I wrote earlier, I did have this feeling of recognition. So it wasn't that. It's just, when you're on the Lower East Side, growing up, going to school, then dropping out to make money . . . when your experience of movies is Don Miller holding open the back door of the cinema for you . . . you just don't see cartoons as much as the average kid. If Bendy was still running a comic strip by the time I started drawing, that would have been different. Those were my whole world.

It wasn't anyone's fault. It was being poor's fault. It was trying to do right by my ma and working twelve hours a day.

And let's be honest here, those cartoons weren't exactly popular in the way they had been. I was barely in the world when the Bendy toons were all the rage. So the little devil wasn't a big deal. He didn't represent anything. He didn't mean anything.

Except he meant everything to Mister Drew.

"This is my point, this is my whole point," he said, standing up and pacing about the room. He still wasn't talking to me but he was talking louder and I couldn't just ignore it now.

"Sorry, sir, what's your point?" I asked.

He looked at me but kept pacing. "What is this studio coming to? What have we come to that a kid your age doesn't know Bendy? This is my point, this is why."

He still wasn't making much sense. It was kind of crazy that a few sentences that made sense could still sound like total nonsense.

You like that, Dot? I know you like that kind of stuff. That funny wordplay stuff.

I hope I'm making you proud.

I hope you read this.

I hope you're alive.

Where was I?

Right.

"Oh, okay," I said. I didn't know what else to say at this point.

There was a silence. He stopped pacing. I stopped talking. And then he clapped his hands together loudly. Sharply. The sound made me jump in my seat. It was like a gunshot; I nearly ducked.

This has always stayed with me: Of all the memories that are getting mixed up a bit in here, in this brain, in this head, this . . . this for some reason just sticks out. Right then when he clapped, the lights came back on. It was like they were waiting for him, it was like he was in control of them.

He wasn't. But I made that connection back then. Somehow it made sense to me that maybe, just maybe, he had the power to do that.

He didn't. And he doesn't. Don't let anyone make you think he does.

Mister Drew noticed the light and laughed a "Ha!" exactly how you'd spell it. Like that: "Ha!" He turned to me and he was smiling again. "Come on, I'll give you a tour, kid."

I nodded and all the strange thoughts I'd had in that short moment disappeared. I was excited now. I was getting a tour of a studio that made cartoons. I was going to meet other artists. This was not at all how I pictured my day when I woke up that morning.

"Great!" I was up in a flash and following Mister Drew out of his office and into the now brightly lit foyer. A woman was sitting behind the desk next to the door. She was compact looking, with jet-black hair formed into perfect curls.

"We're going for a tour, Miss Rodriguez," announced Mister Drew as he passed her.

"Tom's here," she replied, not looking up from her typewriter.

Sure enough there was a tall, broad man sitting in one of the chairs near the elevator. He had one leg folded neatly over the other, holding his hat in his lap. Next to him was what looked like a yellow tool bag with the word "Gent" written on it.

I glanced up at Mister Drew and saw his smile flicker, kind of how lights do before they go out. Then it grew larger and he pointed at the man and said, "Tommy Connor!" It wasn't a question.

The man stood, picking up a long narrow cardboard tube that had been sitting beside him on the chair.

Mister Drew noticed and pointed at the tube but didn't say anything. Then he smiled bigger.

"Yes, sir," said Tom, even though there hadn't been a question. "It is."

What was?

"Sorry about that, Buddy, got to take this meeting. Big plans, kid, big plans," said Mister Drew. "Come back first thing and we'll get you settled in." He didn't look at me but did give me a firm pat on the back as he extended his other arm toward his office. "Right this way, Tommy."

"Mr. Connor," replied Tom as he walked over.

Mister Drew just laughed at that, though I didn't get the joke and they went back into his office, closing the door behind them.

I was alone then.

I walked up to the secretary. She didn't look at me. I didn't expect her to at this point. I also didn't know what to say.

"What did he hire you for?" asked Miss Rodriguez.

"A gofer. Maybe . . . maybe an artist. He said I'd be in the Art Department." I wasn't so sure anymore what exactly my job was going to be.

Miss Rodriguez stopped typing and leaned back, looking down at her desk. She pulled open a drawer and grabbed a thick envelope full of papers. Finally she looked at me as she handed it my way. "Fill these out, bring them with you tomorrow. Come by at nine a.m. and check in with Mrs. Miller downstairs in the lobby."

I took the paper and nodded. "Thanks."

Miss Rodriguez looked at me for a moment longer. Like maybe she wanted to say something. But she didn't. She just went back to typing.

I didn't go home right away. First I had to see Mr. Schwartz, let him know the delivery was made and Mister Drew was pleased with the suit.

Then I had to quit.

Which, well, didn't go too great, but I didn't really care how red in the face Mr. Schwartz got, or how hard he pointed his finger at me. I was going to work tomorrow morning at Joey Drew Studios and no one was going to stop me. The only thing that scared me was Mr. Schwartz might take it out on Ma, might fire her. But he didn't. Ma was too good. I wished sometimes she could just start a shop on her own.

Well, maybe now. Maybe when I was earning enough.

When I was a paid artist for Joey Drew Studios. I grinned at the thought.

I wasn't ready to go home yet after that. I was buzzing with excitement. Wandered a bit through the neighborhood. Got a free doughnut from Ms. Panek as she was closing up the deli, and the Jankowski kids tried to get me to play stickball with them. I smiled and kept going and made it eventually to the East River as the sky was turning a dark purple.

The lights were on in Brooklyn. They looked like stars across the river.

I sat on a bench. Almost in some pigeon crap but I saw it last minute and jumped my bum to the side. The air was less stagnant by the water. And it was cooler now with the sun almost set.

It made me feel kind of calmer than I had been. The vibrating excitement of the day was now settling around me like a blanket. I still felt happy but it all felt a lot more real.

Sometimes things like that happen.

I got home late. Real late. The hall light was on, which was nice of Ma, but I knew I had to shut it off immediately behind me. Lighting bills get high and then Ma has to work more. I hoped now with this new job maybe lights wouldn't be as big a problem. Maybe now she could sit up and read comfortably and not with a candle.

I knew also I'd probably get some speech the next morning about being out so late. She liked to know where I was. Like I was a kid or something. Well, it wasn't my fault for losing track of time . . . it had been a big day.

I opened the door as slowly as I could. Ma slept on the daybed in the sitting area, right there by the entrance. It was all one space, the kitchen, where we ate, where we sat. And the door opened right onto all of it. She was curled up under the sheet, deep asleep, and I slipped out of my shoes, carrying them to my room.

My room was never actually pitch-black. It's funny, but up until this day standing in the dark lobby of Joey Drew Studios, I'd had no idea that there could be different kinds of dark. It never occurred to me that the streetlamp outside our windows made it possible for me to find my bed, toss my clothes into the corner, and crawl under the sheet in my shorts without crashing into everything.

It had never occurred to me that it could be so black you couldn't even see your hand in front of your face.

Back then, I hadn't known about that kind of dark.

I threw the sheet off and lay on the bed for a moment, trying to get cool. I got up and opened the window a crack. There wasn't much of a difference in temperature, but there was something soothing about the hum of the city. I lay back down and closed my eyes.

Sometimes you don't know you've fallen asleep. That's what happened then. I thought I was still awake trying to fall asleep when I realized that I wasn't lying in bed anymore. Everything was still black like when you close your eyes, but I was standing in it and my eyes were open. I was trying to see something but couldn't. So I walked forward into the blackness.

There was something ahead of me.

I could hear it.

Something breathing maybe?

But for some reason I didn't know if it was alive. I think I still thought I was awake at this point because I thought to myself, *You don't have time for this, you have to sleep.* But I kept going forward.

Finally I came to a door. It just kind of materialized in front of me. But I wasn't surprised. There was a knock coming from the other side. This made me take a step back. I felt like I shouldn't answer.

Knock knock.

I took another step back. Somehow the door was still right in front of me.

There was a long silence.

A giant hand burst through the wood, creating a shower of splinters. There was a roar as I stumbled back, but I couldn't get away. It kept grabbing at me, waving around, trying to find me.

I woke up suddenly, facedown in my pillow. The bottom sheet was drenched in sweat. My heart was in my throat.

It was a dream, I told myself. *A dream.*

I rolled over onto my back and stared at the slice of light from the streetlamp as it highlighted the ceiling. There was that crack that ran across the corner in the plaster, water damage. It had bled dark brown once upon a time, and the stain made it look a bit like the Hudson River. Dark. Cold. Filled with all kinds of who-knows-what.

Why couldn't I shake the feeling I was being watched?

I glanced to my right.

A thin figure stood in my doorway.

He glowed in the lamplight. A pale, gaunt face, paper-thin skin stretched over his skull. Eyes wide and soulless. A long white nightshirt covering his skeletal frame.

All I could do was stare. Breathe. Shake the dream out of my brain. He's not real. Wake up and he'll disappear. But he just kept standing there. He didn't move.

He raised his hand slowly and pointed at me. That's when I just couldn't take it anymore. I closed my eyes and yelled. Maybe it was cowardly, but I couldn't move. I yelled again. My whole body was yelling.

The lights buzzed on. The one over my bed did its threatening flicker, the wiring in the walls damaged by the water leak above.

"Buddy, are you okay?" Ma came charging into my room, struggling to pull her pale purple housecoat on even as the right sleeve was trapped under the belt. I'd normally laugh but the terror was still in charge, especially as, even though the lights were now on and the dream long gone, the old man was still there. And he looked pretty much just as scary.

I couldn't answer her, obviously. I couldn't make words.

The figure turned to my mother. It took a step toward her. That helped me find my voice.

"You stay away from her!" I called out, and leapt from my bed. My foot got caught in the hole at the bottom of the knit blanket draped at the edge of the bed and I fell face-first onto the floor.

"My goodness, what's going on?" Ma said.

I was reaching for anything to help pull myself up. I felt like a fool. I pushed myself onto my forearms. A bony hand extended toward me.

"Up?" said a rich low voice with a thick accent I recognized all too well.

I turned my head and stared at the man. His features still seemed too pale and too worn, but his eyes were a light blue and had a spark to them, no longer hollow. I reached out and took his hand. It was warm.

I stood and stared at him for a moment. We were about the same height. He was maybe an inch shorter. He seemed now more frail than terrifying.

I looked at Ma. She'd managed to get her arm through the sleeve and was staring at me like I'd lost my mind. Maybe I had. But on the other hand . . .

"Who's the old guy?" I asked, pointing just to make sure she knew what I was talking about, since she seemed so confused and to me it didn't seem like a confusing situation.

Ma closed her eyes for a moment and smiled. She sighed as she opened them again. "The old guy is your *zayde*."

"My what now?"

"Your grandfather, Buddy. My father." The words caught in her throat a little bit.

I looked at the old man. He didn't smile. He didn't say anything. Just stood staring in that way he had been, framed by the doorway.

"What's he doing here?"

"Look, I'm taking him to bed, I'll come back and we can talk," she said. She murmured something to him in Polish then and he nodded. She took him by the crook of the arm and led him out of my room.

I sat on my bed. It was the first time all day I finally felt tired. Not excited because of Mister Drew, or terrified because of a person who was evidently my grandfather. Just very tired.

Ma came back and sat next to me. She gave me that sort of sideways glance she was so good at. It meant she thought I was funny. It wasn't exactly her laughing at me, but it wasn't not-laughing at me either.

"I'm sorry, I didn't know. How could I have known?" I asked.

"It's okay, it's my fault. Everything happened so quickly. I didn't know he was coming today, I wasn't ready for him myself. At least I didn't put him in your bed—imagine what kind of shock that would have been!" she said with a laugh.

"My bed?"

"You've got the big bed, Buddy, and we're just going to have to make it work for a while." I sighed hard but didn't say anything. My ma was a nice, warm kind of person, but don't let that fool you—you didn't argue with her. You'd never win. "When you didn't come home, I put him with me tonight. I didn't want to scare you."

"I guess that was nice of you," I said, feeling sorry for myself.

"Wasn't it?" said Ma with a wink. "And where were you so late? You don't think of your poor mother at home, worried sick?"

I didn't think it was time for a change of subject yet. I still didn't have enough information. My grandfather from the "old country" was now here in my apartment in New York, and why? The why still hadn't been addressed. But it was late. And also the answer would make her happy. "I got a job," I said, trying not to smile. Trying to make it a casual sort of thing. Like I didn't really care that much.

"What about Mr. Schwartz?" she asked, biting her lip.

"Don't worry, he didn't get mad, you still have your job. But I hope soon you won't have to work for him either. This job is better. It's working as an apprentice for Joey Drew Studios. Who knows where it could lead."

"You get paid for that?"

"Of course. Twice as much even."

Ma smiled then, a small smile, maybe I wasn't meant to even see it, but I could tell something in her had relaxed and that made me so proud. "What's a Joey Drew Studio?" she asked, turning to face me, one knee up on the blanket.

"It's where they make cartoons. Bendy cartoons. I get to be

a gofer but also a drawing apprentice. Learn stuff."

She looked at me funny then. But that wasn't unusual. She always looked at me funny, like there was a whole story going on in her head that I'd never get to hear. Secrets. She smiled again. "So you get to draw and get paid for it." It wasn't a question.

"Yeah."

"And your grandfather arrives the same day you get this job."

"Sure," I said.

"Perfect." She smiled.

I didn't get the connection. And of course she didn't explain it. I didn't ask either. It's funny. I'm just starting to realize how much I didn't ask questions back then. Not until I met you, Dot.

"Well, I'm happy for you, Buddy." She leaned over and kissed my forehead. Made me feel like a little kid. "Now get some sleep. We'll talk about everything tomorrow." That made me feel even more like a little kid.

She left and turned out the light and I crawled back under the covers, and only then did I remember my dream. I wondered how loud I'd been to make that old man wake up and come in. I wondered if I'd completely embarrassed myself.

In front of my creepy grandfather who looked like a ghost.

What a strange day.

And night.

If I'd had any kind of superstitious sense of anything, I

might have seen it as a sign. Something beginning, something not quite right.

But of course I didn't. I never saw the signs until I was past them, down the dark road with no exit. Another metaphor. That one wasn't bad. Hey, Dot, I'm getting better at this.

I'm hungry. Or maybe he's hungry.

I don't know. I just feel hungry.

That's not the point. It just makes writing hard, thinking hard. I'm having trouble staying in my head. Not sure that makes sense. I'll be honest, that last bit about my ma and Grandpa in my room, that was like I was telling someone else's story for a moment.

Was that my story?

Remember: the five senses. The smell of the apartment, old and moldy, but also of meat and potatoes and cabbage rolls. The water-stained ceiling above the bed. The sounds outside in the street, cars, people yelling, even at two in the morning. The itchy blanket. I remember it.

I met you the next morning, Dot.

I guess you could say I was a person used to meeting people, especially as a delivery guy. New people didn't bother me much. I liked looking at them. That sounds strange. What I mean to say is, you meet a new person and you see things about that person. How maybe this guy's shoes were just shined, that guy's got a sweat stain ring around his collar. This lady's hair curlers are singed with black, that lady's lipstick goes around the outside of her lips. Everyone is unique.

I actually first saw Dot from afar. I didn't know who it was then. I just knew the distant human was a short, stocky kind of girl with broad shoulders and a purposeful walk. She was probably around my age, with sweaty dirty-blonde hair that was already falling out of its curls first thing in the morning. Her large cat's eye glasses seemed a bit too big for her face.

After realizing she was also going into the main entrance at Joey Drew Studios, I jogged a bit to catch up and she held the door for me. She gave me the once-over, head to toe. It was quick, but she had made an opinion of me by the time it was over. I know this because we talked about it later.

"I thought you were tall," she'd said.

"Well, I *am* tall," I'd replied.

"You were like a baby horse, all limbs. You seemed off-balance. I liked that."

I still don't quite get why she liked that. But I do know that Dot was always suspicious of swagger: "How can you tell if the person is being real or fake when they act all confident like that?"

After sizing me up she'd continued her determined walk and gave the woman behind the desk a sharp nod before turning down the hall and disappearing around the corner.

I, on the other hand, went up to the woman, who once

again gave me that look of suspicion. Or maybe not. Maybe that's just how her face was. You know, I never asked her. I don't know the answer to that one.

I never asked people a lot of stuff.

"Hey, I'm Daniel Lewek. Uh . . . Buddy," I said.

She kept staring at me.

"I, uh, I'm the new gofer and art apprentice."

She stared.

Someone tapped me on my arm. I turned and was face-to-face with a woman, probably around fifty, with a puffy curl of soft brown bangs and hair framing her angular face. She had a deep wrinkle line between her eyebrows that made it look like she was concerned about something. But I would eventually discover that was just how she always looked.

"You're Daniel?" she asked.

"I am."

She wiped her hand on the apron she was wearing, and stuck it out to shake. I noticed it was stained with ink. Like my fingertips. "I'm Ms. Lambert. I'm head of the Art Department. Come with me."

I took her hand, we shook, and then I was following her back along the hall that yesterday had been so dark and creepy, but was now brightly lit with buzzing lights above. She pulled back the grate to the elevator and we stepped inside. Closing it behind us, she pushed a button and we were whisked up, all without saying anything. Which I didn't mind. I wasn't too much of a talker. Never was. Never will be.

Definitely never will be.

That's sort of funny.

"Gallows humor" is what Dot calls that.

Anyway.

I was also really interested that a woman was in charge of the Art Department and was thinking about it a bit. I don't think I'd ever seen a woman in charge of anything before. Not that there hadn't been a lot of women working the last couple years. I did know about that, with the lack of men and them being all away at war and everything. But actually the boss? No, I hadn't seen that.

I wondered why.

The elevator jerked to a stop and my teeth knocked together a bit at the suddenness.

Ms. Lambert noticed and laughed. "Yeah, it does that." She pulled back the grate, it clanged open, and we stepped out onto the Art Department level. There were artists sitting around the room in their own little nooks and crannies, each bent over a desk and working hard. Each space was decorated with drawings and photographs. There was an organized chaos to it that I liked.

It was also very quiet.

I'd done enough deliveries to offices to know about the hum of conversation and the clicking of typewriters. It was like the sound of the city that way, a background white noise, almost comforting.

But here the only sound I could really focus on was the

scratching of pen on paper. It made me feel like any sound I made would be distracting. Like even my breath was a bit too loud. Like maybe I shouldn't be breathing.

Ms. Lambert didn't feel the same way. "Hey, can I get everyone's attention!" she called out loudly.

Heads popped up, eyes blinked in our direction. One guy sitting by the windows took off his glasses, wiped them, and put them back on again.

"This is Daniel Lewek," she said.

"Buddy," I corrected her. She looked at me. "People call me Buddy."

"Okay. This is Buddy, he's our new gofer."

"Didn't Joey put a freeze on new hires?" asked the guy at the windows.

Ms. Lambert shrugged. "He's the one who hired Buddy."

The man shook his head and turned back to his desk.

"I guess you can take that desk back there. Sorry it's a bit dark but . . . well, it's all we have," she said, pointing toward a dark corner of the room away from the natural light.

"What do I do?" I asked her.

She shrugged again. "I guess just wait until someone needs you to deliver something or grab something." She looked at me looking at her, and her expression softened just a bit. Not a lot, not enough to erase the crease between her eyebrows, but a little bit. "It's okay, Buddy, we'll figure it all out. But I have to get back to work now."

And with that, I made my way across the room. I took

stock of the place as I did. It wasn't too big but there were, now that I could properly look, only four other people in it. The walls were unpainted slabs of wood, but they were covered almost entirely by drawings and photographs of people and animals and places, I guessed to reference for poses and things when making the cartoons.

I sat down at my desk. Yes, my corner was dark, but it didn't seem sad. It almost seemed cozy. Above it were yellowing drawings of Bendy. There were other characters too. A girl in a short black strapless dress with a halo. And something that looked like a tall wolf, ears sticking straight up into the air and wearing overalls.

"That's Alice Angel, that's Boris the Wolf, and obviously that's Bendy," said a warm voice behind me. I turned to see one of the art guys looking down at me. "And I'm Jacob. Nice to meet you, mac." I took his hand and shook. He was dressed in a sharp gray suit and wore a maroon tie with matching pocket square. Snazzy dresser.

"Thanks. I guess I should learn this stuff," I said.

Jacob laughed. "Yes. But don't ask anyone. Especially Mister Drew. You have any questions, stick with the Art Department. Some of the old-timers get sensitive. They don't understand how we didn't know who these characters were before we came here."

"Right," I said.

"Fame is fleeting," said Jacob, pushing his hat back a bit. He grinned at me. Then said, "Can you take this folder to

Story? Need them to agree to the art before I get going."

"Oh, sure," I said.

I took it from him and he made his way back to his desk. I turned back to look at mine, thinking about what he'd said. The wood was worn from years of use, darkened in some areas stained from ink spills. I could also see someone had carved into the soft wood itself. A couple of funny-looking eyes. Alice's halo. And just down toward the edge of the desk, a name. But it didn't look the same as the others. This looked like it'd been carved over and over several times. Deeper. Clearly it was the desk's former owner.

"I'll try to do you proud, Henry," I said quietly to the desk. Then I glanced up to make sure no one heard.

I got up and headed over to Ms. Lambert. She didn't have a secretary, and I wasn't sure who else to go to. She looked up at me with deep suspicion.

"Uh, I need to take this to Story," I said.

She stared at me hard, giving me the impression she had no idea why I was telling her that.

"Uh . . . where is it?" I asked.

"Oh," she said. "One floor down." Then she turned back to her storyboard and I felt pretty much invisible again.

Okay, just do this, I told myself. *Just impress folks and do your job and eventually they'll let you draw. And at least you're not outside in the heat.*

Though truthfully inside wasn't that much cooler. The fans in the ceiling just seemed to push the hot around.

I went down a floor and found myself in a room pretty

much the same as the Art Department. More heads bent over desks. This time there was a young, pretty secretary by the entrance and she looked up at me expectantly.

"Hey, I'm Buddy, I'm new here. Was told to deliver this folder?" I phrased it like a question even though I knew that was what I had to do. I felt like an idiot.

The secretary said, "Take it over to Dot."

I looked around the room. "Who's Dot?" I asked.

Now she looked at me like I *was* the idiot. "The only female writer in the room?" She also phrased that like a question, but it definitely was not meant as one. And it definitely made me feel stupid.

I nodded quickly and looked around for a woman. Finally I saw her, sitting a little away from the rest of the team, next to a window with a low bookshelf underneath it. Her head was bent over so close to the paper I had fun imagining she was writing with her nose.

"Excuse me," I said.

She looked up at me sharply but not in surprise. She didn't seem scared. Just . . . intense.

Of course. I remembered now. The girl from downstairs. The one who'd held the door for me. I think she had a similar moment of realization.

"Yes?" she said.

"I was supposed to deliver this to you." I handed her the file, which she took with one quick, efficient movement.

She looked at me again.

"I'm new," I decided to explain. "Mister Drew hired me yesterday. I'm in the Art Department." Why was I still talking? I didn't normally talk that much, so why was I now going on like this?

"Okay," she said. Then she turned back to her writing and I had no choice but to leave.

It's weird to think now that those two brief meetings made you sure of me. Made you like me. I'll never understand why. But I'll always be grateful you made the decision.

I was lucky to have known you.

The rest of the morning was pretty much a combo of me sitting at my desk for too long and then running deliveries. No one really knew I existed yet, and Ms. Lambert assured me that when the rest of the studio found out there was a new gofer in town, I'd be in high demand. "Enjoy the peace and quiet while you can," she said with a wry laugh. "And take this to Music."

So I did. I made my way down several stories until I ended up on the Music level. This was the first time I really got a sense of what a maze this building was. Unlike in my department, which was just one big room, the elevator now opened up onto a narrow hall. It stretched out in both directions and there were no signs or other markers indicating which way I should go. Also no people. Which was jarring compared with all the other bustling areas of the studio. Almost strangely creepy. My imagination immediately wondered what had happened to all the people. I pictured a giant hand coming out of the floor and scooping up all the people. It was funny, but somehow I felt a little uneasy still.

I put that behind me. Because I was being silly. It was just an empty hallway.

I chose to go right. I wandered along listening to the sound of my own footsteps until the hall opened onto a little space with four rooms off it. Three of the doors were locked; the fourth opened onto an old bathroom that didn't look like it'd been used in a while. I closed the door. The uneasy feeling was still there. Locked doors meant someone wanted to keep people out. But an unused bathroom meant that people hadn't been there for a while. Which was it?

There was another small dark hallway splitting off from this one, but it felt like I was going the wrong way deeper into the maze, so I turned and headed back the other way. I only had the two choices after all. I passed the elevator and this time turned left. I felt more confident. This hallway had posters hanging on the walls, and as I walked along, framed sheets of music appeared and even a few framed records hanging as art.

And then, suddenly, I was in a plain-looking hallway again. I spun around on my heel, but I couldn't figure out how it had happened. I must have missed a turn somewhere. I was starting to feel a little panicked.

It was silly. These hallways couldn't go on forever. This building was wedged between two other buildings. This was New York, a city on an island, always going upward because there was no sideways to go.

Just turn around and you'll figure it out. Eventually.

But.

I couldn't. In fact, I couldn't find my way back to the elevator now either. I was starting to feel that familiar feeling I had delivering for Mr. Schwartz. I didn't want to be known as the late guy, or unreliable. Not here, not at the studio. Definitely not on my first day.

I found myself in a hallway that was darker than the others. I was now genuinely getting scared. I was lost in a maze and at this point my imagination was starting to get the better of me. Each time I turned a corner, my stomach clenched just a bit at the thought of what I might find.

Or who.

I turned another corner, and then I heard something. I strained harder to listen.

Music.

I could hear music. It was faint and thin. Like a slow, high-pitched scream. It grew louder, then faded away. And again, loud and fading. I followed the sound and turned a corner. The lights were brighter here and I came upon a large empty desk next to a door. Above it was a sign: "Music Department." And the music came from behind the door. Someone was playing. That someone was going to help me get out of this maze.

I carefully opened the door and peeked inside. It was a large room, with a ceiling two stories high and a stage at one end. On the back wall, a square of bright white light flickered as if a reel of film had just finished playing. I turned to look up at the wall opposite. There was a projector booth up above, but the light was so blinding I couldn't make out if that guy Norman I'd met yesterday was there, or really if anyone was. So I turned back and walked farther into the room. Chairs and music stands were scattered across the stage. And instruments had been left on seats, open cases on the floor next to them. Looked like everyone had taken a lunch break. Except for the lady on the violin.

She sat in the middle of the stage, surrounded by this forest of music stands, her hair long and straight and unstyled. Her sheet music hid her face and most of the instrument, so I could only see her hand and fingers, claw-like, holding down the strings on the violin's neck.

The music she produced was slow and strained, hardly any kind of melody at all. It shot through my head and made me feel a little dizzy.

"Excuse me?" I said quietly, not wanting to interrupt, but not knowing what else to do.

She snapped her head up and the music stopped instantly. She stared at me from behind heavy hooded eyes.

"Hi, I'm sorry for interrupting, but I'm lost . . ."

There was a sudden loud crash from outside the room. Then an anguished scream. The woman stood up and stared at the door, and I turned to look, my heart pounding fast. "What is it?"

The woman stared, completely still. Then in a whisper said, "He's coming."

I turned back to her. "Who?"

Suddenly the room got dark. I whipped around and saw the projector had gone out. Only a light in the corner lit the room now. I could feel my chest constrict with fear, but it was just a change in lighting. That was all. That was all.

Thud.

I turned slowly back toward the door. I remembered my nightmare then. The darkness around me. The hand through the door. I glanced at the violinist. She stood completely still in her long black dress. Her hair melted into it so she seemed like one long shadow. She wasn't turning away, she didn't run. She just stared at the door.

Thud thud.

Like the sound of someone limping, heavy on one foot. Just outside. Getting closer.

No. I wasn't going to let my brain get the better of me.

Thud thud.

It wasn't a nightmare.

I made my way slowly to the door, took in a deep breath, and then flung it open wide.

No one was there.

"He's coming."

I looked at the violinist. She pointed toward the door with her bow.

"Who?" I asked again.

She said nothing, just kept staring. I was starting to feel more frustrated than scared, and I turned back around with a sharp sigh, only to confront the face of a creature covered in dripping black goo right in front of me.

I stumbled backward, and the folder in my hand fell to the floor, forgotten, as the monster launched itself into the room using the doorframe to push its way toward me. Its whole body was covered in something dark and seeping. It groped at its own face and released a moan of pure anguish as it fell toward me. I hadn't been able to get away. I tripped on my own feet as it fell on top of me, covering my torso in the same sticky wet substance. I pushed hard as I could as it clawed at its face, that horrifying cry from deep within its throat never ending. Every time it opened its mouth the black ooze slipped down its throat, making it gurgle and sputter.

Finally it rolled off me and I staggered back to standing. I looked down at myself.

My hands, trousers, shirt—everything was covered. I looked closely at my hands, rubbing at the black goo.

"Ink?" I said, gasping for breath.

I turned to the thing on the ground and realized then that it wasn't some monster. It was a man. Covered in ink. A man covered in ink, writhing on the floor in agony and rage.

I was down at his side at once. "Sir, sir, can you hear me?"

The man suddenly grabbed at the collar of my shirt and pulled me in close. "My eyes!"

I nodded and pried his clutching hand off me as I stood up. I frantically looked around the room and saw a cloth tucked into an open cello case. Behind that, by the back row, was half a glass of water. I rushed past the violinist still standing there like a statue, got both, and, in a panic, returned. "Water, and a rag," I explained, handing them over to him. He waved his arms around blindly, and I grabbed his hand and wrapped his fingers around the glass. Did the same with the other one and the rag.

I watched as he furiously wiped at his eyes, and it seemed to me he was making things worse. At the same time I wasn't about to tell him what to do—he seemed a bit . . . crazed.

Ink can do that to you.

Eventually he was able to clean enough of his face off, because he calmed down and he dropped his arms to the side and lay there staring at the ceiling.

"You okay, sir?" I asked.

The man stared in silence for a moment longer and then turned his head so he could look at me. His face was smeared and the whites of his eyes weren't white. Instead, they were more like a pale shade of pink. Everything about him seemed pointy. His nose, his chin, even the shape of his eyebrows.

That's when I noticed the red. The bit of blood dripping down his forehead.

"Am I okay?" he asked with a laugh, repeating my question. He shook his head and then blinked at me hard.

"You're bleeding," I said, and gestured toward the spot.

The man touched it, then ran his fingers higher over his scalp. He flinched. And then made a sharp pulling gesture with his hand. He looked at his fingers. In them was a piece of glass. He looked back at me. "Who the heck are you?"

"Oh, uh, I'm Buddy. I'm the new gofer for the Art Department."

He stared at me longer this time. Then he started to laugh this laugh that was all breath and no sound. Almost like wheezing. "Art Department. Okay. Okay, gofer for the Art Department, answer me this: Why are you guys storing ink in my sheet music closet? And why is *Joey* running a pipe through my closet that's apparently filled with ink?"

A pipe? With ink? That definitely didn't sound normal, but then again, I had no idea what was normal for an animation studio. "I don't know."

"You don't know. You don't know." The laughter got bigger even though it was still just breath. There was a clicking sound coming from the back of his throat now too. He pushed himself up so he was leaning back on his elbows, still laughing.

"I . . . don't know," I said, as if repeating it would make it sound like a less funny answer. "I . . . don't even know where the sheet music closet is." I didn't know where most things were. Even now, at this moment, I don't always remember where things are.

But I remember the man getting up and grabbing me by the elbow. And I remember looking at the violinist, the way she quietly stared while he pulled me out of the room. I remember following and not knowing what was going on. And his firm grip. His fingers were as pointy as the rest of him.

I remember.

I remember following a trail of inky footsteps along the floor in reverse.

And I remember the closet.

The door was wide open and the floor was pitch-black and ink was dripping down over cliffs of white paper from high shelves like a waterfall had just been turned off. Broken glass was everywhere.

"*This* is the sheet music closet," said the man, releasing my arm in a way that felt more like a push. I stumbled toward it. My toe kicked a shard and it clinked away into a dark corner. "And *this* is the ink that shouldn't be there." He pointed to a few remaining rows of unlabeled, still intact inkwells. "And *this* is the pipe that is inexplicably running with ink and has managed to burst, ruining untold amounts of my sheet music."

"Okay," I said. I looked at him. He looked at me.

"Okay?" He sounded indignant, but I didn't know what else I could say. All I wanted was to get back to the elevator and my work.

When I didn't say anything, he shook his head at me. Then he leaned in so close I could see the ink that had seeped into each of his pores. When he spoke, I could see his ink-stained gums and tongue. "Clean. Up. This. Mess."

Then he stormed off and I was alone. Again.

I stared into the closet.

This feeling of being lost just wouldn't let me go. This feeling of always being wrong. It wasn't nice. And now, looking at the mess, I just didn't understand. Didn't they have people who cleaned up here? How was this my job?

And how was I supposed to do this job?

How do you clean up spilled ink?

This is a tricky question to answer.

Because the answer is: You don't.

Let me tell you something about ink. It doesn't go away. I mean, you can wash your hands and scrub, and you think you've got it all, but then, a little spot, a small spot will pop up. Something you missed? Maybe. But it doesn't seem like it. So you wait for the layers of your skin to peel off instead, you wait for black-stained skin to flake onto the floor. Then it's gone. Or is it? You think it's gone, but then you find more. Somewhere else. And more.

And more.

Ink never disappears.

It's always there, like it was hiding, waiting to reveal itself. It's always there to remind you. It'll never go away.

At first it's not so bad. You get used to seeing it on the inside of your index finger like that. Maybe it's even a friend. Or a mark of pride. That's how it lures you in.

But it blossoms and burrows. And seeps and sinks.

And drowns and drinks.

It's alive.

It's everywhere.

It's inside me. It breathes for me. I can feel it sloshing about in my lungs.

I can feel it in my brain.

I am ink.

"Buddy?"

I'd been pushing ink around with an old mop I found in the utility closet for probably an hour at that point. Before that I'd cleared away the broken glass and ink bottles. Tossed away the sheet music paper that was destroyed. It had felt like I'd accomplished something. But not now. Now it was just ink swirling but not going away.

I turned.

"Oh, hi." It was that girl from the Writing Department. The one I'd seen earlier.

It was Dot.

Coming to rescue me.

"What are you doing?" she asked. She said it as if she thought I was crazy.

"Oh, uh, that music guy told me to clean this up," I said, holding my mop midair as it dripped onto the floor. More ink. "He was in here and I guess broke some bottles and there was a burst pipe or something."

"Music guy?"

"Yeah. He's . . . pointy." I didn't know much else about him. Not even his name, now that I thought about it.

"Oh," said the girl with a small smile breaking her severe expression. "Sammy."

"Maybe."

"Oh, it was definitely Sammy. He's . . . enthusiastic." She stepped around me efficiently to look at the mess in the closet. "What was all this ink doing here in the first place?" She reached up and touched a sticky puddle on one of the shelves. "Thick," she said more to herself than me.

"Tell me about it," I replied, finally lowering the mop to the floor and feeling the physical exhaustion from all the cleaning come over me.

"Can ink go bad?" she asked, looking at me.

"No idea."

She shrugged. "Well. Doesn't matter. He shouldn't have had you do this. Look at you, you look terrible."

I remembered then I was also covered in the ink. Because of Sammy. Ma was going to kill me when she saw the state of my clothes.

"Come with me, I wanted to show you something."

And because anything was better than pushing ink in a circle, I did as I was told.

I didn't know why Dot was so keen to take me wherever we were going. Okay, so I do admit my first thought was maybe she liked me. I mean, not just liked me, but was sweet on me.

If you're reading this, I know you're laughing, Dot, but I didn't really know any other reason a girl would want to hang out with a guy, especially at our age. It hadn't occurred to me then that we could just be people together.

Friends.

I'm glad I figured that out.

Anyway, I didn't know where she was taking me or why, but anything was better than cleaning up, as I said, and at this point I was so far off task that I wasn't really sure what my job was anyway. And I deserved a break.

I was pretty good at making things make sense in my head that way.

I followed her down the hall, turning this way and that until we came to the elevator. I felt such relief seeing it that I forgot for a moment that I wasn't heading back to the Art Department and was totally thrown for a loop when the elevator starting heading down instead of up.

"Where are we going?" I asked. The cage we were in shook a little, and gears controlling the moving mechanism squeaked a bit too loudly. *This elevator must have been one of the first of its kind*, I thought. A historic artifact. A really slow-moving one.

"I don't want to spoil the surprise," said Dot matter-of-factly.

"Huh," I said out loud. I'd meant to think it.

She turned and narrowed her eyes at me with suspicion. "What?"

"What? Oh, nothing, oh no. You just don't seem like the

type to go for mystery and games and stuff." I slowed down as I said it and she stared at me. It felt stupid all of a sudden. I knew nothing about her. I just knew she looked practical.

But looks could be deceiving.

"Not inaccurate," she said, un-squinting. "But once in a while, you know. A surprise can be neat. Besides, it's hard to explain, better to just see."

"Yeah, sometimes words aren't enough," I agreed.

She thought about that for a moment. "I'm choosing not to take that as a personal insult."

"Oh! No, it's not." Didn't mean it any way at all. Just thought I was agreeing with her. She made me feel on edge, like if I didn't say things perfectly she'd get the wrong idea.

Turns out *that* was accurate.

In a good way.

"I'm Dorothy, by the way." Yeah, I think that's how it went. I think that was our first introduction. *I'm Dorothy, by the way.* "People call me Dot. I call me Dot. Just call me Dot."

Right. I remembered now the secretary calling her that.

"I'm Buddy. My real name is Daniel, but everyone else calls me Buddy."

"Really, why?"

"Well, why are you called Dot?"

"It's a typical nickname people give Dorothys," she replied, as if I should know that.

"Oh."

"For Daniel, usually it's Dan or Danny or something. Buddy is weird."

That took me aback. I didn't really agree with her on that one.

"No, it's not. Anyway, it started as Little Buddy. Everyone in the neighborhood called me that. I was pretty tiny and always doing whatever I could to help my folks, with chores and stuff. Just wanted to be helpful. Running around the neighborhood. I guess people just started calling me that. But then, you know . . ." I looked down at myself, at my narrow legs propped up by my large shoes. Always felt like I was a stick on a stand or something.

"You grew," she said.

"Yeah."

The elevator finally stopped with a jerk, clacking my teeth against one another a bit again. I figured I'd need to get used to sudden stops or else they'd eventually pop out of my head.

Dot pulled the grate open and we stepped into a dark, deserted hallway. We were in the basement, that much was clear. And as I looked around it was pretty obvious no one worked down here, that the space was used for storage more than anything. Large people-sized cardboard cutouts of Bendy were leaning against the wall to the right, and as Dot turned and I followed her to the left, I could see several storage rooms with open doors. Inside the rooms, boxes were piled up on each other.

"Are we allowed to be down here?" I asked.

Dot shrugged.

I took that to mean *no*. She was pretty straightforward answering any other kinds of questions, so I figured: a shrug that didn't actually answer the question? Yeah, that was probably a *no*.

"So can I ask you something?"

She glanced at me with, again, that look of suspicion. I mean, I'd eventually learn that that's how she looked at everyone 'cause she was suspicious of everyone. Still, at first it made me wonder what I was doing wrong all the time.

"Okay."

"I notice there's a lot of . . . ladies working here." I wasn't exactly too sure how to put it.

Dot laughed at that. A single kind of coughing laugh. And she shook her head. "Who you callin' a lady, Buddy?" she said with a small grin.

My face got hot at that. "You know what I mean. Just, you know, girls working here. Like the head of the Art Department. Is a lady. And . . . you know . . ." I kind of faded that thought away and was silent.

"I know what?" she asked, turning a corner. I followed her. She flipped a switch and a few dusty lightbulbs that ran along the narrow ceiling flickered to life.

"I'm not . . . used to seeing so many women doing . . . this kind of work." It was hard expressing what I wanted to say. Mostly because, I guess, I wasn't really sure what I was asking.

"Okay, okay, before you tie yourself into a knot, string bean, let me help you." Dot stopped walking and turned to face me, and I faced her back. "During the war, Mister Drew, like every other employer, lost a lot of his staff to fight the good fight. So like a lot of other companies, he hired us 'ladies,' as you put it. War finishes, not all the boys come back, and those that do, well . . . Mister Drew liked our work. I think it surprised him at first, but then he realized he'd been ignoring a lot of talent without realizing it. Mister Drew likes talent. He doesn't care what gender or age or color or class it comes in."

"Yeah." I nodded, thinking about my interview with him. Not that Mister Drew actually knew if I had any skills. I hadn't drawn so much as a circle yet. Odd, when I thought about it that way.

"Anyway, you get it. The guys who came back, came back. But Mister Drew didn't fire any of us gals. We worked together for a while, some of the men stuck around, others didn't much like being bossed around by women, so . . . we end up where we end up."

"With lady bosses." I got it now.

"Just bosses, Buddy. Women aren't some strange special boss breed. Just people, Buddy, just people." I nodded again. I mean, I knew that. I did. Dot looked at me for a moment. "You're going to have to toss that whole outfit. It's destroyed."

I looked down again at the black ink soaking through my shirt. "Yeah," I said. I didn't want to think about it. That left me with only one other good outfit of a shirt and trousers.

Dot gave a sharp nod and started walking again. I did too. She walked quickly, but her every two strides were one of mine, so I didn't exactly feel rushed. Even though I sort of knew that I should be getting back to work. It was nice to have something make some kind of sense. It was nice to have a friend. Was she my friend? I wasn't sure.

We finally stopped in front of a closed door. Dot glanced around then, and that definitely made me think what we were doing was not allowed. She pulled out a small brass key from within a deep pocket in her skirt and unlocked the door.

"Where'd you get that?"

Another shrug.

She opened the door, turned on the light, and we stepped inside.

It was another storage room. But much bigger than the others we'd passed, which had been barely bigger than a closet. That being said, so much was piled up along all four walls that it gave the impression the space was much smaller than it was. In the middle were a couple of chairs and a table. And what looked like a buncha those little dollhouses you'd see in the toy shop windows were laid out on the desk. My shoulder caught against something sticking out, and I turned to look at it. It was a wheel.

A wheel?

That was when everything finally came into focus.

It's interesting how the brain works. It can see all the things as one thing. It doesn't see the pieces, the individual component parts. You see a car. You don't see a windshield, doors, headlights. You see those second. After you've seen "car."

It's funny how, if you don't look for the pieces, sometimes you never notice them.

The small individual things that make up the whole.

The clues.

The point was that I'd just seen "stuff." But now that I noticed the wheel, I noticed more. I noticed the wheel was attached to a small-looking cart, and I realized it was a lot like the bumper cars at Coney Island. And then I realized that this wall was made of a stack of cars. And more than just that, there was a sign half-hidden with lightbulbs around it. I could read "DY Bumpers" on it. I walked into the room and turned in a circle, and noticed more things. Like a black-and-white carousel horse and a cutout of Boris the Wolf holding a platter with the word "Food" and an arrow.

"Amazing, isn't it?" asked Dot.

I turned and saw she was standing by the table.

"What is all this?"

"Well, let me show you," she said, pointing at the little dollhouses.

I joined her at the table and realized then that they weren't dollhouses at all. They were part of a small-scale model, which made a lot more sense. We both leaned down on either side of the table. I briefly glanced up, and the way Dot's nose and mouth disappeared behind a small model of a building, it looked like she was a giant watching a human flea circus.

I glanced back down. I was hovering just above a tiny sign that read "Bendy Bumpers." I peeked over my shoulder at the real thing, hidden now in the shadows. "I don't get it. Coney Island?" I asked.

"Bendyland," she replied.

I looked up at her and she was looking at me with this kind of knowing look.

"Does this exist?" I asked. But even as I did, I knew the answer. It couldn't, because all this junk was in this room. "Did it exist?"

She shook her head no. "It's Mister Drew's next big project. Been working on it for the last couple years, or at least for as long as I've worked here. But always in secret. Nobody knows about this place, not that I've seen. It used to be just bits and pieces and the model would grow and grow. But then last month, this room started really filling up. Like something is about to happen."

I thought about that man Tom I'd seen yesterday. I thought about the cardboard tube in his hand. The kind of tube that architects and designers carry. Maybe he was working on this.

"I don't know where he's going to store everything because even this warehouse is tiny. Crazy, isn't it?"

I took in the whole scene of the model before me. There were rides and a midway with little booths hosting little games. There was a food area, and even something that looked like a haunted house. It was a whole park. Just for Bendy stuff.

"Mister Drew came up with all this?" I asked in awe.

"Who else?" asked Dot.

"And you don't think anyone else knows?"

"I don't think so." Dot stood upright and crossed her arms over her chest, still looking at the model. I stood up too.

"How do *you* know about this?" I asked.

"Good question, Buddy." She seemed impressed. "Keep asking questions like those here. It's important."

I didn't understand. I mean, I understood what she'd said, I just didn't understand why she'd said it. So I asked. Since, you know, that's what she'd told me to do anyway. "Why?"

"I don't know, Buddy, I don't. I just feel something in my gut and it doesn't feel good. I need to understand it better. I like information. I like details."

Ma used to say the devil's in the details.

"Anyway, don't get distracted, Buddy. You asked me a question and look what I did. I didn't answer it, and we moved on to something else."

I nodded. I was confused, except I wasn't. Which was also confusing.

"So how do you know about this?"

"I sneak around. I want to collect facts."

"'Cause of the gut thing."

"Yeah."

I understood sneaking. I'd done it a lot in my neighborhood. And when I'd spied on the artists in Central Park.

"Where'd you get the key?" I asked.

Dot smiled at that. "Even better question."

"Thanks."

"Wally's always losing his keys. Doesn't mean I gotta return them."

I nodded again, not sure how I felt about the whole stealing thing. Well, I knew how I felt and I didn't like it, but I liked Dot and she seemed so sure of herself, like she always knew the right thing to do. Maybe the right thing this time was the wrong thing somehow?

"We should probably get back upstairs before they notice we're missing," she said. I felt a flash of panic thinking about being late and getting fired, though at the same time, I'd been missing for a pretty long time already and no one really had seemed to care. Then again, no one really knew I worked here. Yet.

"Could you help me find my way back to the Art Department?" I asked as we locked the door behind us and made our way toward the elevator.

"Of course."

I stopped then. Thinking. Dot stopped too. Noticing.

"What is it?" she asked.

"Why me?" I asked.

"Why you what?"

"Why did you come to find me? Why did you show me all this?"

She squinted at me then with that look. You have that

look, you know, Dot? That look that says I should figure this out somehow myself, that I have the key, the solution.

I didn't. I didn't then, I don't now. You put too much faith in me, Dot.

"My gut," she replied.

5

I didn't see Mister Drew at all

that day. That made me feel a little bad. A little worried even that he hadn't really meant his job offer, or that he'd forgot all about me already. When I made it back to the Art Department, though, it seemed like a giant spotlight was shining down on me. I was definitely not invisible anymore.

"When they say throw yourself into the work, they don't mean actually."

"Is this some conceptual art piece?"

"You wanna be a cartoon character when you grow up?"

I think there were other things the gang in the Art Department said, but I can't remember. I remember them laughing. I remember my face getting hot. And I remember just trying to get the little odd jobs everyone asked of me done as quickly as I could with as little conversation as possible until the end of the workday.

The clocked ticked on. Five o'clock. Six o'clock. I was more than ready to go. So much for day one of the dream job. But no one told me when the day was done and no one around me got up. All the heads stayed bent over their desks, their pencils furiously scratching at their papers.

"It's okay, Buddy, you can go," said Ms. Lambert. I jumped a bit—she had kind of snuck up on me.

"I can stay," I said. I didn't want to look lazy. I was a hard worker.

"It's okay. Everyone's pushing toward a deadline, and this is your first day. Besides, it looks like it wasn't exactly an easy one." She grinned at me.

I didn't know what to say or do, and I kind of did just want to run away. The thought of going outside covered in ink like this really didn't make me feel great. But I did as she said and grabbed my jacket and made my way home. I stayed very focused on the sidewalk beneath my feet. Wasn't in the mood to catch folks staring at me.

It was harder to ignore the shouts from the people in my neighborhood.

"Hey, Buddy! You fall into a vat of chocolate there?"

That kind of thing.

I made it home and dashed up the stairs, knocking into Mr. McKenna coming out of the bathroom, that tired old towel wrapped around his waist, his belly bulging over it.

"Watch it, kid!"

I burst into the apartment and flew past Ma cleaning dishes in the kitchen and into my room. I came to a short stop. I'd forgotten.

My grandfather.

He was standing in the small space between the foot of the bed and the wall, staring at the oversized painting hanging there. I suppose the painting itself wasn't oversized, it was the size it was. It just was really big compared to the wall, and it dominated the room, I'd always thought.

"Just need to change my shirt," I announced. But he didn't move or even make any kind of sign he'd heard me. Not even a grunt. *"Koszula,"* I said. My Polish was terrible, I only knew dribs and drabs. I wasn't even sure how I knew the Polish word for "shirt" in the first place.

Telling him that didn't seem to do anything either.

So I edged my way up to him, trying to get him to notice me. When he didn't, I finally just climbed over the bed in order to get at my dresser. I glanced up at the painting as I went by. It was a nature scene, with a mountain and trees. It wasn't really painted realistically like a photograph, more like the artist had slapped paint on thickly and had accidentally come up with the picture. I was so used to it, so familiar with every shape and every line. But I was familiar with more than the picture itself. There was also the heavy gold frame. When I'd been little, I'd asked Ma if it was real gold. It wasn't, she said. I'd said if it was real gold, we could have sold it and gotten a new apartment. And also more food. She had smiled. "The frame isn't what's valuable."

I didn't get what she meant then. But I did a few years later when Tommy Sharp told me he'd seen in the paper that a painting that looked a lot like one of ours had sold for ten thousand dollars at an auction. I didn't believe him, and we'd gotten into a fight about it. But I'd gone home all bruised and looked at it. And it was like my whole world had come into focus then. I noticed the other paintings in the apartment. The ones stacked above each other against the length of the hall. I noticed how they took up space all the way to the ceiling, almost like they were being stored. They were all crooked. Dusty. I'd lived with them for so long I hadn't noticed that the paintings were something to notice.

"Ma, we could sell these paintings," I'd said. "We could have money. You could stop working yourself to death for Mr. Schwartz every day."

"What ideas you have," she said with a laugh, getting up from the table and ruffling my hair like I was still a little kid and not thirteen.

"Money's important, Ma," I said, turning in my seat to watch her.

"Don't tell me money's important like this is not something I know." She leaned against the sink and looked at me. "We aren't selling the paintings."

"They have value. You even told me that once," I said. "Did you see the paper?"

"No." She turned back to the sink. But she didn't do anything. She just stood there. Silently. Tears don't make noise. People think they do because when people sob and stuff they make sounds with their throat, but actually you can cry and no one will know.

But I knew. I always knew.

What I didn't understand was why she was crying. My heart sank into my stomach.

"Is it about Pa?" I asked quietly. We hadn't had a letter from him in weeks.

She turned abruptly, her eyes wide and red. She seemed scared, but not in a way I can really explain. I bet you could, Dot. Then suddenly her expression softened and she said, "Oh, your pa. No, no, it's not about him."

I looked at my grandfather as I made it to the dresser and opened my drawer.

It suddenly clicked in, that memory. "Is it about Pa?" She'd thought I'd been asking about her pa, not mine. She'd always been hiding something there. About her family.

What was he seeing in the painting? Why did it matter? What was I missing?

I pulled out my shirt and grabbed my other pair of trousers and slammed the drawer closed. It wasn't fair, I didn't need this. I didn't need some mysterious old man who didn't speak English in my room, in my space, making everything complicated. I didn't like how he made Ma sad either. She was always so happy except when she talked about him. Why was she letting him into her life like this? Our life like this?

Why was he standing way too close to that painting?

It was all too much. Today had been just too much.

I stomped my way across the bed again, which isn't actually a thing you can do. It's more like you kind of trip angrily and fall off the other side. And I was back in our narrow hall. I stripped and changed my clothes and flung the inky ones onto the bed.

My grandfather didn't flinch.

He just stared.

And kept staring.

6

Working at the studio was not at all what I thought it was going to be. I mean, it wasn't bad. Anything was better than being a delivery guy for Mr. Schwartz, outside in the heat of a New York summer. That being said, I'm not so sure I would have chosen being a delivery guy *inside* in the heat of a New York summer either. Especially in a stuffy, airless animation studio.

That's not to say that there weren't some advantages. Watching the artists at work was a huge one, of course, when they let me. Jacob always allowed me to glance over his shoulder a bit, but Richie, nah, he hid his work from me like he was writing secret messages to the Allies during the war. Also honestly being able to tell people from the neighborhood I was working uptown for Joey Drew Studios was pretty great too. They were impressed. They were jealous.

And the folks I met at work were pretty swell too. Most of them. Ms. Lambert, who ran the Art Department, was a bit severe, and sometimes frustrated me when she told me to sit down at my desk and stop hovering all the time. She also wore men's suits, which I found fascinating and definitely an inspiration for some kind of character I figured I would create. Someday. When she finally allowed me to draw. Which couldn't come soon enough. I wanted to learn, I wanted to be part of the group. Then there was the rest of the team. Richie, Dave, and Jacob, who I'd met that first day. They were like this little gang almost. Their desks sat in a row along the wall under three bright lights. Richie and Jacob looked to be in their twenties and were full of energy. Richie was rough around the edges and always reeked of cigarette smoke. The tips of his fingers were even yellow, which I learned when he passed me some new sketches, looking over the top of his small round glasses at me with suspicion. His clothes always looked a bit wrinkled, and that made me feel better since, after the Sammy incident, I now had only one set of shirt and trousers to my name. Didn't even have a suit jacket.

Jacob, on the other hand, was a snappy dresser with brightly colored ties and matching socks. I didn't even know they made socks in colors other than black and white. Sometimes he'd even wear his hat indoors. He seemed okay enough, though he was the one who teased me the most. He couldn't seem to let go of the whole me-being-covered-in-ink thing. At least when he brought it up he smiled. The fact was he teased everyone, so I tried not to take it personally.

Dave was older than all of us and his skin was as thin and dry as a piece of paper. After Dot had explained what had happened in the studio after the war, I wondered how an older fellow like him felt about taking orders from a woman, if he was stuck in old traditions and stuff. But he didn't seem to care much. He didn't do anything, apparently, but draw and take long lunch breaks. He didn't really talk with anyone. He turned in his work on time and went home on time, except when the department was under deadline.

But because my job was a gofer, as they called it, I got to know people outside just my department. Generally I took things from one person and gave them to another. There was a lot of coordinating that had to go on in the building, and I was the one bringing everyone together. I felt like that alone ought to have earned me a bit more respect, but I was definitely the lowest rung on the ladder, for now. So I brought scripts from the Story Department to the Art Department. Sheet music from the Music Department to the Animation Lab. Receipts from everyone to Accounting, and bills from Accounting to everyone. I got to know the secretaries. I got to know the bosses.

I got to learn that "Sammy" was Samuel Lawrence, composer, award-winning musician, and head of the Music Department. Seeing him not covered in ink for the first time was strange for me. The angles of his body were even more pronounced now that he wasn't hidden under the goopy ink. He kind of looked like a bird. Especially when he'd sit at the conductor's stand during rehearsals. The violinist still gave me the creeps.

I got to know Norman Polk, the guy who'd led me upstairs during the blackout, though he had no interest in getting to know me. He ran the projector, which I learned happened when they needed to synch up sound with a moving image. So there was a projector booth up in the Music Room like I'd noticed that time. And there was one in the Voice Recording Studio too. Norman knew all the actors and musicians, and he watched when they performed, I could tell that. He watched from behind the flashing light of the projector. I didn't know him super well, but the few times we interacted I got the feeling he didn't like me. Called me "Drew's gofer," which wasn't true. But also I didn't know what was wrong with that. It was almost like he didn't like Mister Drew or something. Which I didn't understand. How could you not like him?

I'd only met an actor once in those first few weeks. I'd held the door for her on the way into the building and was struck by how not-like anyone else in the studio she looked. I mean, she looked like she stepped right out of the pictures. On the day when I held the door for her, she was wearing a light gray skirt and jacket with a pink blouse underneath. She wore a small hat with a lace front that covered one of her eyes, but not completely. I have to say, I never understood why she was a voice actress. She was just as pretty as Ginger Rogers. With the same kind of platinum-blonde hair too. We'd ended up in the elevator together, and I'll tell you, she was very nice. Said thank you when I held the grate for her and even asked me my name.

"Buddy." It was all I could manage to say. I couldn't even ask what hers was.

"Well, I'm Allison, which is funny, right?" she said with a smile as we rose.

I didn't want to stare, and I didn't understand why "Allison" was funny, so I just shifted from foot to foot on the floor of the elevator.

"Because of Alice. Allison. Alice. It's so close, see?" I could tell she was looking at me. She wanted me to find it funny and clever. Come on, Buddy, come on . . .

"Oh! You're the voice of Alice Angel!" I said loudly as the elevator landed on my floor.

Allison laughed. "Yes! Well, it looks like this is your stop. Nice to meet you, Buddy." She stuck out her small gloved hand and I took it quickly in my sweaty one, shook once, and practically ran out of the elevator into the Art Department.

Hadn't seen her since then and, honestly, I was relieved by that.

I did get to see Dot more often. Ever since our strange adventure, she'd decided we were friends, and while I still didn't exactly get why she'd decided that, I didn't mind it either. It was nice when she sought me out at lunch. Or showed me a new script she was working on and explained it to me instead of just handing it to me and ignoring me like the other writers did. Maybe it was because we were close to the same age. Maybe it was because even though she got to actually write and wasn't a gofer like me, it still seemed like she was getting the grunt work of the Story Department and was on the lowest rung like I was. She mostly corrected spelling and grammar from what I could tell. But at lunch she'd sit at my desk in the dark corner of the Art Department as the pipes overhead made their grunts and groans, and tell me all about different Bendy stories she'd come up with.

"I've got a great one with him as a cowboy," she said, biting into her sandwich.

"I like cowboys," I replied.

Maybe it was just her gut instinct about me that made us friends.

I didn't really care. It was nice to have a pal.

The one person I didn't see, however, not once the whole time, was Mister Drew. I understood he was busy. He was in charge of the whole thing. I hadn't expected that he would come and check on me in person. Or invite me to lunch. Or anything like that. But I did think that maybe, I dunno, maybe he'd want to follow up at least once after hiring me. Maybe I'd just been imagining things like I did, but I really thought he'd liked me.

"That's just Mister Drew," Dot said.

She'd convinced me to go out after work to the pub across the street. It was a small, crowded hole-in-the-wall down a couple stairs where clearly a lot of after-work types hung around. The place was full of men and even some women crowded against the bar and sitting at the few tables by the door and in the back. The air was so thick with cigarette smoke it made me cough at first. Dot was eighteen, so she could drink, but I was a little relieved when she grabbed a root beer instead. Helped me not feel quite so babyish. We'd collected our beverages from the bartender and found a spot by the wall.

"What's 'just' Mister Drew?" I asked, almost yelling above the noise.

"Disappearing. That's what he does. Just stick with your work, that's all you need to do."

I sighed, but I knew Dot couldn't hear it. I leaned in to talk into her ear. "It's just that—I'm not doing the work I want to do. I need him to tell Ms. Lambert to let me draw."

Dot shook her head and gave me a small smile.

"You don't need permission, Buddy," she shouted back. "Just do it. Draw."

I shook my head. "No. No, I don't have time. I'm running around all day. You know that."

"Then do it at home, draw some Bendy stuff. Show Ms. Lambert."

On what? I asked myself. *With what?* Dot didn't understand. Yeah, I had a pencil and scrap paper, but I needed proper tools. The paper at the studio was thick and crisp and absorbed the ink. I couldn't just hand over the back of a grocery receipt. I didn't want to anyway, didn't want them to see how little we spent on food.

"I . . . can't . . ."

Dot looked at me. I was getting used to the look now. So I just looked back. If she could read my mind, if she could just figure out my issue without me having to tell her, that would be great.

And then, she did.

Not really of course. She just had this way of knowing what people were actually thinking, not what they *said* they were thinking.

She didn't say anything. She just reached into her pocket and passed me her key. "Borrow it. I'll keep it in my desk from now on in case you need it again."

I didn't take it, just stared at it.

"You want me to use this?" I said slowly.

"Yes."

"To . . ."

"Get yourself the right materials, Buddy. Get yourself some paper and some ink."

I shook my head. "That's stealing."

"It's *borrowing*. You're doing this for the sake of the studio after all. On your own time no less. And anyway, you want to show some initiative. This is how you do it."

On the one hand she was right, it didn't seem like that big a deal. It wasn't like I was going to take the stuff and then sell it to the kids in the neighborhood or anything. On the other hand . . .

"Think about it," she said.

I pocketed the key quickly. "You're a bad influence," I said with a little laugh.

Dot shrugged, like she did. "Maybe just more of a pragmatic influence. They hired you for a job. So do your job."

Pragmatic. Didn't know that word at the time. I looked it up later. Pragmatic. Meant dealing with stuff "sensibly." Taking out the emotion. Making a choice because it's practical. Didn't think I agreed with her that that's what this was, but I wanted to.

"I'll think about it."

And I did.

I thought about it all night, lying there in bed next to the bony figure of my grandfather, whistling rhythmically through his nose as he slept. I must have dozed off at some point, but it felt like I had spent hours awake, thinking. Thinking about living like this, with my ma, now with my grandfather. Sleeping here in the big bed. In the big room. In an apartment hardly big enough for a single person, let alone a family. All the other families in my building living with five people or more. This big room that used to belong to my parents. Until my pa died, and then it belonged to me. "You're so tall now, Buddy," Ma had said. "I don't need that much room."

Tall like he'd been tall.

Imagine more rooms. Imagine an apartment that didn't suck in the heat and suffocate you inside. Imagine owning a suit. Couldn't borrow my pa's. I couldn't put it on. I just couldn't.

I wasn't going to have more rooms and a suit as a gofer. I was too old to be a delivery boy.

And anyway, the studio had so much paper and ink it was drowning in it. Like Sammy. Covered in ink. Running through actual pipes apparently.

When I woke up in the morning, I decided I knew what to do. Dot was right. It was the pragmatic choice.

It was the only choice.

The art supply closet was off

down a hallway behind my desk, but I was too afraid of getting caught. So I turned to the only other place that I knew had Art Department supplies, whether Sammy approved of it or not: the sheet music closet in the Music Department. That was an advantage. Being the gofer meant that folks were used to me walking around in different parts of the studio and doing whatever I was doing. I figured this would make my task pretty easy. But I still wanted to wait until lunch when I was alone.

Which I did.

I waited five minutes or so, making sure no one came back all of a sudden because they'd forgot their hat or something. Then I got up from my desk and made my way down to the Music Department, through the winding path of hallways, and to the closet. I glanced back up the hallway and then down the other direction that led . . . well, I didn't really know. I'd never gone farther than the closet before, and I assumed it must lead to some kind of dead end eventually. Then again, this place was so mazelike. Maybe there was something else deep in the shadows. I grinned thinking maybe there was a sphinx or something, guarding a secret entrance, quizzing employees and choosing if it would let them past.

No. No more imagining. Stop it, Buddy! I quickly unlocked the closet door, went inside, and pulled the chain for the light. I leaned down and picked up a small stack of thick, crisp white paper. The difference in quality between kinds of paper was amazing. I hadn't thought much about it before I'd started working here. Then I looked around for ink. There was a cardboard box on the floor, and I opened it carefully. There they were, little glass bottles full of black. I gingerly pulled one out. I still needed a pen. It was while I was searching the narrow shelves that I heard the voices.

I froze in place and listened hard. You'd think with my big ears I'd have a better sense of hearing, but the way they stuck out so much never seemed to make a difference. But I could tell, at least, like anyone probably could have, that the voices were coming from the dark part of the hall, not the Music Department. I was starting to get anxious. I couldn't get caught; if I did I'd definitely be fired. I needed the job, and I was starting to really regret doing this.

I slipped inside the closet and closed the door behind me. Then I pulled the chain for the light and stood stock-still with an arm full of paper in the pitch darkness. The voices got louder and I could hear footsteps now. They were almost right there in front of my door before they stopped. There was the sound of a scuffle.

"Don't grab me again, Mr. Lawrence," said a stern voice I didn't recognize.

"Then listen to me when I'm talking to you!" That was definitely Sammy's voice, that one I knew for sure. It was lower than the frantic cries I'd heard on our first encounter, but it had that same edge to it. Always just a little angry.

"I've heard you, and I don't believe you," said the other voice.

"Why not?" It was almost a squeak the way he said it.

"I've seen you sneaking around my work station. I've seen you at the machine. Last Friday you asked my worker where we kept the ink. So don't you go on about being all innocent. I'm going to Mister Drew."

"Tom, come on, why would I want your ink?" asked Sammy.

Tom . . . I still didn't know who that was.

"It's Mr. Connor," replied Tom coldly.

"Why can't I call you Tom?"

"Because we're not friends. And you will give me the respect I deserve." There was a long pause then. I couldn't decide if I wanted the two of them to move on down the hall already or for them to stick around so I could hear more. When Sammy didn't say anything, Tom added, "What's the matter, Mr. Lawrence? Not used to giving someone like me respect?"

"What's that mean, 'someone like you'?" Sammy's tone had gone from angry to threatening.

"You know what it means," replied Tom.

There was a long pause.

"Leave me alone," said Sammy. I heard the sound of footsteps as he marched away back down the dark part of the hallway.

"Leave my ink alone!" Tom called out after him.

I was suddenly very aware of the small inkwell in my hands. It seemed much heavier than it had a moment ago. I was also aware now of how loud my breath sounded in the small confined space. I had no idea that ink was so important. And that it was so important to Tom Connor.

That man I'd seen only once before, waiting for Mister Drew that first day.

Tom let out a huff outside my door, and finally I heard his boots also stomping off in the direction of the dark hallway. I kept still, straining to hear more footsteps. To see if either of them was coming back. But the longer I waited, I realized, the more likely it was someone eventually would come by, and lunch was probably going to be over soon anyway. So I had no choice. I carefully opened the door.

No one.

Quickly I turned around and grabbed the first refillable pen I could find. And then I was out of there, locking the door behind me, dashing back to my desk, and hiding the supplies in the garbage bin under it. I sat there, still for a moment, and then took in a deep breath. I was more scared than I'd been at first. Sure, stealing wasn't something I was keen on, but I really didn't think that ink was such a big deal. Not like Tom was making it out to be.

I felt the key in my pocket.

I stood and headed for the elevator just as it opened and Jacob came back from lunch. "Hey, Buddy," he said as he passed, all casual, like nothing weird was going on in the studio.

Probably because he didn't know.

Probably because I was overthinking it.

I went down a level to Story and luckily found Dot at her desk, her sandwich unwrapped before her, her head bent so low over her paper her nose was practically touching it.

I wasn't sure if it was right to interrupt her, but she made the decision for me. With one swift movement she was suddenly sitting up looking at me.

"Whoa, you scared me," I said, taking a step back.

"I scared you? You were the one sneaking up on me," replied Dot, matter-of-fact.

"Yeah, I guess."

"What's going on?" she asked, looking at me closely like she was trying to read my brain.

"I, uh . . ." I looked over my shoulder, but no one was nearby. "I wanted to return, you know."

Dot nodded and opened her drawer. I quickly dropped the key inside and she bent over, placing it between the pages of a book. *The Complete Works of Sir Arthur Conan Doyle*, it said in gold lettering on the cover.

"Thanks."

I just stood there. I couldn't decide if I should tell her what I'd heard.

"So did you get what you needed?" she asked after a moment.

"Yeah." I didn't know what to say. Maybe I was just panicking about being a thief now.

"What's on your mind, Buddy?" she asked, leaning back in her chair.

Okay, fine. "Do you know anything about a man named Tom Connor?" I asked quietly.

Dot thought about it for a moment. "I don't think so."

"Well, I just overheard him and Sammy talking about ink."

"Ink?"

"Yeah, it sounded like this Tom guy thought Sammy was stealing ink." I remembered something else then. "And also there was talk of a machine."

"Machine?" Dot furrowed her eyebrows at me. "What kind of machine?"

"I don't know. I just was curious because, well, as you know, I just . . ." I lowered my voice to a whisper even though no one was close by. "I just stole some ink. And I'm worried this could be a bigger deal than we thought."

Dot shook her head. "No, that's silly."

I didn't like that. It wasn't silly. She wouldn't be thinking that if she'd heard what I'd heard.

"I'll look into it," she said.

"You don't have to, I just was wondering if you knew," I said. But I didn't say it too forcefully. Dot was really good at "looking into" things, and I appreciated any help here.

"No, I want to." She glanced over my shoulder then and I turned around. Mike, one of the writers, had just come off the elevator. "Let me know what Accounting has to say, but there's no hurry," she said loudly, and I quickly realized we were pretending now.

"Of course."

I turned around and passed Mike, who gave me a sideways look as he took off his jacket and sat at his desk. He pulled the brim of his hat lower down and tipped his chair back onto its rear legs, picked up something he'd been working on, and began to read it over.

I made it back to the Art Department just in time to be sent on an actual task to the Music Department. The last thing I wanted to do was see Sammy, but fortunately he kept to himself, sitting on his stool at the conductor's stand, looking over notes and muttering. Beside him was a half-empty bottle of ink.

Normally I'd never have paid much attention to something like that, but now, well, now I stared at it for a moment. Wondering.

I shook my head and quickly dropped off the folder I'd been given in the "In" box by the door and turned to leave.

Maybe I should just ask. Maybe there was a way I could ask.

I turned back.

The ink bottle was now empty.

How?

"What do you want, Art Department?" asked Sammy, suddenly looking up at me.

"Nothing! Just left a folder for you," I said, backing away quickly.

"Fantastic," he replied, looking back down at his work.

I left immediately, feeling deeply unsettled. It wasn't just being snapped at. I was used to him being unpredictable. It wasn't even what I'd heard him say earlier either. It was that I could have sworn, when he'd turned to face me, that there had been a small bit of black in the right-hand corner of his mouth.

8

I got home early enough to

join Ma and my grandfather for dinner.

"It's nice to see you, Buddy," Ma said, giving me a big squeeze as she placed my plate in front of me.

"Thanks. How's Mr. Schwartz?" I was trying not to grimace as she ruffled my hair.

"Oh, he's fine. How's the studio?"

I didn't think that Mr. Schwartz was "fine," but then again things at the studio weren't really so fine either. That was kind of what we said though. It was our routine. When life isn't easy and days are long and tough, you don't really want to get into it. So that's what you say. And you carry on.

We sat there then, in silence. A whole lot of nothing conversation. Including my grandfather, who just sat silently scooping food into his mouth.

This was fun.

I ate as quickly as I could and then disappeared into my room. I needed to claim it before my grandfather did. I sat down on the floor and placed my stolen paper and ink next to me. Then I took a sheet and put it on the windowsill. It wasn't as wide as a desk, but it was a solid enough surface, and I'd been using it to draw on since I was a kid. I was lucky the windows went down as low as they did. And that my body was as long as it was.

Time to draw.

Yes.

Dot, you know very well what it's like facing a blank page. I know that writers get the same feeling. It starts off exciting, but as the seconds tick by, the minutes, the feeling starts to turn. To feel bad. You get anxious and you can almost feel like the paper is making fun of you.

Not all the time. But it seems to happen exactly when you really need to draw something. This feeling of pressure.

Not fun.

I cracked my neck and pushed my hair up off my forehead. It stayed standing upright since it had been matted down with sweat. I was ready for this summer to be over. I took off my button-up and sat there in my undershirt. It was cooler. A little bit. A very little bit.

Just start drawing. Draw anything.

Cowboy Bendy.

It popped into my head just like that. Dot's idea. Well, she definitely needed pictures to go with it. And I liked cowboys.

I grinned to myself and started drawing. It was my first time ever attempting Bendy and it surprised me how much harder he was to draw than I'd thought. He looked so simple to do. A round head, two eyes, a mouth. Not even a nose to worry about. Noses can be tricky.

But somehow he just kept coming out a bit wonky.

I stopped. And tried another tactic. I started drawing the horse I wanted him to ride.

That wasn't easy either. Somehow the body was looking stubby and thick, like a donkey or an overweight dog. The legs were too wide too. And the head. I didn't even want to think about what a head like that on a real horse would actually look like.

I tried again. This time the proportions were a bit better. I stopped and looked at my paper. Three awkward Bendys, and two kinds of horses.

It wasn't bad. It wasn't . . . good either.

And then it wasn't there anymore.

The paper vanished from beneath me and I whipped around and looked up at my grandfather standing over me. I had no idea what he was doing and yet for some reason I didn't say anything. I just watched him, noticed that even on a day like today he was dressed in that same long-sleeved shirt, cuffs tightly closed at the wrists, slacks and suspenders, socks and shoes. I had no idea how he wasn't melting from the heat.

He was staring at the paper intently.

He looked at me. Then he pointed at me. "You?" he asked.

"It's for my job," I said. Did he understand words like "job" yet? Did he understand anything? Even where he spoke his own language? I was starting to think maybe the people in Poland might have thought he was as bizarre as I did.

"Riding?" he asked, and pointed to the paper.

"Yes," I replied, nodding.

He smiled. "Cowboy."

I didn't think in that moment that it was neat my grandfather knew what a cowboy was. I didn't even think to question how he knew. I was too hot and too frustrated. I sighed. *Yes, Grandfather, a cowboy. Can I have my paper back? Please?*

He placed it on the dresser next to me and leaned over, looking at it closely. He motioned with his fingers, a kind of grabbing thing, but didn't look at me. I didn't know what he was doing. I didn't have time for this.

"Give give," he said, still wiggling his fingers. It clicked finally—he wanted the pen. He wanted to draw. This wasn't just some game for me, but he was treating it like I was a little kid doing some hobby. I didn't like this at all. But he wouldn't stop. I knew it.

I gave him the pen.

He smiled. "Give." He raised his eyebrows at me. Then glanced down.

I sighed again and passed him a fresh piece of paper.

"Ah!" he said. He started to draw on the page while I leaned back against the wall. This was ridiculous. I looked out the dusty window. Mrs. Bilski across the street was hanging the laundry on the line. Her cat was trying to play with the sheets as they dangled. Never liked cats.

"Cowboy," said my grandfather. He was smiling at me and pointing at the paper.

I nodded.

He tapped on the paper.

So with a groan I pushed myself up to standing and looked at it.

And looked.

And stared.

I turned back to my grandfather. He was walking out of the room. Just leaving, like nothing had happened. Like he hadn't managed to draw a perfect horse. And a perfect Bendy. Just like that. In less than a minute.

I grabbed the paper, following him out into the hall at once. "Grandfather!" I turned into the kitchen. He was sitting already, looking at me like I'd lost my mind. How the tables had turned.

"Buddy?" Ma was standing at the sink staring at me too.

I ignored her.

"How? How did you do this?" I asked him, pointing to the paper.

"How?" he asked me, looking confused.

"How!" I kind of yelled it, which made him flinch in a strange way, and I hadn't meant to scare him, but I was just really fully of energy. He slouched low in his chair, like his frail old body was withering away and seemed to almost disappear in it, but even more than just that.

"Buddy, please," said Ma, her voice full of warning.

"I'm sorry," I said, sitting next to him. "It's just . . . it's . . . good. It's really good."

He looked at me carefully and thought for a moment. "You draw cowboy?"

"I can't."

"You can."

I laughed the kind of laugh that isn't really one. That's more like a frustrated sigh. "I really can't, Grandpa."

He reached out and took my hand gently in his. It was warm and soft. He carefully looked at my fingers, at the ink stains. "You can."

I shook my head. The heat was getting to me now and I was feeling overwhelmed and very tired. And mad at myself. The one thing I wanted to do and I couldn't even do it.

"I teach," he said.

"No." I stood up slowly. "No, it's okay."

What was the point?

I made my way to the door.

"Where are you going?" Ma asked.

"I don't know," I replied. I got deeper in my head with that question. Where was I going? What was I doing anyway?

I went outside but the air was stale. I started to walk east toward the river. I needed to feel a breeze on my face, I needed to not feel completely suffocated. I picked up speed and soon I found I was running. Running away? Running toward something?

The river greeted me and I could breathe again.

For that moment at least.

The next day I sat in my dark little corner, and it was the first time I actually didn't mind being so far from the rest of the team. I pulled the drawing of Cowboy Bendy out of my pocket and spread it out on my desk, flattening it as best I could with my hands. It wasn't just that my grandfather had drawn the perfect horse. It was more than that. It was the expression on Bendy's face, confident and proud. It wasn't just that plastered-on smile that I saw in the large advertising cutouts stored around the studio. There was personality even though there was so little to work with. Just eyes and a mouth. There was a feeling too of movement, like they were riding along at a fast speed. And there was the comedy of his lasso getting all messed up around the cactus.

He'd done so much with so little. I didn't know how. I needed to figure it out. So I could impress Mister Drew.

"What's that?" asked a voice over my shoulder.

I looked up. It was Jacob. He bent down and stared at the drawing. "Hey, mac, that's not bad." He grinned at me and stood up.

"Thanks," I said. I knew I should explain it to him, that I hadn't done it. But it was the first time anyone in this place had actually said a nice thing to me. He nodded but didn't go away, so I felt like I needed to say something else. "I did it last night."

"It's nifty," he said.

"Is that a good thing?" I asked.

Jacob grinned. "Definitely." He turned. "Hey, Ms. Lambert!"

"No, don't," I said, but it was too late. She glanced up from her desk at the other side of the room, unfolded her long legs, stood and marched over to us in a very sharply pressed pair of trousers.

"What's going on?" she asked. The line between her eyebrows seemed extra deep.

"Have a look at what our gofer did last night," said Jacob, pointing at the picture.

I tried to smile in a relaxed kind of way as Jacob moved aside and let her peer over my shoulder. But I was starting to panic a little. What if they made me re-create it or something?

"It's decent," said Ms. Lambert with a frown of approval.

"I did it last night," I said, feeling a little relieved but also not able to say anything much more than that.

"You were here?" She looked at me, puzzled. "I was here."

"No," I said, scrambling for words. "No, at home. On my off time." That sounded good, right? That sounded like something someone who worked hard would say. Even on my off time I was doing work.

Ms. Lambert stood there for a moment. Then she bent over and picked up the picture. But she wasn't looking at the drawing, she was looking at the paper, feeling it between her thumb and forefinger. "Tell the truth, Buddy. Where'd you get the paper and ink?"

Oh. Right. The truth. The truth was . . .

Lots of silence then while I tried to figure out what the truth was.

"I see. Buddy, we were low today on stock, and you know as much as everyone here that money is tight. We're not a baseball team." She passed the picture back to me.

"A baseball team?" I asked. I noticed that Jacob was no longer beside me, but slowly walking back to his desk.

"You don't get three strikes here."

I still didn't get it.

"I'm sorry, Buddy, but this is unacceptable. Stealing is not allowed and Mister Drew is very strict about that. You can't do it, Buddy."

Right, okay. I got it, I got it. I wouldn't do it again. "I won't do it again."

Ms. Lambert shook her head and then stared up at the pipes running across the ceiling over my head. "I'm sorry, Buddy. I have to take you to Mister Drew."

My stomach fell out of my body. I could almost hear it in my imagination, flopping onto the floor with a squish.

All I felt was hollow at how unfair it was. It was just some paper and ink. But yeah, it wasn't like I could afford paper and ink. It had a cost. And evidently a much bigger cost than I'd realized.

"Come on." Ms. Lambert motioned for me to stand. I did

and followed her over to the elevator. I could sense heads turning to watch, but I didn't look back. I was too embarrassed.

We stood quietly in the elevator as it chugged its way up to the top floor.

"I'm . . . I'm sorry," I said. I realized I hadn't said it yet. I meant it, but also maybe it mattered that I was?

"I know. It's tough. Things aren't like how it used to be here. We have to protect every dollar. But even more than that, we have to have trust."

I nodded. It wasn't like I hadn't noticed that there was definitely some penny-pinching going on. If there was one thing I understood, it was that. Grabbing paper from the wastepaper basket to write on, only one janitor for the entire studio, all the empty offices and dusty corners. Yeah, I noticed it. But I still hadn't really got it. Until now.

Ms. Lambert pulled the grate to the side when we arrived at Mister Drew's office and let me out first. We approached Miss Rodriguez sitting behind her desk, typing away at that fast speed just like I'd seen her the first time I'd met Mister Drew.

The only time I'd met Mister Drew.

"Does Mister Drew have time for us?" asked Ms. Lambert.

Miss Rodriguez looked up but didn't stop typing. I would have been impressed if I wasn't feeling so low. "Five minutes," she said. And without stopping her typing or getting up or anything, she called out really loudly, "Ms. Lambert is here with that new gofer!"

"That new what?" Mister Drew called back with that gruff voice of his.

"The kid." She looked back at me, eyeing me up and down. I instinctively tucked my shirt tighter into my trousers, pulled my shoulders back.

"What kid? Never mind, send them in!" Mister Drew called out again.

Miss Rodriguez gestured toward the door with her head and looked back down at her typing. I glanced at Ms. Lambert, who didn't seem to find any of this strange and walked over to his door and opened it.

"Mister Drew, we have to talk," she said.

"Sure, sure, come on in," I heard Mister Drew reply. Ms. Lambert turned to me and gave me this look that I knew definitely meant I should follow her.

So I did.

And we entered Mister Drew's office.

He was sitting behind his large desk with a big stack of papers all over it. Everything seemed even more of a mess than the first time I'd seen it, if that was possible. The shades were drawn on the windows this time, no view out to Broadway now. It made the room feel smaller and cramped and uncomfortable.

Or maybe it was because I was feeling uncomfortable.

"What's all this about?" he said, not looking up, instead focusing hard on a piece of paper in front of him.

It was the first time I'd seen the man since he'd hired me. Since I'd brought him his suit. And now I was about to be fired.

What would happen then? Would Mr. Schwartz take me back? I didn't think so. Ma would be so disappointed in me.

"I'm sorry, Mister Drew, but this new kid of yours was caught stealing," said Ms. Lambert.

"Stealing?" He finally looked up at that. He stared at me. "The kid!" he said, pointing at me, remembering I existed. That didn't make me feel bad at all, being forgotten. Nope, not at all.

"Yes, sir, Buddy Lewek. Unfortunately he was caught stealing and per the rules . . . well, I brought him to you to handle it." She sounded tired, like this was the last thing she wanted to be doing right now. I didn't blame her.

"Ah," said Mister Drew. "Right, well, Buddy, what do you have to say for yourself?" He frowned his forehead at me, and his thick eyebrows met each other over the middle of his nose to have a private conversation. I imagined eyes on them, and lines where their own furrowed brows would be.

Ms. Lambert gave me a small shove. "Go on."

I looked back at her. She didn't seem all that angry, she just had to do this.

"I wanted to draw," I said, turning back to Mister Drew.

Ms. Lambert sighed hard behind me. "He stole supplies and took them home with him. You know we can't afford—"

"Please, Ms. Lambert. Tell me what I can and can't afford, why don't you?" Mister Drew crossed his arms against his chest.

I looked back again at Ms. Lambert and saw her sputter a

bit. She went to say something, but stopped herself. "I was only following your directions, sir," she said through a tight jaw.

Mister Drew nodded. "I do understand, Ms. Lambert. I do. And we can't have the team just taking things. We have stock to keep track of. And of course the fact that he got into a locked cabinet . . ." He looked at me carefully. I didn't like it. For a moment I'd thought maybe he was on my side. Now I had no idea what he was thinking anymore. "You get back to work, Ms. Lambert. Let me have a word with our gofer here."

"Yes, Mister Drew." With that she turned and left the office, her shoes clicking away until it was eerily silent.

Mister Drew didn't move. He didn't say anything. He just kept looking at me in that way he'd been looking at me. "Buddy, right?" he said finally.

"Yes, sir."

He was still for another moment.

Then.

"Okay, let's see it."

"See what?"

"You wanted to draw, so let's see it. Let's see the finished result."

I didn't have a finished result. All I had was my grandfather's drawing in my back pocket.

I reached back and pulled it out, placing it in Mister Drew's already outstretched hand. He unfolded it and looked at it. He looked up at me. "Close the door, Buddy."

I closed the door.

"Sit."

I sat.

"There are things I'm supposed to say and do as a boss. But the thing is, kid, I never planned on being the boss of anyone. I was just a man with a dream. I was just a man who knew what he wanted, and took one step and then another, and soon I was dancing, you get me?"

Not really.

"Yeah," I said.

"I'm supposed to tell you stealing is wrong, and believe me, I don't like it when people steal from me. But is this stealing?" He held up the drawing.

"I . . ."

"Stealing is you taking something from me. Someone who claims something is his when it's mine. I don't have much tolerance for anyone who takes something from me. I don't think any man does. But when you're doing something for the greater good? When you're creating and making things, and taking that extra step on the dance floor . . . that's not stealing. You know what we call that?" He watched me expectantly. But again, I had no idea what to tell him.

"I don't, sir."

"We call that ambition." Mister Drew finally smiled then, and leaned back in his chair. I wasn't sure how or why, but I understood then at the least I wasn't in trouble. I understood that, for some reason, I was actually being praised.

Mister Drew looked at the drawing again. "This is good,

Buddy, real good. I knew you had the skill, but I didn't know you had the ambition. You were impatient. I get that. I've been impatient my whole life. You knew what you wanted, and you took it. I get that too. For the greater good."

"For the greater good," I repeated. This story he was making up about me was part lie. I wasn't that skilled. I couldn't draw like that. I felt guilty for a moment until I realized that the stuff Mister Drew was impressed with was actually in the lie too. He just didn't know it. Showing him the picture my grandfather had done had helped save my job. It had been for the greater good.

"I like you, Buddy. I'm sorry I haven't been around much, I've been working on a project. It's been . . . tricky. Not everything works on the first try, you know?"

That I definitely did know. "Yes, sir."

"Been a lot of late nights, and meetings, and investing in technology I'll admit I don't entirely understand. You gotta believe me that when I first saw a movie I thought it was magic. That's how I am with new inventions. It's all magic to me." He sighed. Then, as if he'd made up his mind about something, stood. "So don't take my absence to mean I don't like you, Buddy."

"I don't, sir." I didn't mention how he'd totally seemed to forget who I was a moment earlier. Probably because I didn't want to think about it. I wanted to believe him.

"Good. Come with me. I have something to show you."

I stood and followed him out the door. I thought we were

heading for the elevator, but he turned down the hall past Miss Rodriguez's desk. I followed him to a small storage closet that he unlocked with a grin, and he pulled the chain for the dim dusty lightbulb in the ceiling. There were a couple novelty cans of bacon soup on a shelf to the side and a cutout of Alice Angel. Against the back wall was a pile of boxes stacked to the top, and that was what Mister Drew started to move aside.

"Help me out there, would you, Buddy?" he said, passing a box to me. It was large, but light. Almost like it was empty. I placed it to the side and took the next, and the next, and that's when I noticed a hole behind them. As we cleared the last box, Mister Drew turned to me with a finger to his lips and then motioned for me to follow him. He disappeared through the hole into the dark beyond.

I admit, I approached it carefully and with a bit of concern. I should just have trusted him, I guess, but it was such a strange thing to be doing. To just casually move some boxes in a closet and then walk through a giant hole in the wall. And getting closer I could hear strange sounds from the other side. They were hollow and echoey. Voices?

But I couldn't just stand there doing nothing. I thought about Dot. I thought about all the stuff I'd done already. I could do this. Besides, when your boss tells you to do something . . .

I stepped through the hole and out onto a small, wrought iron landing, kind of like a fire escape. I stared down between my feet. The floor was far below in the dark. I could see the shadows of gently swinging ropes below me.

Ahead was a catwalk and brightness in the distance. Mister Drew gave me a look and I followed him along it, holding on to the railings on either side and not looking down. I didn't really have a height thing, but maybe I had *a bit* of a height thing. The voices I'd heard got louder now, and I realized they were coming up to us from below, but I still kept staring straight ahead at Mister Drew's back and at what was around us. There were a lot of ropes now, and cables here too. A dark curtain ran along next to us.

We stopped.

"They close next weekend," he said quietly, and looked down. So I finally looked down again too. And that's when I got it.

We were standing above a stage. I stared down through the lighting rig to the stage below. Far beneath us, maybe fifty feet down, I could see two actors walking around on a set that looked like a fancy living room. It was neat because where we were standing we could see the top of the back wall of the set, so you could see both sides: the front part covered with fancy wallpaper with a large window cut out of it, and the back part plain plywood with wooden supports propping it up. The actors were under very bright lights that contrasted sharply with the darkness on the other side. In the shadows were two stagehands sitting on apple boxes, dressed in black and not doing much.

"I like watching them like this," said Mister Drew.

"Yeah, it's neat," I replied in the same quiet voice.

"Oh, it's more than neat, Buddy," he replied.

"It is?"

Mister Drew leaned on the catwalk railing, still staring down through the twisted maze of cables and ropes. "They have parts to play. They do it the same way every show. Every pattern they make on the stage is repeated." The audience laughed just then, a muffled wave against the short curtain in front of us. "Did you hear that?"

Of course I did. "Yeah."

"The audience laughs every time at that same part. They are under the spell. They don't know that they're going to laugh exactly at that point in the play, but they will. It's their fate." It was Mister Drew's turn to laugh.

It was interesting to listen to what he had to say. It was true. And a different way of thinking. A twisting kind of way that I wasn't really used to.

"Who's in control?" he asked me, turning then for the first time to look at me. I looked back at him. He was in shadow and his expression hard to read. I wasn't sure if the question was supposed to be answered, but I tried my best.

"The actors?" I asked.

Mister Drew shook his head and looked down again. "Not the actors, Buddy. They need to be told where to go. Remember?"

I remembered. "Okay, um. I guess then the person who tells them?"

"The director," said Mister Drew.

"Yeah, the director."

We watched the actors a bit more. One of them fell over an ottoman without spilling his drink, and then suddenly a trap-door opened under him and he vanished under the stage. The audience laughed and applauded.

"Joy. Fun. Pleasure. All of it is coordinated and carefully planned. Everyone knows this and everyone works together. It works because they trust the vision."

I nodded.

"You know what that is?" he asked me.

"What, 'vision'?" I replied.

"Yes."

"Sure."

"What is it?"

I looked at him and he was staring at me hard. "Oh, uh, it's having a dream, I guess. Wanting something and seeing it like it's real. Like when people talk about visions they've had, sometimes religious or sometimes they're sick and see things, and . . ." I stopped because I could tell I was rambling. I knew no one liked my rambling.

"Go on."

"But, uh, the way you're talking about it is like seeing something in your imagination and wanting to make it happen."

Mister Drew smiled then and snapped his fingers at me. "Exactly. Making your dream a reality."

"Dreams come to life," I said automatically. I'd seen it on the Bendy poster enough times.

"They do, Buddy. They do." He looked down at the stage again, so I did too. "But they don't happen without work. And ambition. You gotta fight for your dreams. Fight hard."

Now I couldn't tell if Mister Drew was talking to himself or not. But then he stopped talking entirely, so I didn't have to worry about which it was. At first his silence made me uncomfortable, but I got used to it and began to enjoy the fact I got to watch more of the play. I didn't know what was going on, or who the actors were pretending to be, or even why the audience laughed. But there was something really fascinating in watching from this angle. It also made me have that empty sort of feeling, that one where I realized that I'd missed out on something I didn't know I'd missed out on.

I'd never seen a play. I'd always thought the lights on Broadway and Times Square were enough. Kind of like a painting, I guess. But inside the buildings there was also magic. I'd never thought much about it. Until now.

Suddenly my whole body lurched forward, my hands losing their grip on the bar and my feet slipping from under me. I thought that I was going to fall to the stage. Crack my skull on one of the lights, land on the ground, my legs twisted under me. It was such a vivid thought that, for a moment, I thought it had happened. I screamed out, from fear and the pain that I wasn't actually feeling, and then the world came back into focus and I realized I was still on the catwalk. Mister Drew was laughing, really hard. I noticed then his hand gripping the back of my shirt. Holding on to me.

I looked down. The actors were looking up at me. Or at least into the darkness. The magic had stopped. Everything had ended. For that moment.

"Sorry, Buddy, terrible prank. I shouldn't have done it. But you see now what I mean?" asked Mister Drew, offering me his other hand and pulling me upright.

"What?" I asked. I was out of breath even though I hadn't gone anywhere. I was still trying to understand the nature of the prank.

"When everyone is working together it all goes smoothly. When one person doesn't, everything stops."

"Did you push me?" I asked.

"Nah. I yanked you around a little bit, all in fun, Buddy. Like an initiation. You know."

I didn't, but I felt better that it'd been a joke and he hadn't put me in danger, even though it felt like he had. It was kind of funny actually, now that I'd calmed down. I imagined I must have looked pretty silly thinking I was about to fall to my death and screaming like that. When I was safe.

So silly.

"I bought this theater," he said.

"You what?"

"This. All this is mine." He gestured with his arm at the dark space.

"That's impressive," was all I could think of saying.

He nodded and took a step toward me. "It's still a secret, so don't tell anyone. I gotta figure some stuff out, but everything's changing, Buddy. Everything." He placed a hand on my shoulder and looked at me intensely.

"That's a good thing," I said, but I kind of meant it as a question.

Mister Drew smiled and nodded. "Oh, yes, Buddy. It's a very good thing."

9

I couldn't believe at first I hadn't

been fired. Ms. Lambert couldn't quite believe it either, when I came back downstairs and sat back at my table.

"Well, I don't get it," she said, standing over me. "Guess he likes you, huh?"

I nodded.

She nodded too. "Okay, well, I get how it is. And you might have Mister Drew's trust, but it's going to take some time to earn mine," she said, clapping her hands together.

I nodded again.

"Right," she said. "Check in with Story and see if they have the new script."

I was up on my feet in a flash, ready to show that Mister Drew's faith in me wasn't misplaced. Ready to show Ms. Lambert that I wasn't someone she should be worried about. "Got it," I said. I immediately made for the elevator.

"Buddy!" she called out after me.

"Yeah?"

"You keep working on Cowboy Bendy," she said. "It better be worth all this." Her expression was as severe as ever, and yet finally I was getting my first art assignment. I was terrified at making it good since I couldn't even really make it in the first place, but I was so excited not to be fired and to get to draw that I couldn't help but grin wide.

"Yes, ma'am!"

The rest of the day was spent doing gofer duties, which I really didn't mind because I couldn't actually work on Cowboy Bendy. I was thrilled that I was finally going to get the chance to draw, to do more than just run around like this, but at the same time I couldn't do what my grandfather did, and wouldn't people notice the difference in ability if I started drawing my own stuff?

"So, you're in a bit of a pickle," said Dot after I'd explained it all. She took a sip of root beer and leaned back in her seat. I hadn't wanted to admit any of it to her, but she'd heard about my almost-firing and had demanded we go to the pub together again so she could pass me her Cowboy Bendy script and hear the whole story. Which I told her. I couldn't seem to keep stuff from her.

"Yeah," I said. "I need to practice, but I don't think I can get good overnight."

The door behind us swung open, and I glanced up to see Jacob, Richie, and a couple guys from Accounting come into the bar. I hunched my shoulders a bit. I didn't really want to be seen by them. I didn't know why. Maybe I was a little intimidated. They disappeared into the crowd by the bar and I looked up at Dot.

"So I've been looking into this Tom fellow," she said.

"Oh!" I'd forgotten I'd asked her about that.

"Yeah, so it's very interesting. He works for a company called Gent. Seems pretty high up in the company. It looks like he's working directly with Mister Drew on some kind of machine."

"With Mister Drew?"

"I don't know what it is, couldn't figure out *where* it is even. But I'm going to keep looking for it."

"What kind of machine?"

Dot shrugged and sipped her drink. "Maybe a more efficient way of filming cartoons?"

I nodded. "Maybe."

"Look at you two so cozy!" Jacob was suddenly sitting next to me, slamming his beer down so the foam slipped over the edge and splashed onto the table.

Dot rolled her eyes. "In this heat, I wouldn't want to be getting *cozy* with anyone. No offense, Buddy."

"Ain't that the truth," replied Jacob, taking off his hat and mopping the sweat on his brow with a paisley handkerchief. "So, Buddy," he asked, "how're you liking working at the studio?"

"It's been interesting," I replied.

"Well, I'll say it: I'm glad you weren't fired. And I'm glad you drew that picture. Because sometimes it's hard to get noticed. Trust me, I know. People will underestimate you at every turn, mac." He looked at Dot. "Right?"

"Absolutely." She nodded.

"If anyone knows what it's like to be ignored it's the woman, and the black man. Trust us on this one." He raised his glass to Dot and she clinked hers with his. It was as playful as I ever saw her get. But it wasn't actually playful in a way.

"You have a girl, Buddy?" Jacob asked after taking a swig.

"Nah," I replied.

"Really? A good-looking kid like you?"

"I'm not too focused on that stuff right now," I said. The fact was I wasn't focused on that stuff at all. Sure, there'd been a few girls in the neighborhood I'd been sweet on, but I didn't have the time to ask them on a date—didn't have the money to either. And now with this new job and everything . . . Besides, it felt really uncomfortable talking about this with work people. With any people.

"You can focus on more than one thing at once, you know," said Jacob.

"I know, I just . . . need to get some stuff in order." And I live at home with my ma. And my grandfather shares my bed. And I need to become a pro artist overnight.

"How's your dating life, then?" he asked, turning to Dot.

She didn't say anything, just looked at her drink.

"You look sad there, Ruby Slippers. Did I say something wrong?"

She laughed a little at that and looked at him. "Don't call

me that. And no, it's just I don't date. I'm not ready."

"Ready?" I said.

Dot sighed hard. "You two. Boys. Pushing, always asking questions. Don't like to answer them, but you love asking them."

"I'm sorry," I said. At this point the whole conversation had got away from me. I didn't really know what I was doing or supposed to say.

"Come on, Dot," said Jacob, nudging her with his elbow.

"I said no, Jacob," she said firmly, staring him down.

"Okay, okay, I know when I'm not wanted." He stood, picking up his beer, and took a swig. "See you two in the funny pages." He shook his head like we were both nuts, and then he slipped into the crowd back toward the table with the other guys.

Dot looked at me for a moment, then leaned her elbows on the table and hunched over a bit. "I don't like talking about that stuff."

"I don't blame you," I replied.

She took another pause, then a sip of soda. She looked back at me. "My husband died in the war," she said matter-of-factly.

"You were married?" I asked. I knew that wasn't the point. I also knew I shouldn't have been that surprised. Many of the girls in my neighborhood, the ones I'd grown up with, had already settled down and were keeping house. But there was something about Dot that just seemed like . . . well, not like them.

"Not for long. We were sweethearts in high school. Then he turned eighteen, they conscripted him. We married at the courthouse just before he had to leave." She swirled around the remains of her soda in the bottom of her glass slowly. "A month later he was dead. A month after that the war was over."

I didn't know what to say. I didn't know why she was sharing this with me. Especially after everything she'd said about boys pushing too much.

"My pa died in the war. Early on. In '42." It was all I could think about saying. Even if I didn't want to think about it in the first place.

She looked up at me then and gave me a sad smile. "I'm sorry, Buddy."

"I'm sorry for you too. Do you want to—"

"Nah, I don't want to talk about it right now."

I felt really awkward. I didn't know how to carry on with a conversation like things were normal. I didn't know if Dot wanted me to. I didn't know anything. How did someone just change a subject like this? Did you just . . . change it?

"So what do you think I should do?" I asked, giving it a shot.

Dot looked at me for a moment. Then: "You mean about Cowboy Bendy?"

I nodded, relieved we were on the same page. Relieved it had worked.

"I think you just need to practice. I think you should also ask your grandfather if he can teach you."

"I can't do that," I said, shaking my head and finishing my Coke with a gulp.

"Why not?"

"He barely speaks English."

"What does he speak?"

"Polish."

Dot thought about that. "I don't know if you have to speak the same language. I mean, it would be different if this was about writing, but art . . . it's universal. Couldn't he just, you know, show you?"

I shrugged. I didn't know. Maybe he could. But that wasn't the biggest problem. The biggest problem was that he was there at all. That he creeped me out, took up my space, that my ma hadn't even told me he was coming. That we had one more mouth to feed. That I resented him. It was hard asking favors of someone like that.

But maybe she was right.

Maybe it didn't matter how I felt about him.

Stick to your vision. Be ambitious. Dreams come to life.

Do what you have to do.

"I'll think about it. He just got to the States and he's all confused. He might not be able to help me even if I asked."

"You're Jewish, right, Buddy?" asked Dot.

I felt that very familiar tightness in my gut. That protective shield unfurl over my spine. I sat up a little straighter but tried to sound even more casual. "Yeah. Is that a problem?" I didn't sound casual. I sounded angry, and I knew it.

"Of course not," said Dot. "It's just, you said your grandfather was from Poland."

"We're Polish," I snapped back. Obviously we were.

Dot held up her hands. "Never mind. Sorry. I don't want to get personal."

"Well, I already told you my dad died, and that I'm Jewish, but yeah, let's not get personal." I couldn't not feel angry. I just knew she was judging me. I knew it. Like the bullies in the school yard when I was a kid. Like those same bullies all grown up. Calling me names as I walked through their neighborhood. I hated it.

Dot shook her head. "I get it. I'm sorry." She pushed her glass away from her across the table. "I'm going to go now." She stood up then, just like that. And then turned and was gone.

I felt bad. The defensiveness vanished and I was up on my feet chasing after her outside. She was already halfway down the block walking that fast way she did. I caught up finally and grabbed her shoulder. She whipped around and gave me a look of death.

"Oh," she said, her expression softening, "it's you."

"Look, I didn't mean to make you upset," I said.

"I know."

I looked at her.

She looked at me.

"Are you still angry with me?" I asked.

"I'm not angry at all. I feel bad. I upset you. I thought I should leave. Besides it's getting late." She looked at me like I was the one who was doing something strange.

"Oh, I just thought you'd stormed out."

"No."

No. Okay then.

I said good night and she said the same and that was the first time I learned about her directness.

Your directness.

You once said to me that you liked writing subtext in your scripts but had no time for subtext in real life. I always remembered that.

So just in case I haven't been clear yet, Dot, and following your always amazing lead, I'll just say it plain: You have to save them.

You have to stop him.

It was the weekend, not that that mattered much to Ma. She was sitting by the window at her sewing machine next to the kitchen table, putting together a suit jacket for Mr. Schwartz. I had to admit I was still getting used to the idea of taking the weekend off myself. I'd spent the last couple weeks doing chores for Ma instead, getting the groceries, paying the milkman, that sort of thing.

I was thinking about what Dot had said when my grandfather passed by with his worn jacket and hat on.

"Where are you going?" I asked.

He looked at me in that way he did.

"Where's he going?" I asked Ma.

She didn't look up from her work. "Probably the library."

I turned back and Grandpa had already opened the door. I just had this "it's now or never" feeling. "Hey, Grandpa, I'll come with you."

Ma did look up at that. She gave me a smile, and it was small but so full. It was a thank-you. I didn't get it, but she appreciated it.

I didn't bother putting on my button-up if we were going to the library. That was just up the block and everyone else would be in their undershirts too. It was too hot to care. I slipped on my shoes and held the door for him. He stared at me a little as he walked onto the landing. Then nodded.

As we stepped out into the thick midday air under a hot midday sun, I still wasn't really sure if I wanted to ask him for help. Obviously my gut thought it was a good idea, and Dot did say to trust your gut. But at the same time how would it even be possible for him to help me?

I reminded myself he had offered to "teach." That maybe I should respect that. But still.

We crossed the street to avoid the open fire hydrant spraying water on the local kids, and I never thought I would be one of those people to cross the street to avoid that. I guess that meant I was getting older.

"Fun," he said, pointing at the kids squealing and laughing in the water.

The library was a four-story brick building on the corner. A mom and her little girl were sitting on the steps leading up to it reading a book of nursery rhymes. The girl waved at me as

I walked by, and I waved back. Inside, the air was a little cooler thanks to fans in the ceiling that rotated slowly above us, and the tall white walls made of stone. It was a nice relief.

The quiet was also soothing. You couldn't even hear the hum of the city. It was like when Ma would turn off the radio when it was time to go to bed.

I followed my grandfather to the back of the stacks. He seemed to have a purpose. We made it to the children's section, and that's where he stopped to look through the collection. He carefully examined each book as he pulled it off the shelf, flipped open the cover and went through the pages, then carefully and neatly put it back where he found it. It was a time-consuming process but it was fascinating to watch.

He eventually collected a small pile of books. Three picture books (including a Curious George book) and Pippi Longstocking. It was when he looked at me and nodded, satisfied with his collection, that what he was doing finally clicked.

He was teaching himself English.

Of course.

If he could teach himself something so difficult, then I shouldn't be afraid to ask him. That's at least how my train of thought went.

"Grandpa?" I whispered, as we made our way to the librarian's desk.

He glanced in my direction.

"Could you teach me how to draw better?" He stopped walking and looked at me. "You know," I said, motioning with my hand, pretending I was drawing on a piece of paper. "Art."

He smiled. "Art."

"Yes. Could you help me?" I asked.

He didn't nod or say anything. He just placed the books on the checkout desk and said to the librarian behind it, "Keep for me?"

She nodded. "Certainly, Mr. Unger."

She knew him. Of course she did.

"Come," he said to me, and I followed him. This time he made his way to the stairs and we climbed them very slowly.

We climbed to the second floor, and we walked along the stacks and then stopped. We were in the art section. I should have known. Once again my grandfather carefully appraised the books, in no rush. He smiled at them and touched them as if he had a fond memory of each. Then he started to pull books off the shelf. And pass them to me. One after the other after the other.

The stack got heavy in my arms, and as I looked at the titles, I wasn't exactly sure why I was holding them unless I wanted to learn all about art history, which I didn't. Ancient Roman. Ancient Greek. Renaissance. Da Vinci. Monet. Not a single book on how to draw. Nothing like that.

Grandfather stopped and looked at me. Then he said, "Good." And turned toward the stairs.

"Grandpa, this is swell and all, but I don't really want to be an artist-artist. I just want to learn how to draw the cartoons." I said it all knowing he probably didn't understand.

"History. Good," he replied.

History good.

By the time we made it home I was a sweaty mess, but Grandpa was just starting. He sat at the kitchen table and looked at me. "Paper," he said.

So I grabbed the paper and pen and ink from our room and brought them to him.

He pushed over a thick, small book with "The History of Art" written on the cover. I opened it. The writing was small and densely packed into each page. It looked impossible to read. I was bored just flipping the pages.

"Read and practice. Today, circle." He reached over to one of the larger, glossier books and opened it. He found a page with a glossy photo of a painting. A woman sat, looking kind of depressed, holding on to a puppy in her lap. My grandfather looked at me and pointed at the painting. Then he started to re-create the painting on the page with circles. And ovals. And other geometric shapes. She had no facial features, hands, or anything. It was almost like she was a shadow of herself.

"You see?" he said.

"Ah, circles," said Ma, looking over my shoulder. I looked up at her. "Starting with the basics." I nodded. "Water?" she asked.

I nodded again.

As she went to the sink she said, "You know, I always said that you'd inherited your artistic ability from your grandfather."

"To who?" I asked, watching my grandfather draw.

"To everyone," she replied, placing two cloudy glasses of water on the table.

"Not to me," I said. "I don't remember you saying much about him ever."

"I did," she replied. "Maybe you don't remember."

"You didn't." I was feeling annoyed again. Reminded of how she had just invited this stranger to stay with us without even talking to me about it. Without even warning me about it.

I heard her sigh. "I'm going to buy groceries for dinner." She turned on her heel and left.

"Buddy," said my grandfather, and I looked back then, shocked. I'd never heard him say my name before. "Okay, work now."

He passed me some paper and pushed over the book, flipping to another page. It was strange seeing these colorful paintings in black and white. They felt like only half the story.

"Work."

He passed me the pen and looked at my page closely. I finally nodded.

"Circles?" I said.

"Yes. Circles."

10

It was fun. It was. Learning from Grandpa. Sure it was frustrating, and sure sometimes even boring, everything was so technical, I didn't get to draw what I wanted to. But, yeah, it was also fun. And the more excited he got when I learned something new, the better. In a few days he added more to the lessons. We were still doing circles but moved on to lines. Lines that helped with perspective. Don't ask me how he knew that word, he just did.

We drew a buncha lines that ran beside one another to the middle of the page. Then we drew things like rectangles for buildings or cones for trees along the lines. We made them shorter as we got closer to the center of the page. And it worked! It looked like the "trees" were getting farther away.

"Pyramid," Grandpa had said. "Perspective."

He was pointing to a painting by da Vinci. Of the Virgin Mary sitting on some rocks holding Baby Jesus.

I nodded. "Pyramid," I said back.

We kept practicing after work together, on the weekends,

and during my off times at the studio I practiced too. I didn't have any more Cowboy Bendys to give to Ms. Lambert, and I could feel her sometimes looking at me, judging me, doubting me. I really wanted to prove myself to her. Almost more in a way now than to Mister Drew. I felt like she didn't think I had saved my job because I deserved it. I felt like she thought that Mister Drew just liked me. A boys' club thing.

I thought that because she'd said it once. Just "the old boys' club" and not really at me, but I heard it. And thought about it. Thought about how Mister Drew had dismissed her that day in his office. I was so confused. Which was it? Did he respect talent or not? Or maybe he did, but he was more forgiving toward people who looked like him? Who *reminded* him of himself?

No, no. I didn't want to think that way.

Anyway, I figured it was time to start actually doing some Bendys and had planned on asking Grandpa at home to help. I was feeling excited, and was rushing through the lobby at the end of the day when I heard a familiar voice: "Buddy!"

I skidded to a stop and turned. Mister Drew was standing by the front desk, a big grin on his face.

"Sir!" I said, shocked. I instantly made my way over to him.

"Where you rushing off to so fast, have a date?" he asked with a laugh.

I felt my face get hot like it did whenever people asked personal questions like that. "Oh no, sir, don't have a sweetheart."

Mister Drew nodded at that. "Probably for the best. Right now it's important for us to focus on the work."

"Yes," I said. I supposed. That wasn't really it, but it was also it. When would I have the time?

"Have something for you. Apologies for the delay, but gave you a little something extra to make up for it." He handed me a white piece of paper.

I looked at it.

My paycheck.

My first paycheck.

It'd been three weeks and, yeah, I guess it was late, but I'd been so wrapped up in everything going on with drawing, and lying, and then doing my best to cover up for the lying that I guess I'd kind of forgot. The reason for all of this in the first place.

The money.

Forty bucks.

Forty whole dollars.

In my hand.

"Hope it's enough; we never actually talked about how much Schwartz paid you. Good lesson, Buddy. Always talk numbers."

Always talk numbers.

Forty bucks.

I felt like I couldn't breathe.

"It's good," I managed to squeeze out.

"Good!" replied Mister Drew. He gave me a hearty slap on the back and I coughed. "Come on, we're celebrating!"

We are?

Without even waiting for me to say anything he made his way to the door and I followed him outside into the blazing heat. Somehow it didn't seem totally overwhelming for once. Somehow it felt kind of good.

I caught up to Mister Drew and stepped in beside him as he walked fast along the sidewalk. "Where are we going?" I asked.

"To celebrate," he replied, grinning again.

Yes, but how and where, I wanted to know. I didn't ask it again. I wasn't supposed to. I just had to trust him. And I did, trust him.

We walked along a couple blocks and turned south. Eventually we came to a restaurant with a bright red awning. The word "Sardi's" was written on it.

"I think I've heard of this place," I said as we passed through the doors into the dark red interior.

"I should hope so," replied Mister Drew with a laugh.

"Ah, Mister Drew, usual table?" asked the host at the stand.

"Absolutely," replied Mister Drew, and as he reached out to shake his hand I noticed a flash of a dollar bill pass between them.

"Right this way!" he said with a bright smile.

We followed him through toward the back of the restaurant and to a table for two right under a wall full of caricatures of famous people. "That's Sinatra!" I said as I sat down.

"Someday, kid, that'll be us," said Mister Drew.

"Well, you at least," I replied. I didn't notice how Mister Drew reacted to that, I was too wide-eyed looking around. There were drawings of famous people covering the walls everywhere. And I was pretty sure there were some actual famous people sitting in some of the booths too, not that I recognized them. Men in suits, women in dresses, having dinner before seeing a show.

I looked up above my head at the caricatures there. I recognized Lauren Bacall. It was really neat. I didn't actually have this desire to be in one of the drawings, but the idea of having one of my drawings up there? For everyone to see? That made my stomach get excited.

A waiter in a red jacket approached us. "Drinks, gentlemen?"

"Get me an old-fashioned," said Mister Drew. "Buddy?"

He looked at me and I could tell if I wanted to I could have ordered the same. But I just couldn't. "A soda?" I asked the waiter. "Coke?"

The waiter smiled at me like I'd just made the most perfect choice anyone had ever made before and swooped off to get our drinks.

"Buddy, you gotta start drinking like a man," said Mister Drew.

"I, uh, I have some stuff I have to do when I get home. Gotta have a clear head," I replied. I found it weird. How did what I drink make me more of a man or not? Wasn't I just a man because I was one?

Still, somehow I felt bad.

The waiter was back with our drinks and gone just as quickly.

"How's Lambert treating you?" asked Mister Drew, picking up his glass and taking a sip. He closed his eyes and sighed. "That's beautiful," he said to the drink.

I sipped my Coke through a straw.

"Oh, she's swell. Letting me work on Cowboy Bendy," I replied.

"Good, good. Well, if she gets too big for her britches you let me know. She can be a handful," he replied.

I didn't think that about her exactly. Just serious.

"Well, I believe you have great potential, Buddy, I really do. I see how hard you work. The way you dash around the studio. Bet you see all kinds of things." He gave me a wink.

"Uh, not really, sir, I just like getting the job done."

I didn't exactly know what he meant by "lots of things" but I took a long sip of Coke, trying to calm my tightening throat. It wasn't a lie anyway, I hadn't seen anything. Just heard things. Heard conversations.

About machines.

And ink.

Mister Drew leaned forward across the table, kind of like he was going to tell me a secret. "You see anything . . . interesting . . . or something you think I should know about, you let me know."

"Sure." Of course then I felt like I should just tell him

everything in that moment. Especially about Tom and Sammy. But that would involve Dot. And she liked secrets. Felt that it was necessary. She had to have a good reason even if I didn't understand it. But in this quick moment I just knew I couldn't tell him.

Not yet.

"Good," said Mister Drew. He leaned back as the waiter approached our table.

"Ready to order?" he asked.

I looked at the menu I hadn't even opened yet. "Uh . . ."

"We'll have the steaks, medium rare, and don't skimp on the fingerling potatoes," announced Mister Drew, handing back his menu. The waiter laughed like Mister Drew had made the best joke he'd ever heard. "And another," said Mister Drew, tapping his empty glass.

"Another Coke for you, sir?" asked the waiter, turning to me.

I was only half done with the one I had.

Mister Drew laughed. "Come on, Buddy, live a little!"

"Okay," I told the waiter.

"Very good, sir."

And he was gone in one of his swoops again.

As we waited for the food Mister Drew started talking. I don't mean talking like we'd been having our conversation before. But *talking* talking. The way he had up in the theater. The way he had the day he hired me. I was starting to get used to it, listening to him go on. He had a lot of personal life philosophies. He had a need to share it. I could listen, even if I couldn't always understand what he was going on about.

"It's why I wrote the book. It's all an illusion, see. Life. Living. It's all in here." He tapped at the side of his head and took a long sip of the new old-fashioned that had materialized in front of him. "People think that there are rules, but rules are things that are man-made. Trying to keep society in order. That's not bad, but it's also not something people like us have to worry about."

He always did that, said "us." I wasn't sure I was people like us. But I liked the sound of it.

"I don't get it," I replied.

The steaks arrived just then and I stared openmouthed. I didn't mean to, and when the waiter laughed I clamped my jaw shut, feeling embarrassed. But they were huge. The biggest pieces of meat I'd ever seen. This could have easily fed me, Ma, and Grandpa for one dinner.

"Looks fantastic," said Mister Drew to the waiter, who beamed and then left. Then he turned to me and smiled. "Don't be scared, Buddy, dig in!"

"I'm not scared," I replied as I picked up my fork and knife. But honestly, I kind of was.

I cut a piece and ate it. It was the most incredible taste I'd had in a very long time. Soft and juicy, just the right amount of flavoring. It seemed almost wrong that food could taste this good and not everyone had the chance to experience it. No. Not almost wrong. It was wrong.

"They say rules are meant to be broken," said Mister Drew,

chewing hard. "But I say, why not rewrite the rules? Why break them when you can control them? It's all about having control over our own destinies."

I nodded as I scooped up the potato. It tasted different, had a zing to it.

"Horseradish," replied Mister Drew without me having to ask. "Amazing, isn't it?"

"Yes," I replied with my mouth full.

And then he went on. It was a dinner where Mister Drew wanted to talk deep stuff I didn't really understand and where all I wanted to do was to taste. I wanted to savor. Keep it all in my memory. I barely listened to him, honestly. I heard the word "vision" again. And more stuff about illusions. But after his third old-fashioned I was pretty sure even Mister Drew wasn't really keeping up with what he was trying to say.

By the time we hit the cheesecake for dessert, I didn't think my stomach could hold any more food. And I certainly didn't think my brain could hold any more of Mister Drew's speeches.

Finally the marathon was over and we were both leaning back in our chairs. Mister Drew had stopped speaking, I had stopped eating. We both just kind of sat there. Full.

"Now *this* is living," said Mister Drew.

"Or a good illusion of it," I replied, not really thinking. But I guess all the stuff he'd been saying to me had managed to get into my brain somehow.

Mister Drew pointed at me and started to laugh, hard.

Harder than I'd ever seen anyone laugh before. He leaned forward and bent over and was laughing so hard tears were coming out of his eyes, but the sound of laughter wasn't. "Oh my, oh, Buddy," he said, wiping his face with the napkin. "You're good, kid. You're a good one."

I smiled too, though I felt more unnerved than anything.

The waiter approached with a thin black book.

"Whenever you're ready, sir." He handed the book to Mister Drew.

"Great, yes. Buddy?" said Mister Drew, extending his hand over the table.

"Yes?" I asked.

"You have to sign the check over," he explained.

I stared at him. He stared back.

Then it hit me.

I slowly pulled my paycheck from my pocket as the waiter handed me a pen. "Uh, how much is it?" I asked.

Mister Drew opened the little black book. "With tip, let's say fifteen even."

I stared. Fifteen dollars. For one meal.

"Money comes with responsibility, Buddy. That's how it works."

"Yes . . . s-sir," I stammered, still staring at the number "fifteen."

"Come on, kid, we both have places to be," said Mister Drew. The tone of his voice had gotten serious now, almost annoyed.

I slowly took the pen from the waiter and signed the back of the check. I handed it to him. "Very good, sir," said the waiter. "I'll bring you your change."

I stared back at Mister Drew, my heart pumping fast. I hoped he couldn't see the panic in my eyes.

"Now that's what I call a celebration, right, kid?" he asked with a wide smile.

"Yes, sir," I replied softly.

"Now don't go spending like this every time you get your pay." He laughed. "That's not responsible."

"Yes, sir," I said again. I could barely say the words.

Mister Drew looked over his shoulder. I could tell he was getting impatient. He sighed hard. "Look, Buddy, do you mind if I head back to the office? I'm meeting someone in half an hour."

He was just leaving me? I mean, I guess why not, right? Dinner was done. I didn't need help getting home or anything. "Oh yeah, sure."

Mister Drew threw his napkin on the table and stood with a sharp nod. "Excellent. Keep up the good work, kid. I'll see you tomorrow." And with that it was his turn to swoop away, shaking hands with the waiter and the hostess as he left.

Everyone laughing.

I really didn't know what was so funny.

"Your change, sir," said the waiter, coming over and handing me the little black book.

"Thanks."

I opened it. Twenty-five bucks cash. It was still a lot of money. But it had been more. Much more.

I shoved the bills into my pocket and got out of that restaurant as fast as I could. Took the subway home, keeping my hand in my pocket. Didn't need anyone swiping the rest.

I got home just as Ma was clearing the table. Grandpa smiled at me from the sink and waved a soapy hand in my direction.

"Buddy! Thought you'd be home for dinner," Ma said when she saw me.

"Me too," I replied. *Buck up, Buddy, you can't let them know how guilty you're feeling.* I looked at the dusty curtain, the pile of dirty dishes, the old daybed that Ma slept on. Nope, that wasn't helping the guilt. "Uh, Mister Drew took me out to celebrate. I got paid today."

"Finally!" said Ma. She smiled at me. "I was getting worried."

"Yeah, me too. Anyway, here." I quickly put the pile of crumpled bills on the table.

"Oh wow, Buddy," said Ma, staring at it.

That made me swallow, hard. "Yeah, twenty-five bucks. It'll be more though, now that he trusts me." A lie. It'll be more now that I won't be having any fancy dinners. "It's all yours."

Ma picked up the cash carefully, smoothing out each dollar. She held out a ten for me to take. "You need something, new clothes. Maybe take one of your new friends for a piece of pie."

I wanted to run away I was so ashamed.

"No, Ma, please. Not this time. Maybe next time," I said. And then I went to my room as fast as I could. Hid inside. My heart wasn't racing but it was hurting.

It was a kind of shame I'd never felt before. I was so angry at myself. And at the world too. All those people in that restaurant, they could all afford to eat there, weren't having an episode because of one meal. It wasn't fair. It just wasn't fair.

Never again, I told myself. Not until at least I could afford it actually. Not until I could take Ma, buy her a fancy dress. Take Grandpa too, of course. Get him a new suit. A new long-sleeved shirt since he liked them so much.

Never again.

Until.

It was because of the pipes.

I know that now. My little corner of the Art Department that no one wanted to sit in. The one far away from any light source. It wasn't just that it was small and cramped. It was that the pipes in the building ran up the wall and overhead. They made a clanging sound when the temperature changed or when a valve was turned somewhere. But it wasn't something I thought I should find annoying. After all, our apartment was nothing but slow creaking noises, the constant adjusting of the building's foundation. I always kind of thought when I was little that the apartment was alive, that it was breathing and sighing, cold in the winter and sweating in the summer.

So the pipes making the odd noise as I sat and worked in my corner that night really didn't even make me blink. Didn't make me look up.

Until they did.

It started with a bang. Like the saying. But this time literally. I was hunched over, working on perspective. Drawing lots of lines. It wasn't going too well; it had been a long day and I was tired. But I was determined. I'd stayed late after everyone else had left. Determined to get this right. And every time I got a little tired or bored, I had this vision of Mister Drew pushing me over the edge of the catwalk. Yeah, maybe that wasn't exactly the best thing to see, and maybe folks would say he had a strange way of motivating staff, but I sure as heck didn't think he'd meant it that way. After all, we'd gone out to dinner last week, talked like real friends. It was just a joke.

That's all.

But still, it did work. It'd shaken me up, refocused me. And so there was a moment I was drifting, my eyes getting a little heavy, when suddenly I imagined that I was falling toward the floor of the stage, and at the exact moment I hit it, a loud, force-ful *bang!* clanged over my head. It threw me back so far in my chair I almost tipped over. My heart was pounding, and as the shadows in the Art Department became clear again in my vision, I really couldn't tell if I'd imagined the sound or if it had been real.

Until it happened again.

I stood up instinctively. This wasn't a furnace feeling frus-trated. This was something else. What it was, though, I had no idea.

Well, the one thing I did know was that it was none of my business. So I sat back down and focused on my paper.

That's when the moaning started.

It wasn't like wind in trees. Or like the creak of floorboards when a neighbor needs to use the bathroom. It was like an animal, like when a starving dog howls in the alley. But not like that exactly. Like that, but also like when a cat sees an enemy and releases that sound from deep inside its gut.

And maybe also the hint of a single low note played on a violin.

It was not like anything I'd heard before.

And I was curious.

I also remembered what Mister Drew had said. That taking initiative was important. It was late, dark-outside-in-the-summer late. Others had gone home, and Ms. Lambert had to turn the lights back on when she realized I was still here. I was doing it on purpose, of course. To show Mister Drew and everyone that I had drive. And with that in mind, if I was the only one left in the building and something strange was going on in Mister Drew's studio, this studio that meant so much to him, then surely it was my duty to investigate.

I sat for a quiet moment, listening. Then there was that determined banging noise again and I was up on my feet. I wasn't going to overthink this, I was just going to do it. Even if it creeped me out a little.

I wasn't exactly sure where to start, but I figured the furnace room was as good a place as any, and I made my way over to the elevator. As I descended into the basement, I realized just how alone I was. Each floor was empty, a single light lit, deep shadows otherwise. Maybe this was too ambitious. Maybe I had stayed too late.

Too late.

The basement was pitch-black and I had to feel along the wall for the light switch. The knot in my stomach eased a bit when the hall lit up, looking very normal. And I felt more confident as I walked toward the furnace room.

I'd been there once before, to seek out Wally the janitor because one of the toilets was overflowing. Wally had set up a makeshift kind of office down here, so that's where you found him if he wasn't making rounds. But it was after hours now, so of course when I tried the door handle, it was locked. I hadn't really thought this through.

There was a loud bang again. I looked up, and only after did I realize that I'd gone too deep. It seemed the sound wasn't coming from the furnace after all. Which was good news, seeing as I couldn't get access to it. Instead, it sounded like it was just above me, one floor up. And almost to confirm that thought, there was another *bang* right over my head. Some dust floated down toward me from the boards in the ceiling.

A wail snaked its way down to me now. Like the moan, but more distressed. It sounded far less like an issue with plumbing and far more like an issue with something living. That made the hairs on my arms stand up, but it also spurred me to action even more. If this was someone in trouble, not just a pipe acting up, then I needed to hurry. I needed to help.

I flicked off the switch as I leapt back into the elevator. I felt nervous watching the walls drop down slowly as I rose up. As the floor of the next level materialized, I noticed my breathing was shallow. And when the elevator lurched to a stop, I was already wondering how sure I was of my plan. But I stepped out into the dark hallway and flicked on a switch. Again, the brightness made me feel a little less unsure.

The wail came floating toward me again. It sounded like it was coming from farther down the hall. Knowing that I was on the right track made my stomach flip. I couldn't be sure if it was fear or excitement.

Probably fear. There was something about being on the Music level that would not, could not, ever make me feel anything other than uneasy.

There was a loud thud. I waited. Then the moaning began again.

Well, I was definitely on the right floor this time.

Wasn't sure that was a good thing.

As I followed the sound I remembered my first time down here, lost in a maze of hallways. When I turned a corner and came upon a set of stairs heading downward, I felt a sense of dread pour over me.

Hanging at the bottom of the stairs was a sign with the word "Infirmary" written on it. An infirmary? Didn't know the studio had one.

I walked slowly down the stairs as they creaked beneath my feet and into the Infirmary's foyer.

The room was fairly large with hard wooden chairs, a bed off to the corner, and a desk covered with charts against the wall. The walls were generally bare except for a yellowing poster placed without much thought near the waiting area. It was a picture of Bendy dressed as a doctor, Alice Angel in a nurse's uniform, and Boris the Wolf lying on a stretcher, with the title "Bedpans and Bedlam" written across it in that typical Bendy cartoon font.

Crash.

This time louder and coming from the hall upstairs. That shook me back into focus. I didn't know what was more unnerving, the sound itself or having no idea what the sound could possibly be. I hoped it was just some wonky plumbing. I really hoped it wasn't trespassers. I wasn't much of a tough guy, didn't think I could fend anyone off.

Still. I followed the sound. I immediately switched on the lights for the hall and saw a set of doors running along each side. I waited. And waited. But of course now, when I needed it, there was no sound of clanging, no wail. No nothing.

I decided the only thing for it was to check out each room. If they were unlocked. Didn't trust they would be. But the first door opened, revealing a small office with some desks and a chair.

I checked two more rooms, each the same. Then there was a bigger office. This one had a couple of framed diplomas on the wall, and now I was wondering who it belonged to.

I closed the door behind me. It made a loud sound, louder than I expected, and then, right away, I heard it. The wail again. But this time it was more like a cry. As if whoever it was had heard me. Was alerting me.

It was toward the end of the hall.

Behind a door.

With two long pieces of wood crossing over the top of it making an "X." Like the door was being protected from a storm or something. Except of course this door was on the inside of the building.

Suddenly something threw itself against the door. It shook. There was a large bang, and a shadow appeared and then disappeared in the crack beneath the door.

Definitely someone was being kept inside. Or was it . . . something? I noticed I'd been holding my breath and I let it all out now, gulping for air after I did.

Something? Like an animal? Like a . . . ghost?

That was stupid. I just needed to see it with my own eyes, know that whatever it was made perfect sense. Stop my imagination from making things into a bigger deal than they were.

The wail began again, this time definitely coming from behind the door. Up close there was something to it that felt different. Almost sad, almost like crying. But not human crying. Animal crying. It sounded helpless, and I felt bad for it. About as bad as I felt scared of it.

I reached down slowly and tried the door handle. It was locked. Of course it was. Who would keep a door unlocked with something like that behind it?

The lock should have been a sign. Not even a sign, really. It wasn't magic, it wasn't a message from a higher power. It was a locked door. And a locked door means "Keep out."

Unless you have the key.

I thought about Dot. I thought about her key.

It didn't seem likely that a copy of the key to *this* door would just be lying around anywhere. Especially not when all the other doors were unlocked. This was a room you weren't *supposed* to get into. I wondered. I'd never actually asked her, but the fact that Dot could just unlock a room in the basement, and then a storage closet, seemed to mean that this was one of those keys that could open many locks: a master key.

There were a lot of thoughts running through my head in the following moments. There were worries, and, of course, that feeling that I shouldn't be doing this, but at the same time—I can't tell you why—I felt this drive. I didn't even feel like it had anything to do with Mister Drew anymore. I needed to sniff this out.

As I found myself in the Story Department, going through Dot's desk, I figured she'd be impressed with me and wouldn't mind me doing this. She'd probably have encouraged me if she had been here. Probably would have brought the key along, just in case a situation like this happened. And there it was. In her bottom drawer in the pages of a copy of *The Complete Works of Sir Arthur Conan Doyle*.

I don't remember how I made it back to the door with the "X" across it. I don't remember the thoughts I had. Maybe I once remembered them, but the way my mind is now, all mixed up, I don't really know.

I just know that I was there.

Outside the door.

With the key.

Whatever it was inside heard me again because once more it threw itself at the wood and seemed to shake the whole hallway. The wailing was more insistent now.

I fit the key in the lock, and *bam!* Again, it threw itself against the door, threatening to shatter the whole thing and shaking me to the core. I swallowed hard.

I turned the key.

Click.

Silence. Not even the wailing. Nothing.

I took in a deep breath, turned the door handle, and pushed. The door creaked open a crack, and I pushed harder until I just decided to go for it and shoved the thing wide open.

I immediately flicked on the light switch.

I stood there in the doorway, staring into an empty room. It was like a mini-surgery. And everything was all over the place. Garbage on the floor, the bin knocked to one side. Strange surgical tools were lying splayed across the counter, and a wooden chair broken into pieces was in the corner.

What there didn't seem to be was . . . anyone or anything.

"Hello?" I said. That's the thing people tend to say, I've noticed, when they are unsure entering a place. Even if maybe getting a "hello" back is not really something you want.

At this moment I wasn't sure what I wanted. But the empty room was definitely not on the list.

I entered the room cautiously and then, quickly, checked

behind the door because that's always where people hide, behind the door. But no one was there. No one was anywhere. So I stood just in front of the open door, confused, alone, and feeling even more uneasy. I felt a shiver go up my back, like a cold hand was slowly walking its fingers up my spine.

That's when the lights dimmed. Or I shouldn't exactly say "dimmed." I'd say it was more like shadows began spilling into the room. They started slowly, so I thought maybe the light-bulb was about to go out, but then I looked down and saw darkness seeping in around my feet. I picked my foot up, think-ing it was something wet, but it was just a shadow.

Just a shadow.

I looked up and watched as it crept up the walls. Along the ceiling. Covering the room in dripping blackness. Like a room full of spilled ink.

I turned around to look into the hall, and sure enough the blackness was oozing its way out the door.

I held my breath and stood very still. I was in a state of frozen panic. I'd never seen anything like this, and I didn't think anyone else probably had either. I didn't know what it meant or how it was happening, but I did know one thing.

It felt threatening. Dangerous.

Like the dripping shadows were evil itself.

I don't know how to explain what evil feels like. I just felt it. I just knew.

My blood ran cold.

All the light went out. In the room. In the hallway. The

shadows had won and I could barely see the doorframe, only a few feet in front of me.

I should have just left.

But fear held me rooted to the spot. Fear of the darkness. Fear of the shadows.

And a growing crawling fear. Tickling at the back of my neck.

Fear that something was in the room with me.

A soft watery breathing. Quiet and calm, but distinct. Somewhere behind me. And now I could hear the sound of scraping across the floor too, like a dragging, halting, limping footstep.

Then silence.

There was a sudden crash as something landed on the counter behind me, then the tinkling of metal hitting the floor. *The surgical tools*, I thought. Sharp, precise blades on the floor. Still I couldn't move. I had the thought that if I didn't move, if I didn't make a sound, maybe whatever it was wouldn't see me.

The scraping against the floor began again. It got louder as whatever it was got closer. And then, as I stood there trying to be invisible, I could feel its presence. Not just hear it. I could *feel* it just behind me. It leaned in.

Hot wet breath against my cheek.

And then a different kind of breathy sound. Quick inhalations.

It was smelling me.

I wasn't invisible. I needed to run. I needed to run faster than I'd ever run in my life.

Come on, Buddy, run.

Run!

I moved toward the door, uprooting one of my feet like I was pulling it out of thick mud. I reached with my arm for the doorframe, to try to pull myself farther. I didn't understand; I wasn't physically stuck. But my mind was making my body act that way.

The thing behind me made a strange grunting noise then, as if it had realized something. I felt it pull away from me.

There was a sudden weight on my back, pushing me forward, followed by the sound of heavy footsteps running past me. I'd been shoved and fell hard to the ground. It had the same force that I'd seen against the door, and it knocked the wind right out of me. But I didn't stay face to floor for long. I was up quick. Finally my mind unstuck my feet and I ran out into the hall after the sound of footsteps.

In a daze I looked up and down. One side was a dead end. The other was the corridor that led back to the waiting area. There was nothing. I ran down toward the main desk and skidded to a stop in front of it.

Again.

Nothing.

It was then that I noticed the brightness around me. The lack of inky shadow. I turned around and sure enough the hall was brightly lit too. Panting slightly, I walked slowly back to the room. No shadows.

Nothing.

I rubbed my hands together, realizing now they stung

from the fall, and noticed the torn knee in my trousers. Now I was one shirt and two sets of trousers down. I only had the shirt on my back that was clean and put together enough for work. That shouldn't have bothered me just then, out of all things. But it did.

A wave of exhaustion wrapped my fear up in a hug.

Wandering through New York City at night, my only thought was to get home. Staring into the dark shadows down alleys and through grated storefronts, I felt a sense of dread unlike anything I'd ever known. I didn't understand what had just happened. Nothing had been in that room and yet something had been breathing on me. Had pushed me.

Had it been a trick of the mind? Was I that tired? Had I fallen? Had I tripped over myself? It wouldn't have been the first time. "Clown feet," they'd teased me in school.

But what about the sounds? The rattled door? The growing shadows? That had been real. More than real. Those shadows were alive, I was pretty sure. Breathing, existing.

It wasn't a dream. It wasn't a lie. I had heard sounds. I had seen the door shake. And I had been pushed to the floor. All of that had happened. I knew it had. I wasn't going to doubt my mind.

I was so sure of my mind back then.

I remember that feeling.

It's almost like I'm feeling that feeling again.

I walked all the way home. It took me just over an hour, but I needed it. I needed the time to settle my nerves, to get into that familiar rhythm, to see other people just being people and not being nightmares. The shadows stalked me, but I was a fast walker. And by the time I got home, the dread was very small and the exhaustion had taken over. This was good. I just needed to sleep.

I climbed up the stairs and slumped into our darkened apartment. Everyone had gone to bed. Good. I didn't feel like talking with my grandfather or trying to make Ma feel like everything was okay.

I carefully opened the door to my room so that I didn't wake the old man. Lying there on his side of the bed with the streetlight illuminating his face, he looked almost like a corpse. I wondered if he was breathing. I couldn't help myself—I held a hand over his nose and mouth and felt a slight warm air against it.

Thank goodness for that. I sat down on my side of the bed, facing the closed door, and had an image again of the locked door at the studio. No. I shook my head; I wasn't thinking about that anymore that night. I slowly pulled the suspenders from my shoulders and rolled them back, arching my neck and hearing a very satisfying crack.

I sighed.

Then something grabbed me hard from behind.

I leapt up with a cry and turned to see my grandfather sitting up, staring at me with those hollow eyes, wide and haunting. His mouth was open in what looked to be fear or anguish.

"What?" I asked a little too loudly, but my heart was racing fast. "What is it?"

He raised his hand slowly and pointed. Pointed right at me.

"Grandfather, it's me. It's Buddy. Daniel." I placed my hand to my chest and tapped it. "It's just me. Your grandson."

He kept pointing, his index finger shaking slightly. His expression stayed frozen.

I bent over to try to, what? To comfort him? I thought maybe he couldn't see too great, so if he could see me close up . . . "See, it's just me."

With another sudden movement he was holding me by my collar with both hands. His speed amazed me. He was pulling at my shirt. I could hear the seams along the shoulder starting to rip. "Stop it, Grandfather, stop it!" Pulling back only made it worse, and his long skeletal fingers only grabbed tighter. "Stop it!"

"Off!" he said hoarsely.

"What?"

He managed to finally pass a button through a button hole.

"You must see, you must see." He was determined now, but I finally understood and I placed my hands over his shaking ones.

He wouldn't let go and as I tried to stand upright, I relented and unbuttoned my shirt as I did. He kept pulling at me until finally I could flail my arms out of my sleeves, disentangling myself from the fabric and staggering back toward the door.

Grandfather held the shirt in his lap and looked at it.

I stared at him, wide-eyed, in my yellowing undershirt.

"What is wrong with you, old man?" I wanted to shout it but didn't want to wake Ma, so I whispered it through a hiss.

"Look," said my grandfather. I looked down at myself. All I saw was me. And the hole in the knee of my trousers.

"No. *Koszula*."

I looked up. He held my shirt bundled in his lap, and then with aged shaking hands and pencil-thin fingers, he held my shirt up for me to see.

And I saw.

And I stared.

"Look," said my grandfather.

The light from outside shone through the shirt, making it see-through. Making it so I could see the back of the shirt easily. So that I could make out the dark shadow imprint on it.

I reached out and took the shirt from him. He let me have it easily.

"You see," said my grandfather, sounding satisfied and lying back against the pillow.

A handprint.

Exactly where I had been pushed.

On the back of my shirt.

A large, black, ink-stained handprint.

Today I didn't know what this was.

Today I looked at these pages and forgot why it was here. What this object was supposed to be. It confused me.

I had to dig deep into my mind.

The five senses:

Touch: rough edges to pages.

Smell: ink and paper.

Taste: not tasty at all.

Sound: hollow quiet.

Sight: words on pages.

Words on pages. Buddy. Dot. Ma. Grandpa.

Joey Drew. My story.

This isn't just my story, it's your story too, Dot. I wish I could tell it from your point of view sometimes. I wish I knew why you believed me and sought me out that first time. I wish the answer was more than just your "gut."

I wish I understood you the way you seemed to understand me.

Maybe it was all a lie.

But you were never a liar. That was the whole thing, wasn't it? You chose not to lie.

People can make that choice.

I wish I knew why you believed me when I told you about the Infirmary. About the creature in the darkness. About my shirt. I'd been stupid not to bring it in to work the next day with me, but it hadn't mattered because you believed me. It wasn't just some dark fairy tale.

It was real.

You came with me to the Infirmary hallway at lunch. I showed you the room. There was nothing there, of course, but that didn't make you not believe me. It just made you want to investigate more.

You, Dot, always asked questions.

She really did. In case this is someone else. In case this isn't her reading this. She was great at asking questions.

"What about Sammy and Tom?" she asked, quickly pocketing her master key after I handed it back to her. She didn't seem to mind at all I'd taken it, but maybe it was because she was so interested in what I'd found.

"What about them?"

"What about that conversation you overheard? About ink?" I shook my head, I wasn't sure what to think. "Come on, Buddy. These guys are being secretive about ink in this odd way, and then you end up with an ink-stained handprint on your back. Might be no connection, but does it really feel like there isn't? I don't think so."

True.

There was something I hadn't told her. Because it made me sort of uncomfortable. I didn't totally trust what I'd seen and I hated jumping to conclusions, looking stupid. But if anyone would listen to me it would be Dot. So I told her about after the conversation. About going to Sammy and seeing the ink bottle beside him and the black smudge at the corner of his mouth.

"Like he'd had his pen in his mouth?" she asked.

I felt now even more conflicted saying this bit. "Maybe, but I feel like I remember that the bottle had more ink in it and then it had less ink in it when I looked again." I didn't want to say it outright.

I worried she'd look at me funny, but instead she immediately asked, "Do you think he drank it? That'd be *toxic*, wouldn't it!?"

She asked the question I hadn't dared ask myself.

"I dunno."

"Well, it's a place to start. First Sammy, and then that Tom person."

I nodded.

"One thing at a time," she said.

I nodded again.

At the end of the day, Dot and I decided to go to the Music Department to take a look around. It was the first time I'd felt truly on board with one of her plans, mainly because it was a plan we made together. At that point I could have pretended nothing had happened. So many others at the studio did. If they knew anything strange was happening at all. But I couldn't. Part of it was definitely wanting to impress Mister Drew and let him know something was going on in his studio. But part of it was my own curiosity. My own need.

There was also something about my friendship with Dot, watching her interact with people, all the blunt questions she asked. It made me wonder why people didn't talk like that more. Why people weren't so direct all the time. Dot had made me start asking questions, and now I wanted to know the answers.

So there I was, back in the Music Department. Dot glanced at me as we passed the hall to the stairs for the Infirmary. Like we had a secret. Which we did. I tried to return the look with a similar one, but I just kind of frowned. I couldn't do it. There was something that would always make me feel uncomfortable about the Music Department. The hallways seemed unnecessarily dark and empty. The musicians weren't there all the time recording, so the large space needed for them once a month just seemed creepy and hollow the rest of the time.

Also, I could never shake that first meeting with Sammy from my mind. If you could call it a meeting. His body drenched in ink. Writhing around on the ground like that. Ink in his ears, in his mouth, in his eyes.

"You okay, Buddy?" Dot asked as we walked into the large

room. The stage was littered with instruments like always. But now for some reason the sight disturbed me more. It gave the impression that the musicians had been there and then suddenly just vanished. Out of nowhere. Into nowhere.

"Yeah." I tried to give her a reassuring smile and then remembered I was terrible at giving people reassuring smiles. "What do you think we're looking for?"

"I don't know." She wandered over to the desk against the far wall. I'd never seen Sammy sit there, I realized, as she started to open drawers and look through paper. I'd only ever seen him by his music stand at the edge of the platform. "There isn't much in here," she said.

"Maybe in the supply closet?"

Dot stood upright and closed the drawer and nodded.

"Good point. You want to look while I finish up here?" she asked, hands on hips.

I remembered trying to clear up that ink, I remembered Sammy yelling at me, I remembered the hot wet breathing on my face from last night.

"No," I said.

Dot looked at me for a moment. Then said, "Okay, I'll do it. You see if there's anything else that looks suspicious here." And she marched off in her purposeful way back out into the hall.

I stood there admiring her bravery. Then I realized: "Dot!"

She poked her head around the corner. "Yes?"

"Do you want me to . . . I mean . . . going alone . . ." I

couldn't even get the offer to come protect her out 'cause already the expression on her face made me feel silly. Of course she'd be okay. She was always okay.

She shook her head and sighed. And then disappeared once again.

It was when I turned and looked around that I remembered that being alone in the Music Room didn't make me feel particularly good either.

I carefully stepped up onto the stage and maneuvered around the instruments, glancing into their cases, trying to see if anything looked out of place. But I wasn't a musician. How on earth was I supposed to know what was normal and what wasn't? All I could tell was what looked creepy and what didn't, and while the stage boards creaked under me and my footsteps echoed in a way that made it seem like someone was in the room with me walking at the exact same speed, nothing looked strange.

It's just . . . everything felt strange.

I eventually made it round to Sammy's conductor stand. I thought maybe he had a little thing of ink off to the side, or anything, maybe even a spill. But all he had were his music notes. I knew that's what they were because he had scrawled "Music Notes" on the front of the book. It was hard enough to see, black ink on a black cover. I tilted the stand a little more upright and the ink glinted in it. Which intrigued me. Because usually the ink wasn't glossy like that. Maybe it was still wet. I touched the end of the "M" very carefully. I was so tired of being covered in ink, from Sammy. From the handprint. I didn't need more of it. Especially not as I was wearing one of my grandfather's shirts now, having totally run out of my own.

Dry.

I tilted the stand even more, but slowly just to see. I noticed something in the bottom corner. I picked up the book and looked closer. I was feeling bold now. It looked like . . . it looked like a pair of Bendy horns. Like the top part of Bendy's head without the circle. It was so hard to tell. The drawing of them glinted and disappeared in the light. And looked like it had almost slipped off the cover.

I couldn't help myself, I had to see more.

So I opened the book.

Inside were rows of lines with music notes running across them. The title "Bendy and the Pirates" ran across the top. That's what Richie was working on upstairs. There was nothing unusual except seeing the music like that. I'd never seen a score before. It was interesting. But not strange.

I flipped a page. Now it read "Alice's Song."

Another. "The Butcher Gang Jig."

And another. "Nightlife Boris."

I'd forgotten I was even looking for anything in general until I flipped the page again and almost dropped the book. The staggering difference between the regular music and this was like a punch to the gut. So shocking.

It was, if I was to put it in a nice way, doodles. But it was so much more than that. It was more like deep scratch marks, hastily drawn images with ink splatters and smudging, and it came across like whoever had done them was a maniac. Like he was rushing like crazy. Had to get the images onto paper before something happened. I understood that feeling.

I didn't understand what I was looking at.

In the center of the pages was a large sketchy symbol I'd never seen before, a circle with a piece cut out and a buncha lines framing it and with another circle around all that. Sammy had drawn over it so many times that the paper was torn near the middle. The ink glistened like the ink on the cover, but it was similarly dry. That's not what chilled me to the bone though. Taking up the full right-hand page was what I could only describe as a drawing of a deformed Bendy. But it had very little in common with the cute cartoon character. Its limbs were long, almost praying mantis–like, with hands that had claws on them, not cute white gloves. Worse still was his face, half obscured with—what was it? Was it blood? The drawing was in black and white; it was hard to tell what everything was. All I could see was how much longer his devil's horns now were, how his smile was filled with sharp teeth. His eyes completely hidden behind a dripping black ooze.

Blood.

No.

Ink?

The pages were full up of other sketches, things I couldn't quite recognize. And words too. "Dreams come true," like on the Bendy poster. And also "Set us free." That one I didn't remember seeing before.

More symbols, and everything seemed to be slipping off the page. Like Sammy had been drawing it while being pulled away from it.

Like the images were also falling away.

I looked down. The illusion of things dripping off the page was so intense I couldn't help myself.

I stared at the ground for a good long moment. Nothing. Of course nothing. Just a worn wooden floor covered in scratches. I looked up and shook my head, going to place the book back on the stand. And that's when I saw the symbol on the music stand. More than just one. And then just circles and lines, disjointed but everywhere, covering the wood. Covering, I saw as I bent to look, all the way down. I stood back up. And I noticed a little sketch of Bendy too. And the words "He will." I placed the book carefully back on the stand where I found it.

"He will."

And it lined up perfectly with "Set us free."

"Buddy, I need to show you something."

I nearly jumped out of my skin. I turned and stared at Dot, wide-eyed. Fear was flowing through my veins, and she could see it. I knew she could see it.

"What?" she asked.

I couldn't speak, I just pointed at the book. Dot stepped around me to have a look. There was a quiet moment as I watched her delicately trace over the images with her fingers, bent over, examining the paper carefully. "What are you up to, Sammy?" she said to herself.

"It's strange, right?" I finally was able to say.

"It's beyond strange," Dot replied, standing upright and meeting my stare. "Come with me."

I nodded and followed her just like I always did when she said that. We made our way down the hall toward that supply closet. My stomach clenched like someone had reached down my throat and squeezed it when I saw the wooden door. The simple brass doorknob. I glanced down. There was still black ink seeping out into the hallway where I couldn't get it clean. The hand inside me squeezed tighter.

"It's okay, Buddy," said Dot. "It's safe. But you need to see this."

She opened the door.

And we stared.

There before us, from inky floor to ceiling, covering all the dyed black shelves, were bottles.

Clear, glass, *empty* ink bottles.

"Hey! What are you guys doing?"

I'd never seen Dot turn in surprise before. Nothing ever seemed to faze her, but she was disturbed this time and quickly closed the closet door as she spun around. Jacob was striding down the hall toward us. He didn't look angry, but he had this intense look on his face. Maybe even concern.

"Trying to find Sammy," I said when Dot said nothing.

"Okay, well, Buddy, they need you in the lobby," he said, not really caring about our answer.

"Me?"

"Oh yes," said Jacob.

"Why?"

"I . . ." He stopped. He looked uncomfortable. Which wasn't really the usual look for Jacob. In fact I'd never seen anyone more comfortable in his own skin really. The change in him made me feel uncomfortable too.

"What is it?"

"I think it's your grandfather," he said, reaching behind his head and scratching at the back of his neck.

The hand grabbing my guts released me instantly, but instead of feeling relieved I felt like I was breathing too freely now. I saw bright stars in the corners of my vision before shaking them off and immediately rushing toward the elevator. I could hear Dot and Jacob coming up behind me.

Once inside: "Are you sure?" I asked.

"No," said Jacob, "But he's old, and asking for you, and he . . . well, he looks a bit like you."

I didn't want him to elaborate on that. Not with all the insults that had been shot my way as a kid.

"Okay," was all I said.

I hadn't prepped for the sudden stop, and my teeth banged together again. First time in weeks that had happened to me.

I was annoyed with myself. But I didn't really have time to be. I rushed down the hall and into the lobby.

"Buddy!" said a happy, loud, and very familiar voice.

He was there, being held by the crook of his elbow by Wally, who didn't exactly look like any kind of scary security guard. He was even holding on to his broom with his other hand.

"Grandpa, what are you doing here?" I asked, rushing over to him. "You can let him go now. What do you think he's going to do, take over the place?"

Wally shook his head at me. "You never know," he said with a shrug.

"You okay?" Grandpa asked, looking closely at me. Examining my face carefully.

"Sure, of course, I'm swell. Look, you can't be here. How did you even . . ." I sensed Dot at my side.

"Buddy," she whispered.

"Not now, Dot."

"Buddy, he's here."

"Who . . ." I looked up and standing by Ms. Lambert at the front desk was Mister Drew. He was leaning back, arms folded over his chest. His expression was unreadable.

"Mister Drew!" I said, startled.

"What's all this?" he asked. He smiled, but I wasn't sure it was a happy smile.

"It's nothing, it's just my grandfather . . ." I said quickly. It was my turn to grab him by the arm. But as I did Grandpa slipped through my grip and walked over to the poster of Bendy on the wall. He stared at it. Then he went up to it even closer.

"What's he doing?" asked Dot.

"He's . . . looking. That's how he looks."

Grandpa turned to me and then pointed at the poster. "Cowboy!" he said.

I took in a sharp breath. No, no. I needed to get him out of here fast. Before he somehow let it slip that he was the real artist. Somehow. With his three-word vocabulary.

I quickly went over to him and grabbed his elbow. "Come on, Grandpa, time to go home."

Grandpa looked at the poster once more, then over at Mister Drew. Then back at me.

"Boss?"

I nodded.

Mister Drew heard that and slowly pushed himself off the desk and came over, suddenly beaming brightly. "Hello there, sir. I'm Joey Drew. It's nice to meet you. Your grandson is very talented." He stuck out his hand to shake.

My grandfather looked at his hand for a moment, then took it. But he didn't shake. He brought the hand up to his face and looked at it closely. He turned it over and touched the inside of Mister Drew's palm. Mister Drew glanced at me with a baffled smile. I smiled back and hoped that was the right choice. What was my grandfather doing?

Finally he looked up at Mister Drew. "Boss," he said again. Mister Drew nodded. And at that point finally Grandpa shook his hand.

Then he dropped it, almost like he'd forgotten he'd been holding it, and turned to me again.

"It's nice to meet your family, Buddy, but we don't do this here. Time for him to go home," said Mister Drew. He turned and left, making me feel uneasy again. Like something had gone wrong. Like I was in trouble.

"You better take him home," said Jacob, watching Mister Drew go. "Before Ms. Lambert busts your chops."

"Yeah, go on, Buddy," said Dot.

"What about . . ." I stopped. I obviously couldn't say what I wanted to say. Not in front of everyone. But we'd only just started our investigation.

"We have time," said Dot.

I didn't really think we did, but then again, what choice did I have? "Come on, Grandpa, let's get you home," I said. I could tell Ma about it, get her to explain why this was not a thing people did in New York. Just show up places. Of course that was kind of his thing, wasn't it? Just suddenly showing up.

Grandpa nodded with a smile and then turned to look at everyone. "Good to meeting you," he said.

"Nice to meet you too," said Dot.

He smiled at her, then looked at me and winked.

Oh no, old man, no. It wasn't like that. Still, I could feel my face get hot.

I escorted him out of the building onto the busy street. He stopped and stared at the traffic for a moment and then looked up at the buildings towering over us. I looked up too.

"This way," he said. He turned left, which wasn't the way. It was north.

"No, Grandpa," I said, but suddenly he was walking quickly. Which surprised me because usually he took his time going anywhere. I assumed it was because of how frail he was. But now I had no idea. Because this man was *fast*. I had no choice except to follow, and when I caught up to him I tried to get him to stop.

But he wouldn't.

He turned right. I had no idea why and no clue what his plan was. If he even had a plan. We crossed over Broadway, all blinking lights and honking horns, and continued to walk in silence for what felt like forever but was probably no more than ten minutes, until we stopped. For some reason.

Grandpa smiled. "There," he said, pointing. He liked to point.

I looked at the façade in front of us.

It was striking how it stood out from the buildings around it. Very modern. There wasn't any other description for it. A solid rectangle made up of rectangles of glass within rectangles of concrete. I couldn't decide if it looked good. I just knew it looked very different.

"Where are we?" I asked.

Grandpa looked at me like I was crazy. He shook his head and then led me inside the quiet foyer.

"Art," he said quietly as our footsteps echoed on the cement floor.

Art?

Finally my eyes landed on a sign. The Museum of Modern Art.

Oh.

Art.

I didn't have time for art.

"Come on, Grandpa," I said. My voice was quiet but it sounded so clear and loud. I glanced at the woman sitting behind the information desk.

But he didn't stop walking, and I had no power to stop him. It seemed no one did, because no one said a word even though I assumed we had to pay to get in. We simply kept going.

I was feeling even more antsy. This wasn't the plan. Didn't he understand that serious things were happening? He had to, that's why he'd come to check on me. Because of last night. Because of the handprint. And yet . . .

Finally we stopped and he sat on a bench in front of a painting.

I sat next to him.

In front of us was a canvas. It looked to be a bank of a river or something. It was strange. It was what it was, but it was also . . .

"Dots?" I asked.

"To make art must make new thing," said Grandpa. "See world different way. Understand?"

I nodded. I supposed. Maybe? I didn't know what it had to do with cartoons though.

"Not pretty picture. Big picture. History. Thinking. Mind. Soul." He was trying so hard to communicate. And I listened. Of course I did. I felt stupid. Not just how much I didn't know about art or even the world, but how much I didn't know about Grandpa. Not just of his life in Poland and all of that, but also how he thought. And what he thought.

"Grandpa, I have to go."

"Boss," he said with a nod.

"Yes."

"Ink."

"What?"

He took my hand and pointed to the ink on my finger. He held up his hand and showed me the exact same spot on his. From helping me, I assumed. "Ink," he said.

I nodded. "Yes. I'm still practicing."

Then he placed his hand on my back. Spreading his fingers wide. "Ink," he said again.

My breathing got thinner, feeling him touch the same spot as last night. Feeling his hand push against my back. He smiled softly and took his hand away and held it up in front of me. "Not this hand, boss hand," he explained.

"Okay," I said, not fully getting it.

"Ink."

I nodded. Sure, yes, Mister Drew had ink on his hands too. He was an artist too. At least . . . that's what he'd implied when I'd first met him. I mean, he'd invented Bendy, hadn't he?

Hadn't he?

"Boss ink same ink," said Grandpa.

"Same ink?" As what? As the handprint? No, that I knew was definitely not Mister Drew.

"Ink bad."

I stared at him. I wanted him to explain. I needed to understand. A few days ago this all would have been nonsense to me. I would have looked at him like a crazy old man.

But not after what had happened last night.

Not after Sammy's notebook.

"Ink bad," I said.

Grandpa lowered his hand and nodded solemnly.

Ink bad.

13

I didn't see Dot the rest of the day. By the time I came back to the office, there were only a few hours left before quitting time. And I did have actual work to do. I stayed late, but not as late as the previous night. I wasn't staying in the studio alone anymore, that was for sure. When I saw Richie lean back and crack his knuckles above his head, I knew it was time for me to pack it up as well. And I was happy to.

By the time I got home, Grandpa was sleeping and I had to sneak by him to look at our drawings. I thought maybe it was time to try just a horse. Maybe. I stood over the dresser, hunched a little so my neck ached, and copied a horse from a painting, first as circles and then slowly drawing over the top of them. Turning them into actual features.

It kind of worked.

It worked better than my old-donkey-fat-dog-horse creation from that first attempt. But it still felt like I had so much further to go than ever. Especially after the visit to the art gallery.

The more I learned, the more I realized I didn't know.

It felt a bit the same about the studio.

About the ink.

The next day I was exhausted—I'd barely slept. Thoughts wouldn't leave me alone, and I hated that. I hated thinking so hard. The harder I thought, the more jumbled up the thoughts got. Kind of like how the harder I'd looked at that painting in the museum, the less I saw the actual picture.

I couldn't see the big picture anymore.

I was grateful that I didn't have too many deliveries to make around the studio. It almost seemed like Ms. Lambert could see how not up for it I was. Like she was giving me a break. I decided to practice drawing Alice today. Because I hadn't really tried at all. And she was cute. It was fun to draw her.

I needed some fun.

Did I ever.

I was the first one to see Sammy.

He came charging down the narrow hall that was next to my desk, and I immediately went from exhausted to terrified. I figured he'd found out that Dot and I were looking into him. That he knew we'd seen the weird drawings on his music, the empty bottles in his closet. That he was coming to pick a fight. And I didn't know what I'd do then, because, for one thing, I didn't think fighting was considered professional or anything people did in uptown, but also because I'd been a lousy fighter my whole life. I only managed to win a few scrapes because it was so hard to tip me over.

Instead he stormed right past me, didn't even seem to notice me sitting there in my dark corner, and burst into the brighter room of the Art Department.

Ms. Lambert got up slowly from her desk with a frown. She could read the rage on his face. It wasn't hard to see. You'd probably be able to spot it from the top of the Empire State Building.

"Mr. Lawrence," she said carefully.

"Abby," he replied.

She bit her lower lip but didn't say anything. I remembered Sammy calling the man from Gent "Tom" and not "Mr. Connor," and I wondered if this was a habit of his. If this was what he did with everyone. Or maybe . . . how had Jacob put it in the bar about women and black people not getting the same respect, having to work twice as hard? I thought about it as I swiveled in my chair to watch what happened next.

"How can I help you?"

"Where's my ink?"

I sat upright in my seat.

"Your ink?" asked Ms. Lambert.

"The ink. Where did it go?"

Ms. Lambert's expression now no longer looked suspicious but concerned. "Are you asking to borrow some of the Art Department's ink? You can just say that, Mr. Lawrence; you don't need to act so entitled."

Sammy huffed loudly and shoved his hands in his pockets. He shook his head violently no, and, after a few times pressing his lips tight together, said, "The ink in your supply closet."

"We don't keep ink in the supply closet."

Okay, so that was odd. We *didn't* keep ink in the supply closet? Then what was the Music Department doing with a closet full of it when the people who really needed ink, the artists, kept it under lock and key? But I didn't think it made sense to bring it up now. I certainly didn't want to remind her of that whole stealing thing. Not after I had got my second chance. Besides, maybe she was lying to keep Sammy out of our stuff. He really did have a strange ink thing. Clearly.

Sammy made to say something, but then didn't. He seemed to be struggling with how to speak. A strange gurgle came from him, like the words wanted to come out but he was holding them down.

"Look, we keep our ink here, under my desk in the safe. I can give you a bottle if you'd like. But you need to calm down. This is not worth getting so angry about."

Sammy shook his head, his neck so tight that his whole body turned frantically from side to side. Then he stormed off past me and back down the dark hallway. And was gone.

"What on earth was that about?" asked Ms. Lambert.

Jacob stood up, his eyes wide and eyebrows raised. "Man's gone off his rocker. You want me to check out the supply closet?"

Ms. Lambert nodded. "Yes please, thanks."

Jacob gave her a bright smile and then made his way past

me. He then gave me one, and I thought for a moment how impressive it was that he could smile so big and at everyone and it still seemed real. Like he was genuinely happy to see you. My smiles just made it look like I was in pain. Or had gas. I watched him go down the hall and held my breath. I didn't hold it on purpose, and I didn't know why I was holding it in the first place. I didn't know what I wanted him to find. Either way, I figured, was strange.

He came back pretty quick and smiled as he sat down at his desk. "Nope, nothing. Guy's off his nut."

My stomach knotted tightly. I didn't understand what was happening. Why wasn't there ink in our closet? Why was it all in the Music Department?

"Buddy," said Ms. Lambert, calling me over. I got up a bit too fast, and my feet slipped around under me as I forced myself not to fall.

"Fancy footwork," said Richie, laughing.

I nodded but said nothing.

"Grab that Cowboy Bendy sketch on your way," said Ms. Lambert.

Again I nodded, and reached into the desk, picking up the piece of paper and hurrying over to her.

"So we're going with the Cowboy Bendy idea, and Story would like a few sample sketches for inspiration. Think you can handle that?" she asked. There was a glint of a smile in her eye that made me think she was maybe actually proud of me. Or excited for me. I was definitely excited for me.

"Sure," I said as calmly as I could, and I handed her the paper.

She looked it over and nodded. "Yup, something like this, but make sure to center the image. We need the whole horse, don't want to be missing the hooves or anything. We can make decisions on how much we want to show later. Okay?" She passed the paper back.

I nodded okay, but I was a little confused.

"So give me maybe half a dozen different Cowboy Bendy ideas."

I nodded again.

"That's all." She dismissed me and I returned to my desk.

I was nervous now. I'd practiced a lot in the short time since my grandfather had first drawn Cowboy Bendy. But six different Bendy moments? Was I able to do that?

And what did she mean about the "whole horse"? Had my grandfather forgotten a bit?

I placed the drawing on my desk and looked at it. Odd. She was right. The drawing was right at the bottom, the legs cut off. It didn't make any sense. Was I remembering wrong? I thought for certain he'd drawn the feet. I thought for certain it had been right in the middle of a page, like a single cel of an animation series.

It's amazing how often we make the assumption that our mind is playing tricks on us. That when things happen that are strange and impossible it must be that somehow we are wrong.

But sometimes things are strange and impossible.

And we don't make some connections until it's too late.

I didn't make the connection then. I did make it later, and I don't know if I should tell you that now or wait until it happened. What's the point in waiting?

No. I can't jump around too much. If I jump forward in the story I might forget to go back. The memories might change. I worry I've already changed them. Did I really go to the art museum and stare at the Seurat painting with my grandfather, or did we talk about that painting in the kitchen, looking at one of his books?

I know he came to see me that day, and I know he'd been worried. But maybe he just went home after.

Maybe that makes more sense.

Maybe the horse wasn't slipping off the page.

Maybe I thought of Sammy's notebook then, not later. Remembered how the pictures in there looked like they'd been slipping too.

Maybe I made the connection then.

Not everything makes sense to me anymore.

I do remember this though. I remember sitting and staring and feeling scared and confused and then hearing: "I'm never going to get sick of that cowboy, makes me smile every time."

I turned a little too fast, straining my neck to see Mister Drew standing over me.

"Mister Drew!" I said quickly, and stood up.

"Hello, son. Excited about Cowboy Bendy?" he asked with a grin.

"Absolutely, sir. Thank you."

"A good idea is a good idea." He just kept smiling at me, and I wasn't sure if I was supposed to say anything back to that because, well, there wasn't much to say except for . . .

"Thank you. But it's really all from Dot's script—"

"So! You worked for Mr. Schwartz there for a while. Your mom makes his suits for him, you mentioned," said Mister Drew, leaning against the wall by my desk.

"Yeah." What?

"So you know suits," he said. It wasn't a question.

Hadn't thought about it that way. I felt like I knew the bags that you carried suits in way more. But I supposed I'd seen Ma put together enough of them to have some kind of knowledge.

"Sure," I replied. It felt like the right thing to say. Wasn't exactly a yes. Wasn't exactly a no.

"Great, come with me," he said, clapping his hands together.

I looked over at Ms. Lambert, who was watching us closely. She nodded slowly despite a disapproving look, giving her permission, even though there was no way I could have said no. She knew that too. Of course.

"Yes, sir," I said.

It was a strange feeling following him into the elevator, everyone watching us. Jacob looked like he was about to burst out laughing, and I figured that probably had something to do with my expression. I knew I looked stunned. I felt stunned.

"Your grandfather okay?" asked Mister Drew as we made our way down to the lobby.

"Oh, yes, he's fine."

"Family can be difficult," he said with a laugh.

"Yeah, I mean, it's different. Having him around now."

"He just move in with you?" asked Mister Drew.

I nodded.

"Ah, yeah, obligations. I get it. But don't let them hold you back. Old people make you feel guilty, but they lived their dreams, didn't they? Why shouldn't you?"

I thought about it. "Yeah, he did." I tried to remember what Ma had told me ages ago. "My parents tried to convince him to come here with them to the States back when I was just born. He refused. Had his own stuff to do, I guess."

Mister Drew tapped his finger against the wall of the elevator. "Exactly." He paused for a moment, and we listened to the strained sound of the chains lowering us. "Well, he seems like a nice old man. Just can't have him interrupting the workday like that again." He laughed. Like it was a joke.

But he meant it.

"Yeah, of course. He was just worried about me," I said. Then flinched. Because of course the next question was going to be:

"Worried?"

Shoot.

I stood there thinking hard. I was ready to lie about

something, but then again, why didn't I just tell Mister Drew what I'd seen? He'd appreciate it. Maybe.

Why did I feel like he maybe wouldn't?

"It's personal," I ended up saying. It sounded so stupid.

"I get it, kid, I get it. But I'm always here," he said placing a hand on my shoulder. "If you need to talk about anything, my office door is always open."

I suddenly felt like maybe I did want to talk to him. About my ambitions and maybe what I could do as part of the company in the future. But not just about that. I wanted to share about my grandfather, and how I felt confused that my ma just dumped him on us. And why it wasn't fair she had to work so hard. And how I was now forced to wear his shirts because I couldn't afford anything more. I was too guilty still to spend any more money on myself. Not yet at any rate.

I didn't say any of that, of course. I just followed him through the lobby and into the car waiting for us. It was really clean on the inside and smelled like leather. The seats were soft to the touch. There was also so much room I could almost stretch my legs out full.

"Nice car, isn't it?" said Mister Drew, smiling at me.

"Very nice car, sir," I said.

He gave me a wink and then leaned back in the seat, turning his head to look out the window. So I did the same and watched as my city went by in an unusual, new kind of way. I hadn't been inside too many cars in my life. Sure, the back of Zip's truck for a block or two, even riding the bumper of Nick's old beat-up jalopy. And I'd taken a cab once in a while, but not that many times and always on someone else's dime. So to see the world from the street, to be part of traffic for once, not just dodging it, made me feel real big, you know. Made me feel good.

We drove up Fifth Avenue and pulled to a stop in front of a shop across from the park. Stepped out onto the sidewalk. A woman in a big hat almost walked right into me, her little white poofy dog almost crushed under my big clown feet.

"What do you think?" asked Mister Drew as we looked at the front of a small, swanky suit shop. In the window was a perfectly tailored pin-striped suit with shiny black loafers that glinted in the afternoon sun.

"I think why'd you ever go with Mr. Schwartz," I replied.

Mister Drew laughed and gave me a slap on the back. "Come on in, Buddy," he said.

We went inside. It was dark, but I couldn't see any dust at all floating in the shafts of light. Instead everything shone, even the wood shelving. There was a glow to it all.

A balding man with small round glasses in a simple navy-blue suit came over to us. He had a measuring tape draped around his neck, and it looked so good I thought maybe this was a new trend people were wearing out on the street.

"Mister Drew, come in," he said. "Let's see how this tux fits you."

I understood better then. Mr. Schwartz did not do fancy dress wear. He didn't have enough clients.

I waited as Mister Drew changed into a crisp black tuxedo,

and I marveled at how neat and clean it was. He stood there with his arms out wide as the tailor measured him with the tape, making little notes on his pad as he did.

"Taking the measure of a man," said Mister Drew with a chuckle.

"Always, Mister Drew," replied the tailor.

"Learn anything?"

"Some folks have really long arms," replied the tailor.

Mister Drew laughed heartily at that. Then he turned to me. "How's it look, Buddy?"

"Really good," I said. I felt a pang in my gut sitting there in my grandfather's itchy shirt. And trousers with the hole sewed shut in the knee.

"We're hosting a party, the studio. Big fancy shindig. Hotel rooftop. Dancers. The works." Mister Drew grinned widely.

"Sounds great," I said. Because it did.

"Gotta look good. Gotta make them all think . . ." He paused. "Gotta make them all *know*, Buddy. Know we mean business. Expansion in all ways."

"The theater," I said, remembering.

Mister Drew looked at me and nodded. "Exactly."

"So the studio is doing well," I said, feeling relieved.

Mister Drew looked at me kind of funny. "What do you mean by that?"

"Oh, well, you know. People are saying that . . . well . . . you know . . ." I stopped talking because the funny expression had turned into something less so. More severe.

"Who's been saying?"

I glanced at the tailor, who had propped himself up on the counter for a moment to scratch out some things on his pad. His eyes flicked up to me and then down.

"Uh, not really anyone. Just, when I was caught taking stuff from the closet and I was told we couldn't afford to waste supplies and . . . well . . . you know . . ."

"Ms. Lambert? Yeah, well, she's a good worker, but she's a woman, Buddy," Mister Drew said, looking front and cracking his neck to one side.

"What does that mean?"

"It means they don't always understand business."

I wasn't sure I believed that. Ma was pretty great with money and she worked hard. And Dot seemed to know everything going on at the studio. Sometimes even more than Mister Drew himself seemed to know.

"Look, here's the truth, kid," continued Mister Drew. He was staring at himself in the mirror now, and it was almost like he was talking to his reflection. "There are always going to be people who are trying to bring you down. Maybe it's sabotage— that's easy because you can see it, right there in front of your eyes. Maybe it's whispers and gossip. The worst is betrayal, Henry, that's the worst. When you think someone understands the plan, when you think someone is part of the team. When you take someone in and share with them all your visions for the future. That's like sharing a part of your soul, kid."

"Vision is important," I replied, remembering the time on the catwalk in the theater. But I couldn't ignore the strangeness of being called "Henry." People slipped up all the time—heck, even I mixed up the names of my friends in the neighborhood, and I'd known them since I was born. But that name . . . the same named carved into my desk. It creeped me out a little.

Mister Drew turned to me. It was as deep a look as anything. Looking through my eyes, not even into them. "Exactly, you get it, you do." He stepped off the little platform he'd been on and came over to me. "Buddy, you're coming to this party."

"I am?"

"I'm inviting you. You need to see what we're doing. You need to be a part of it."

I wanted to be, and I was excited to be. I didn't know if I needed to be, but I was all for it. "Know what else you need?" asked Mister Drew.

I shook my head. I had a list of needs in my life: money, security, food. But I didn't think that's what Mister Drew was talking about.

Mister Drew grinned at me. "You need a tux."

I'd never been fit for a suit before. Well, that wasn't entirely true. Ma always let out my hems and had a magical way to extend the life of all my clothes, making me stand there like a dummy in a shop window. But I hadn't had a tux before, and I most definitely hadn't gotten one from a swank shop on the Upper East Side. The tux wasn't made from scratch, like

Mister Drew's was. It was one that had been returned to the tailor for some reason, one that he was reselling. So he let out the hem of the trousers, which always happened with me, and brought in the waist a bit, and did it so quickly Mister Drew and I barely had to wait before I was handed a fancy black bag with a hanger popping out of the top.

I was used to carrying these kinds of bags for other people. But this one was mine.

And that made all the difference.

"What do you think, kid?" asked Mister Drew as we climbed back into his car.

"I think it's amazing, thank you, sir." I was still in shock from the whole thing.

"It's nothing," said Mister Drew with a wave of his hand. "So, kid, where do you live?"

I didn't know what to say at that moment. Not that I didn't know the answer, it was just . . .

"Hey, Buddy," he said, placing a hand on my shoulder. "I know what it's like. You don't have to be ashamed."

I looked at him. It was hard not to be. It wasn't just growing up in my neighborhood or being poor. That was bad enough. It was living in a tenement apartment that I shared with my ma and grandpa. Where all the apartments on my floor and the one below shared one small bathroom. Where the water was shut off for random reasons sometimes and the lights buzzed too loudly.

How could I be proud of that?

"Lower East Side," I said.

"Great!" He leaned forward to speak with the driver and I leaned back, wanting to disappear into my seat.

Soon we were off, and Mister Drew was talking about how New York was the greatest city in the world, and that Los Angeles had nothing on what we were doing here with animation, and the actors were so much better, and how he loved seasons and hated palm trees. And I couldn't agree or disagree because I'd never left the city, and anyway my stomach was in knots the closer we got to my neighborhood.

Which we eventually did get to. I hated the ugliness of it. How tall the buildings were. How they looked like they might fall over onto one another. The laundry hanging from windows, the food stalls along the narrow street. And the people. So many people shouting at one another. Even if they weren't angry. Just the noise and the heat and that smell. That smell I told you about. Of piss. And vomit. And sweat.

"Which street's yours, Buddy?" asked Mister Drew.

"Are you sure?" I said. I really wasn't excited about showing him that.

"Don't you want to show these people what real success looks like? Don't you want them to see what hard work gets them? They should be in awe of you, Buddy," said Mister Drew as we drove past Singer's Butcher Shop.

As far as I knew, everyone in my neighborhood worked hard. As far as I knew, they worked themselves to the bone.

That's why we were a neighborhood of hunched backs and tanned skin and thin angular faces. That's why it never got quiet here. Folks were hustling even at two in the morning. But I did get his point. The point was I had managed to get out, and that was something to envy. I sure as heck envied those who had escaped before me. There was a difference between good hard work and bad hard work.

At least . . . that's what I felt then. In that moment. In that fancy car with my new tux I felt—well, I'm ashamed of it now, but in that moment I felt . . . superior.

I directed Mister Drew to the front door of our building. It was tough to get there with the folks who had started gathering, and his driver had to make his way slowly. Heads poked out of the windows above, and I noticed Timmy Sharp come running out of his father's shop to peer into the car. I gave him a wave and he stood upright, calling out, "Buddy Lewek's in that car!" Well, that only drew the crowd closer, and I could see the expression on Mister Drew's face was now no longer quite so happy. It looked concerned. Maybe he was worried we might hit someone with the car.

Nah, that's not it. That's what I told myself then.

But this is my story, and I don't have to make up lies anymore. Not after what I know now.

It wasn't worry.

It was disgust.

We pulled to a stop. "Well, you better get out, Buddy. Your

fans are waiting," he said. He was smiling, but he seemed impatient now. And I was confused because, after all, this had been his idea.

I nodded and grabbed the suit bag and slipped out of the car. Almost the moment my feet hit the pavement, Mister Drew was driving off. I didn't blame him for wanting to get away from all this. It made me even more ashamed.

"Hey, Buddy, can I order three of those?" asked Timmy, pointing after Mister Drew's car.

I smiled but didn't know what to say. I wasn't great with joking around.

"Who was that, Bud?" asked Molly O'Neill.

"My boss," I replied, trying to push my way through folks to get to my door.

"You work at that fancy studio, right?" asked Timmy.

"Yeah."

"You'll remember us when, won't you?" called out Mr. Goldman from across the street. "Hey, Buddy, you'll remember us when!"

I waved at him and smiled. I passed through the door. "Billy's having a party on Saturday, you should come," said Molly.

"Maybe," I said, but that wasn't happening. I wasn't going to go to one of Billy's shindigs where folks got sauced and fights always broke out.

I closed the door then. I guess you could say I closed it in their faces, but they weren't backing away and I was feeling overwhelmed. I'd always wanted to impress the neighborhood, but I hadn't realized just how many feelings it'd make me feel.

Mostly all I could think about was Mister Drew's face and how quickly he drove off. It gave me a headache.

I made it up to an empty apartment, and I was grateful for that. I didn't feel like talking to anyone, explaining "how my day was." I didn't feel like practicing drawing either. I just wanted to lie on my bed and stare at the ceiling. I carefully hung the tuxedo in the wardrobe next to Grandpa's two faded suits.

I walked over to the bed and stared at it. I looked over at the dresser. At the pages of drawings on top. I crawled over my bed and grabbed a fistful before turning over and lying flat on my back, staring at the water stain overhead. As a kid I'd pretended it was a river and created little towns in my imagination that lived along it. Designed houses and even chose one for me, Ma, and Pa. Someday we were going to live somewhere where there was room for everyone. Room to breathe.

I picked up one of my drawings. One of a chubby angel from some ceiling somewhere in Europe. It had started as circles but now it looked pretty much like the picture. I'd never thought I'd ever be drawing chubby angels. I never thought it was necessary. But I was understanding better now. The simple lines that made up Bendy were still based on human figures. On classic angles. I was able to draw him walking and it looked like actual walking.

I noticed one of my angel wings was half off the page then.

That didn't make sense to me. Why wouldn't I have drawn the wing entirely? That was part of the exercise.

I sat up. It reminded me of Grandpa's cowboy from that afternoon. The way it had been slipping off the page.

I looked at the next page in my hand, and the next. Was I going loony? Did they all seem just a little different? Were all the pictures slipping?

Or was it just my mind? Was it just my mind that was slipping . . .

I tossed the pages onto the floor beside me and held my forearm over my eyes. Everything felt hot. My arm, my head, my brain.

I just needed everything to cool down.

Everyone to cool down.

Of course that wasn't going to happen.

From the frying pan into the fire, they say.

Right into the flames.

Time passes. Folks say that when

things are going well time goes faster; when things are bad it goes slower. I can see that. But sometimes I think time makes its own decisions about things.

I can't tell you how much time has passed here. In the dripping dark. I can't tell you what time has done, if it all just happened yesterday or if it all happened years ago. Or, I dunno, if it hasn't happened yet.

I want to tell about Sammy. About when he disappeared. I want to get to that part of the story. But the thing is, we only notice someone is gone when time has passed. It's like the clock is ticking all normal, then it skips a beat. And we look up. And we didn't actually hear anything happen. But something inside us noticed it. Something made us sit up. And wonder.

It wasn't quite like that with Sammy. Not exactly. It wasn't a small missing beat. Though for a musical director that would have made some sense. In a funny way. But this wasn't funny.

It started two weeks after I got my tuxedo. After Mister

Drew had invited me to the party. I was on my way down to my least favorite part of the studio, the Music Department, when I ran into that strange violinist I'd met on my first day. I'd never learned her name. The musicians weren't around much and, anyway, she gave me the willies. She always looked haunted.

Her hair was still a sheet of black, and she wore that long black skirt and sweater, even though, yeah, maybe the weather was a degree cooler now that it was September, but it really wasn't that much better. She didn't stop. I wasn't even sure she noticed me. She sidestepped me and kept on going, and that was it.

But later in the day I heard Dave of all people talking about how the musicians had been locked out of the Music Room.

"What's the big deal?" Richie had asked, pushing up a wrinkled sleeve and scratching his bicep. "Get a master key."

"They did. Seems like something was barricading the door," Dave replied. We all looked at him. The old man never spoke, never seemed to remember we were here. "All I know," he added, and then, like a switch had shut off, he was back to work, flipping between his two pages, making sure the change in the drawings of Boris's arm from cel to cel was just right.

"There must be more to that story," Jacob said to me.

Something to do with ink, I imagined but didn't say out loud. Because that was a bizarre thing for someone to say.

Three days after that, when enough time had passed, but not so much that people really noticed it, Toby from Accounting mentioned that Sammy hadn't come in for his paycheck. Again, us workers only knew anything about this because Mister

Drew himself was storming around the building, angrily muttering about it. Interrogating folks he met as he went. I didn't feel like the rage matched the situation, but then I figured maybe he had something more on his mind than just a missing music director.

"It's the machine," said Dot as we were eating lunch.

"What about it?" I asked. She always just said things out of the blue like that.

"Something's not working right. I heard him yelling at Tom."

"He's yelling at everyone," I replied.

"Yes. But trust me. We want answers? We need to find that machine," she said.

I couldn't exactly tell her how I wasn't interested in investigating any further. How the creature near the Infirmary didn't make me curious anymore, just made me want to stay away. After going to the suit shop with Mister Drew, all I wanted was to draw and show Mister Drew what I could do. I just wanted to work.

But then Sammy went missing.

Officially.

He'd been gone for over a week. But when the police showed up and started talking to folks, that's when we realized it was more than just someone taking a day off.

The questions were straightforward. "When was the last time you saw him?" and that's when I remembered that the last time was the time he'd stormed into the Art Department looking for ink. That made me very uncomfortable.

But then things took a turn.

I remember coming to work and the police were outside and the studio was shut down. I remember being told by Richie that someone had broken in and messed the place up. That they were looking into a possible burglary. I remember Mister Drew rushing from his car and shouting in the detective's face something about sabotage. How seeing him shout like that was worse than seeing Mr. Schwartz lose his temper. Than seeing even Sammy lose his temper. It was jarring and a little scary. Especially compared to how he usually seemed.

I remember finding Dot in all the mess. Or maybe she found me.

"Do you think it's burglary, Buddy?" she asked.

"Of course not," I said, sounding more sure than I felt.

"So you'll come with me, tonight, when everyone's left. To check it out," she said. She didn't even ask. If she'd asked I'd probably have said no. Then again, I still could have told her I didn't want to. She had no power over me.

The fact was, despite my concerns, I was still curious. But it was more than that. Seeing Mister Drew so upset, seeing him shake with rage, and locked out of his own studio. Well, it made me want to fix things. And if Dot and I could figure out what had happened, solve the mystery, he'd appreciate that. I had ambition after all.

And Dot had a key.

*   *   *

The police barricades were still up that evening. There were no police though. No one around to guard the studio.

"Do we really want to do this?" I asked. I couldn't draw a more ominous-looking scene if I tried. Which at this point, well, I was beginning to figure my efforts at drawing weren't all that impressive. Still: The dark looming exterior. The "Do Not Enter" sign. The fact even that the streetlamp overhead was dark. A burnt-out bulb or something.

Dot didn't really care about atmosphere, in the real world that is. "Ready?" she asked. She slipped easily under the tape crossing the front door and had the door unlocked before I even made it across the street running after her. She was little, but quick.

Inside, the studio reminded me a lot of the first time I'd seen it. When there had been that blackout. It made me feel strangely better because it was familiar. But it didn't make me feel all that safe or anything.

Dot turned on a flashlight.

Because she'd brought a flashlight.

Because she always thought ahead like that.

"I don't think we should turn any lights on. We don't want to draw attention to the building," she said as she started walking. "And keep away from the windows, okay?"

"Yes," I said, which wasn't quite the right thing to say, but I was feeling so uneasy now. I knew Dot was confident that Sammy was behind everything strange and creepy in the studio. And I wanted to trust her, like I did with most things.

But I couldn't forget the breathing on my face.

The large handprint on my shirt.

It didn't make sense to me that any of it was . . . well . . . human . . .

It also didn't make sense to me that it wouldn't be either.

I didn't want to scare her though. And I didn't want to scare myself. But I was afraid of what hid in the dark corners.

We stepped into the elevator. It was a strange experience. Feeling the motion, but seeing only Dot and part of the ceiling lit. It was hard to believe we were moving at all. Dot didn't say anything, but looked as determined as ever holding the flashlight just below shoulder height. Her glasses created large shadows around her eyes, framing them so it looked like she was wearing a mask. She was a superhero.

The elevator clanged to a stop and we stepped out into the dark hall. *Here we go again*, I thought. We walked that familiar hallway and Dot shone the light around to see more than just where we were going.

"Buddy, look," she said. Her light had caught the glint of something on the wall. She got closer but didn't have to. I knew what it was. "Ink," she said. She traced it with her flashlight down the wall farther away from us. The light grew and revealed thick trails of ink, like a hand had been dragged along it, but bigger. There were larger spatters toward the end of the wall, like someone had thrown buckets of ink at it. Dumped it on the ground and splashed it everywhere.

"No wonder they shut everything down. I don't even know how they'd start to clean this up. This is someone who's angry," said Dot.

"Do you think Sammy did this?" I asked.

"Who else?" She started walking again.

I didn't think Sammy did this.

I was feeling more sure by the moment. Sammy hadn't done all this and then just disappeared. Something else had done this . . . and then done something to Sammy.

Just as I had that thought, I heard it.

Now I wonder if it did actually happen that way. That I thought it and then heard the breathing. Maybe I had heard the breathing first. That would make more sense. I'm not that clever.

At first I thought it was my mind playing tricks on me. Like the ink slipping down the paper. But then Dot stopped and said, "Shh." And I knew. I knew she heard it too.

We stopped walking and stood in complete silence.

Except we couldn't stand in silence.

Not with the sound of wet breath stalking us from somewhere behind. Not with the sudden *thump* on the ground. And another.

I noticed then the light of Dot's flashlight was dimming. What a moment for the bulb to die. I turned to look and saw

Dot's face illuminated by the glow, staring in horror as the shadows started to creep into the beam. It could have been water pooling around us but I knew it wasn't.

Another *thump* and another.

The breathing got louder and louder.

The light got dimmer and dimmer.

"Run!" I whispered loudly, and gave Dot a push. I didn't even think about it, I just did it. And she ran. Didn't ask why, didn't try to come up with a better plan. She just ran. And I ran.

The light that was left bounced off the walls, making it hard to tell which direction we were going. It glanced off a poster and suddenly Bendy was grinning at us like he'd jumped out from behind the corner. I gasped, but the poster was soon behind us. Just like the breathing that was getting louder and louder. Panting. A large heavy animal chasing us. And catching up.

I barely saw the word "Music" before Dot called out, "Over here!"

We launched ourselves at the door to the Music Room and—however we got inside, however we got through—we were in, and the door slammed shut behind us. I leaned hard against it, out of breath, terror flowing from every pore.

"Buddy, look," said Dot quietly but urgently. She was pointing the flashlight at my feet. I looked down. The shadows were seeping their way under the door and her light flickered again.

I pushed myself away from the door fast, tripping into the room and into Dot, who stumbled a bit. I grabbed her hand instinctively, to keep track of her. She didn't fight me. Her light flashed up to the wall, still flickering.

More ink.

Then she turned to shine her light on the room.

Broken chairs and stands. Instruments scattered all over the place.

And ink.

Ink everywhere.

"Can you hear it?" she whispered. "I can't hear it."

I strained my ears to listen for the wet breathing, for the footsteps.

"No. Aim at the door again," I whispered back.

She did and gasped. We both staggered back instantly, still holding on to each other. The black shadows were even longer and seemed to be reaching now, almost like they were climbing up the beam of the flashlight. Like fingers trying to grab us.

"Turn it off, turn it off!" I said in a panic.

I could hear her fumble with the flashlight and then there was a click. We stood there, in the pitch dark. The only breathing I could hear was hers and mine. I clenched my body tight, bracing myself for the shadows to find us, to wrap themselves around us.

Nothing happened.

"What *was* that?" Dot asked in a frantic whisper.

"It was the thing. It's the thing from the Infirmary," I whispered back, trying desperately to answer and also not make a noise.

"I don't understand," whispered Dot, her hand shaking in mine. "It doesn't make sense. The shadows, the sounds."

"Shh!"

She was quiet instantly. I didn't know what I'd heard, but something, something, had sparked my senses. I closed my eyes. Even though it was pitch-black, I closed my eyes. Trying to hear through the darkness, as if the darkness itself was thick and muffling sound.

So quiet.

Too quiet.

"Do you think it's gone?" asked Dot.

Crash.

We both screamed.

"Turn on the light!" I said, and there was a panicked movement from behind me as Dot fumbled with the flashlight. The beam was dim, so dim, as it fell upon the floor.

But there was enough to catch the figure covered in thick ink on the ground in front of us.

"Buddy," gasped Dot.

I leaned down. I had done this before. I was experiencing the same thing before. In the Music Room. Bending over a figure covered in ink.

The head jerked and I fell back into Dot. She stumbled and the light wavered for a moment.

I stared at the figure.

It was propping itself up by its hands, its elbows bent and

shoulder blades protruding. A curtain of hair fell over the face, dripping now in ink, like the hair itself was ink.

I knew that hair.

"He's here," rasped a familiar voice.

The head twisted suddenly and then its body collapsed in a sickening thud against the wood.

"What is that?" asked Dot, her voice high and shaking.

"The violinist," I replied, barely able to get the words out.

"Who?"

I reached toward Dot; I needed the flashlight. I needed it. I was in full panic and all I knew was he was here. *It* was here.

Somehow Dot understood and put the flashlight in my shaking hand. I aimed it around the room wildly, barely taking a moment to see that the corners were empty, ignoring the reaching shadows, the dimming of the light, the flicker. Every direction, every way possible. I aimed down, and all around, and back to the door, and the chaos in the room just made it all like a fever dream, like I was dizzy.

Nothing. No one.

I stopped, the faint beam landing again on the violinist.

"Where did she come from?" whispered Dot. "She couldn't have just appeared."

I shook my head. No idea. "It's like she was just . . ." I didn't finish my thought.

There was a pause and then Dot completed my sentence, ". . . dropped."

Slowly and with a deep intake of breath I turned the flickering faint beam up above us and looked.

Something wet. Black. Dripping. A figure. With something sharp that glinted in the light. Like teeth.

And then the flashlight died in the shadows.

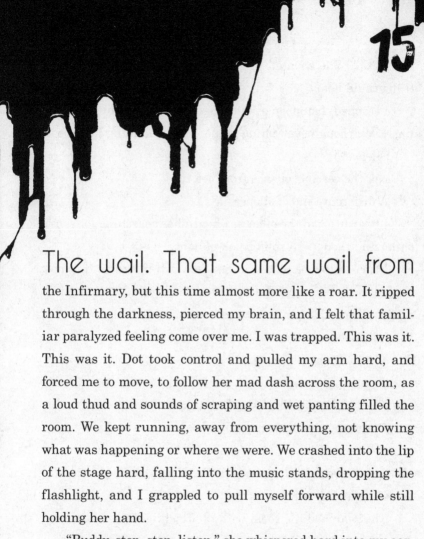

15

The wail. That same wail from the Infirmary, but this time almost more like a roar. It ripped through the darkness, pierced my brain, and I felt that familiar paralyzed feeling come over me. I was trapped. This was it. This was it. Dot took control and pulled my arm hard, and forced me to move, to follow her mad dash across the room, as a loud thud and sounds of scraping and wet panting filled the room. We kept running, away from everything, not knowing what was happening or where we were. We crashed into the lip of the stage hard, falling into the music stands, dropping the flashlight, and I grappled to pull myself forward while still holding her hand.

"Buddy, stop, stop, listen," she whispered hard into my ear.

I couldn't stop, I didn't dare stop. We had to get away, somehow.

"Listen."

I scratched at the stage, feeling splinters under my nails.

"Stop!" She shouted it. Out loud. Loud so anyone or anything could hear.

I stopped. I stopped even though my whole body was shaking. Even though everything in me was demanding I flee.

Silence.

Not the terrible silence from before.

A different kind of silence.

I heard Dot in the silence. I heard her searching for something and then . . . A solid beam of light.

I turned to look at her, at her face still in shadow but now visible in the fringe of the light. It was so good to see her face again. She nodded at me, to tell me she was okay, and then turned the beam.

The violinist was gone.

The thing was gone.

All that remained was a black inky stain.

Dot shone the light up.

Nothing.

Just more ink. Dripping a little. Now I could hear it. The faint single drip every so often.

She searched the room with the flashlight one more time, but even as she did I knew we both knew that whatever it was, whatever that thing was, it was gone. The shadows were gone.

Finally Dot turned, the beam aiming down again, and said, "Are you okay?"

I didn't know how to answer that question. I wasn't hurt. But the fear, the horror of what we'd seen. It felt like I was.

Like I was on the inside. Like when a person is bleeding on the inside.

Light suddenly blasted through the room, blinding me. I held up my hand to my face. What was happening now? My heart was racing and I couldn't swallow. Terrified of the beast.

"Norman?" called out Dot.

I moved my arm away from my face. It was still too bright to see much, but I could make out Dot beside me looking up toward the back wall. So I did too. All I could see was a bright white circle of light above me. Glowing.

"Norman, is that you?" Dot hollered again.

"Hey, little lady," said a familiar voice from upstairs.

"What on earth are you doing here?" She shielded the light from her eyes, so I did the same.

"Well, now, I could ask you the same question," he said.

I stared at the bright light. It felt wrong, almost like we were talking to the projector and not a real person.

"Did you see it? Did you see what happened?" asked Dot.

There was a pause.

"You two alright?" he replied.

"We're alright. Did you see what happened?" asked Dot.

"Not this time," he said. "Heard it though. That's why I came."

Dot turned to me. "Let's go talk to him." I immediately shook my head. The entrance to the Projector Booth was outside the door. No way. No way was I leaving this room, not now, not with that something out there. "Come on, it's safe," she said in a soothing voice. "We just need to watch the light."

"Safe?" I asked. I couldn't believe it. "Are you kidding me? We have to get out of here!"

"You two should probably wait a bit before heading back to the elevator, just in case," said Norman. "She's right about the light."

"How do you know?" I asked, turning abruptly. I shouted it at him, angry. What did any of us really know about that . . . thing? It didn't make sense in the first place, so how could they know we'd be safe out there?

"I know," said Norman.

"Come on," said Dot. I shook my head again but of course I couldn't hold Dot back. And I was definitely not staying behind. I followed her to the door and she opened it carefully, shining her flashlight around the corner. She looked back at me. "All good, steady beam." And then there I was, heart in my throat, racing out of the Music Room following Dot, up the stairs and into the small balcony area that served as Norman's Projector Booth, slamming the door fast behind me.

A wave of relief washed over me, but in place of the fear, the reality of everything that had happened to us really hit me. That thing. That inky thing. The violinist. Her body on the ground. Lying there. It was too much, too much. I stared out of the booth at the room below, holding tightly on to the railing. The flashing, blinding light of the projector made a perfect rectangle on the back wall of the Music Room. It flickered and lit the room, revealing the chaos in even more detail. The ink on the walls, the floor.

That spot on the floor. Where the violinist had been. I

leaned over the railing and looked closer. The ink stain looked smeared, like her body had been dragged . . . somewhere. Until the ink got fainter and fainter and then vanished.

"Hi, Norman," I heard Dot say. She sounded as exhausted as I felt. I turned and watched as she sat on a box filled with metal film reels. I had nowhere to put myself, so I leaned uncomfortably against the railing.

"Y'all happy with yourselves now? See what happens when you sneak around all the time? You two and your sneaking," he said, shaking his head. He took a sip from a mug, but I wasn't certain it was coffee in there.

"You've been watching us?" asked Dot.

Norman laughed to himself. "Never seen a pair of teenagers sneak around so much like you two and yet not fool around at all."

I choked on nothing then and started to cough.

"Sensitive boy, ain't he?" asked Norman, looking at Dot.

"That was a pretty rude thing to say though," she said back.

Norman shrugged.

"Do you know what's going on?" she asked.

Again he shrugged.

Dot sighed hard. "Norman, you invited us up here. I thought you wanted to talk."

"Well," he said, slowly taking another sip from his mug and leaning back in his chair. It seemed so casual and not at all how I was feeling. And it only made me get more tense.

Norman thought for a moment, and in that moment I

realized how much he looked like a character from a comic strip. An old gentleman sitting on his front porch. He had a cravat instead of a tie. "If I say you're right, what happens next?" His lined face glowed in the flickering projector, and his bushy eyebrows had such a steep point in the middle it made him look almost devilish.

"Next, you tell us," said Dot.

Norman glanced at me, gave me the once-over. Like people did that first week I was here. But it was like he hadn't really looked at me before now. "Is that what you want to know?" he asked me.

"Of course." It was an easy answer. I felt tense, and pretty sure we should be getting out of here immediately, but still, if we were going to wait this out until whenever, then, yeah, of course we wanted to know what the heck was going on.

"Of course," Norman said to himself. He took another sip. "He says it like that, knowing that he's the one who brought this creature upon us. Of course. Of course."

I felt cold then, like the temperature had dropped and it was winter. Like if I talked my breath would freeze. "What do you mean?" But I knew what he meant. He meant the Infirmary. The thing in the room with the locked door. The door I'd opened.

I'd let it out.

Me.

It was all my fault.

"What do you two know about the ink?" Norman asked instead.

"We know Sammy is obsessed with it," said Dot.

"So not much then," said Norman.

"How much do you know?" I asked, trying to hold it together.

"Everything."

Dot shifted in her seat, and I couldn't tell if it was because she was excited to get the truth or annoyed he was being so cagey.

"Tell us," I said.

"How much?" he asked.

"All of it," I said.

"Yes," said Dot with an edge to her voice.

"Okay, okay, calm down. You're acting like you've somewhere to go. When we all know no one here in this studio has anywhere to go."

I didn't know what that meant.

"The beginning, Norman," said Dot.

Norman nodded. "The beginning." He leaned back with his mug and put his feet up on the edge of the table holding the projector. "How familiar are y'all with Henry?"

16

Henry.

The name that had been haunting me since day one. The
name etched in my desk. The name Mister Drew had called me
when we were trying on tuxedos. That name I'd just assumed
was some former employee, and who really needs to know
about that anyway?

"Mister Drew's former business partner," said Dot. "Helped
fund Joey Drew Studios. He created Bendy."

"He created Bendy?" I said, shocked. "I thought . . . I
mean . . . I always assumed . . ."

"A lot of people assume that," said Norman. "It ain't like
Mister Drew corrects them."

That made me feel uncomfortable. The implication there.

"He created the big three, didn't he?" asked Dot.

"Bendy and Boris. Even Alice, though they didn't start fea-
turing her until after Henry left. Yup. He was a gifted artist.
Decent fellow too. As far as people go."

"Coming from you, that's quite the compliment," said Dot.

Norman barked out a laugh. "I guess."

"But what does Henry have to do with the ink?" I wanted to get on with the story, I didn't need to know about Henry and Mister Drew.

"Well, Henry left. Y'all know that. He left, wanted to spend more time with his wife, Linda. You get that, this job can be . . . consuming."

"Sure," said Dot.

I nodded, but swallowed hard. I thought about all the late nights. I thought about trying to prove myself. I thought about how I hadn't had a good conversation with Ma in a long time.

"How do you think a man like Joey Drew takes that?"

"Takes what?" I asked.

"The leaving. Mister Drew had the vision. But Henry, he had the talent. Talent's gone, what now? It ain't personal, but maybe Mister Drew takes it like it is. Maybe he decides he don't need Henry. Never did. Just needs the talent."

None of this was making any sense, and with everything that had just happened, the thought of some monster outside the door, and this feeling, this pit-in-the-stomach feeling hearing the word "vision" . . . I just couldn't put it all together.

"Okay, so Mister Drew hires talented people, we know that," said Dot.

"And we know the cartoons do okay for a while, after Henry leaves. Alice was popular for a beat. So was the original actress, Susie. You ever meet her?" asked Norman to Dot.

"Once," she replied.

"Cute kid." He finished up his drink and placed the mug on the table. "But still. It doesn't last. All the talent in the world, and it doesn't last. He starts spending money on that amusement park he ain't never going to build."

Of course Norman knew about that too.

"And the theater," I said, almost more to myself.

"What theater?" asked Norman.

"The studio starts to fail," said Dot, getting us back on track.

Norman nodded. "He needs something, anything. To get the studio back in the papers again. Get investors excited again."

That's when it finally clicked. "The machine," I said. "Tom Connor."

"Yes," said Norman, looking at me. "So you know about the machine then," he said, like he approved.

"Kind of," I said. I couldn't help but glance over my shoulder, just to check if the light was still as bright.

It was.

"We know that there is one. We know Tom Connor is working on it," said Dot.

"Was," corrected Norman.

"Was?" I asked.

Norman raised an eyebrow at me. "Was."

There was a silence where I suppose we were meant to ask

him why. But then Dot asked a different question. Getting us back on track. As she always did. "What does the machine have to do with the ink?"

"It needs ink to work."

"The pipe," I blurted.

"What pipe?" asked Dot.

"I thought it was strange, that first day, when Sammy was covered in ink and I had to clean it up. It was from a burst pipe in the closet. The pipe was flowing with ink. But how does it—"

Norman cut me off. "I don't know how, and I don't know what's going on. All I know is that all this ink goes in and comes out and when it comes out it's different somehow."

"Different ink." I thought about it. Now that the pieces had started coming together things were making more sense in my messed-up mind. I could solve more problems. "The ink Sammy was looking for . . . was crazy for . . ." I said carefully, making eye contact with Dot.

"Yes," she said. "Of course. Why would he care so much about regular ink? It's everywhere. We are an animation studio; we have it everywhere."

"Everywhere," I said.

"The machine," Dot said, turning back to Norman and leaning forward. "You said Mister Drew needs the ink for the machine. Norman, what does the machine do?"

I held my breath waiting for the answer. I almost felt like I didn't want to know it.

Norman just shook his head. He took his feet off the table and sat up. "I wish I knew. I only watch what I can see. And Mister Drew and that Tom Connor fellow, they were more sneaky than you two. I just know that Sammy isn't Sammy anymore. The ink, well, I don't know, but it seems to me like the ink is taking him over. I think it's the ink that took him."

"You think he's alive?" asked Dot.

"I don't know, but I'll tell you one thing. That ink has a mind of its own. Goes where it likes . . ."

"Slips off the page," I said, thinking about my Cowboy Bendy. Thinking about Sammy's notebook. Thinking about . . .

A kind of panic I'd never felt before, not even when the monster was chasing us. Something animalistic and deep down, something past my gut and right into my spine, overtook me in a moment of pure white-hot realization.

"I have the ink," I said. "I took a bottle from the supply closet, from Sammy's stash."

"Well, by now the studio is overrun with it. Mister Drew saw to that," said Norman.

"No, he didn't, that's not fair!" I shouted, but even as I did I thought about my grandfather looking at Mister Drew's hand, the words "Bad ink." No, it wasn't that. It couldn't be that. "You said it yourself that he hires people with talent," I said to Norman, "that he's the one with vision, so none of this was his fault. It's that Tom Connor. Or maybe Sammy." I was shaking now. All my feelings were mashed together as fear. I couldn't pick them apart. I couldn't split my realization about the ink from the conversation about Mister Drew or from the creature and the violinist and the shadows. The grasping, clawing shadows. All of it was just one big ball of fear.

"Buddy, calm down," said Dot.

"I can't, you don't understand. I have to go!" I did, I had to go.

"It's okay, Buddy, we should wait a bit longer," said Dot, standing up and coming over to me, placing a gentle hand on my shoulder.

"I can't! Don't you understand? I have the ink. I have the ink at home. It's in my apartment." I pulled her hand off me and ran out of the Projector Booth. I didn't worry if I'd hurt her. I didn't worry if Norman thought I was crazy. And I also didn't worry that the creature might find me and catch me. I didn't worry about any of it because I wasn't thinking. I wasn't processing. I was just doing.

I was running home.

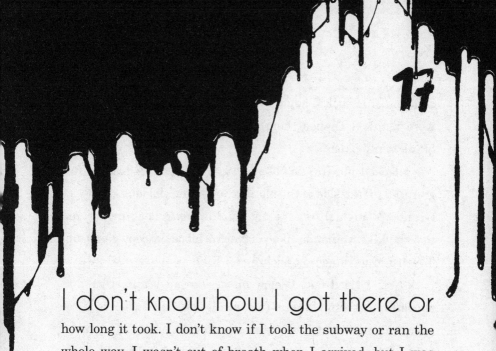

I don't know how I got there or

how long it took. I don't know if I took the subway or ran the whole way. I wasn't out of breath when I arrived, but I was slicked with sweat, though whether it was from my fear or the heat I couldn't say.

I don't know.

I just know that I was home. And I burst into the dark apartment. And I couldn't hear the silence or the sound of my hard feet hitting the wooden floor, just my heart pumping my blood through my body, thumping in my ears.

I burst into my room.

My ghostly grandfather lay as he always did, flat on his back, the streetlamp making him seem so pale, all skin and bones. I made my way around the bed to his side to look at the drawings. They were how I'd left them, scattered about on the floor, as I'd frantically gone through them, seeing the changes, feeling anxious.

I got to my knees to gather them up. But as I did, my fear

came pulsing back. They were blank. All the pages on the floor were blank. I flipped them over, examined both sides. Just blank white paper.

I looked up, frantic. That's when I saw it. A trail of ink running up the side of the blanket, up along the long sleeves of Grandpa's nightshirt, tracing up his neck heading for his mouth. Like veins, or like a river of blood, except going up. Toward him. Fingers. Reaching for him.

"No!" I cried out. I leapt up beside my grandfather and shook him. Pulling him up to a sitting position. His eyes burst open wide and he started thrashing about, clawing at my arms holding on to his. He screamed out in terror, or in pain. Or both.

"It's okay, it's okay!" I said, but he wouldn't stop moving, and it wasn't okay. He was still covered in the ink. I reached up, trying to wipe the ink off his neck with my hand, but he grabbed my wrist and pushed at me hard then, harder than I thought a man his age could push. I fell backward.

"What on earth!" Somehow Ma was in the room, on the bed, reaching for her father. "Papa!" She held his face firmly but gently between her hands. "Papa, *wszystko w porządku!*"

I could only watch, panting a bit as the old man finally calmed down and stared into my ma's eyes. He slowly reached up and held her face in his, so they were both cradling each other's.

"Irena," he said softly.

"Tak, Papa, tak," she said. "Irena."

He smiled slowly then. And nodded. He looked over at me. "Buddy."

I smiled back, rubbing my wrist where he'd twisted it. "Yes," I said.

He nodded again.

"Everything's okay," Ma said finally in English. She looked over at me. "What happened?"

Then I saw the ink on Grandpa's cheek. "The ink," I said, coming over. "We need to clean off the ink."

She saw it then and looked down at her hand. There was ink on it too from when she'd grabbed him and then transferred it to his face.

"What on earth . . ." she repeated quietly. She looked back to Grandpa, and that's when I knew she saw it, the ink running up the sheets, up his hand, his shirtsleeve, his neck. "What is all this, Buddy?"

"I'll explain as we clean him off. Let's get this nightshirt off." I motioned to Grandpa to raise his arms.

She nodded and explained to him what we were doing. It was a lot easier to communicate with him when you could communicate with him.

We peeled off the nightshirt, and sure enough, the ink had snuck in underneath, leaving a fine trail of ink from his neck all the way to his fingers. I picked up his forearm and looked at it, at the glossy, living blackness. I rubbed my thumb and smudged it. That was good.

I grabbed the nightshirt itself since it was ruined and began to rub at the arm.

"Buddy, don't," said Ma.

But I didn't listen because it made no sense. We didn't have time. We had to get all the ink off.

All of it.

There wasn't time to lose. "Get a wet rag, Ma," I said, still wiping.

"Buddy, stop!"

She held my shoulder. I looked at her in confusion. She looked at me and then at the arm. I stopped.

And I looked at his arm too.

The ink had been pushed away, but beneath it more ink revealed itself.

Numbers.

A tattoo.

When we learned Pa died, Ma didn't tell me till that night. I didn't know she'd spent all day just living her life, doing her work, her chores, taking care of me, with that heavy weight on her heart. That a man in uniform had come to our door. That he'd been direct to the point. That he'd told her the truth.

She told me at night in bed so she could make me feel better, tuck me in, lie beside me, and stroke my hair. Because she wanted me to be ready to be sad. But you can't always prepare for sadness. You just have to live with it.

I remembered this now, sitting with her, the clock ticking on the wall, my shoulders heavy, my back aching after scrubbing all the ink off Grandpa.

Under the single bulb above the kitchen table, the shadows

on Ma's face made her look much older than she was and very tired. I figured if there was a mirror I'd see the same with me. It felt like the summer had lasted a lifetime, and maybe it had. I don't know. I'm not sure time works the way I always thought it did.

"Why didn't you tell me?" I said finally.

"There was so much to tell, and you had this new job, and I never saw you. And I had work too. And then you two seemed to be bonding and what's the point anyway?" she said. I noticed her long, winding sentence mirrored my long, winding thoughts. I came by it honestly, I guessed.

"Start at the beginning."

Start at the beginning.

Like there is such a thing. There isn't a beginning. There is only a moment that makes the moments that follow matter.

Ma shook her head because she understood that. "Do you know how many times I've tried to figure out the beginning?" She sighed. "Oh, Buddy. It's so sad."

I leaned over and took her hand. "It's okay, I can handle sad."

"Your pa wanted to come here. He wanted opportunity. So many people do. I came with him and brought you, this little bundle in my arms, because he was my husband. Because he made me believe in the adventure. I wanted your grandfather to come with us. But he had his job, his students."

"He was a teacher?" I asked.

"Can't you tell?" She smiled.

"Art . . ."

She nodded. "Then . . . then when things started getting scary over there, I begged him to come, I begged him. He was my only family left, and I thought he needed me as much as I needed him. But he refused. He wouldn't come. He needed to stay for his community, he said. But he did send us his art collection. That he wanted to protect, not himself." She looked angry and sad and still so very tired.

"I don't understand. Because they're worth something? What's so important about these paintings?" I looked at the one hanging just below the clock, its gilt frame, its bright abstract pattern.

"To him art is more than just a pretty picture. It's history. It's . . ."

"Your soul," I said, remembering now.

"Yes. The Germans had invaded, and they were taking everything. He wouldn't leave anyone behind, but he didn't want them to get their hands on the work. I was so angry at him at the time, but I understand now. When I hear about over there, when I hear about everything that was destroyed . . . He was right to send his art. But I can never forgive him for not sending himself." Her eyes were misty with tears.

"I understand that." I took her hand in mine.

"Then he disappeared. And I didn't hear from him again." She looked down at the table, her head bent so low. "I was mourning your father, I was taking care of you, I was working to support us, and these paintings haunted me. I was angry, and I thought he was dead, and I was hurting. So I didn't think to look any deeper." A tear fell onto the stained wooden table-top. Right in the middle of a ring made from a damp glass.

"This all makes sense, Ma," I said. I wasn't used to reas-suring her. To being the one who comforts. I'd always wanted to take care of her, but that was about making money and her not having to work as hard. Taking care of her sadness, her fears, that was something I wasn't so prepared for. It was hard. My throat ached. "You shouldn't feel bad."

"I tell myself this. But I do. Because I should."

She squeezed my hand and looked up at me.

"When the war ended, your father's brother was looking for family. Because that's what good children do. He learned so much. What they had done, where they had sent people like us. Such horrible things. I am so ashamed. He found Grandpa. A family in a town near the camp where he had been impris-oned was taking care of him. A family, not his family. Not me." She took in a sharp breath and quickly wiped her cheeks. "Your uncle helped me bring him here. And you know the rest."

"Ma, you should tell me these things," I said.

"Like you're telling me things about your work? Like you and your grandfather don't have your secret projects?" she said, smiling through her tears.

"That's different, and you know it," I said. I took both her hands now in mine.

"Oh, Buddy, I feel so much shame. But you must learn from my mistakes. You have to fight for the people you love. Okay?"

"Yes." Of course I would. I always would fight for her, for Grandpa.

It was so easy in that moment to make that promise to her, to myself. It seemed so obvious. So clear that of course this would be a thing to do. I had no idea that in a short twenty-four hours, that promise would be tested.

Once more I didn't know how I got to where I was going. But it wasn't from full fear or panic now, but from never having felt so completely overwhelmed before. I had been told so much in such a short span of time. Experienced so much. My eyes had been opened wide to things I'd never even imagined, and my own guilt and confusion pressed down hard on me.

I reached the East River, coming to realize two things: I had judged my grandfather so horribly, and, in the end, it turned out I knew nothing about him or my own family. And that I also knew nothing about Mister Drew, so how could I possibly understand his motivations, what was happening at work? I needed to know his story.

Everyone has a story to tell.

Even if it's fictional.

I tossed the bag with the papers, pen, ink bottle, rags, and my grandfather's nightshirt into the black water in front of me. It bobbed for a moment, and then slowly sank.

I didn't feel good about it. Just more unsettled. The water looked like ink.

18

There was nothing in me that felt like going to a party. It had been everything I was looking forward to for the last few weeks, and now it loomed like a dark cloud on a sunny day. I'd been almost hoping, with all the chaos at the studio, the thing would be canceled, but the studio reopened two days later and everyone went back to work as if nothing had happened.

Of course for most people it hadn't been such a big deal, two days off, a little holiday. But what Dot and I had experienced? What we had seen? Going back into the building was a terrifying thing. I wasn't in any kind of position to quit—I had to keep making money for my family. But I also knew that I was done searching in the dark corners. I was keeping my head down and leaving before it got dark. Focus on my work.

And if Mister Drew thought it was safe enough for us all to go back inside, well, I trusted him.

Still.

Mostly.

Mister Drew gave a little pep-talk in the lobby. "I know it's been a tough few days, but we've reopened and the work goes on! Let this be a lesson to anyone who thinks they can mess with our studio!" He laughed heartily and everyone applauded, and I exchanged a look with Dot. She made her way over to me as the crowd scattered.

"Hey," she said. "How are you?"

I couldn't make eye contact with her. I didn't want to talk about anything, I just wanted to pretend like none of it had happened. There was real life to focus on. I was done with monsters.

"I have to get to work," I said, and pushed past her.

She didn't chase me. Dot didn't really chase after people.

Funny that I'm sitting here writing this, hoping to reach her.

The party was Friday, and as the day approached, the storm clouds gathered in my mind. The Music Department was still shut down, and no one had heard anything from Sammy. Dot and I hadn't even talked about that night because I'd been avoiding her. I don't think she understood why. I mean, why would she? Well, she probably thought I was still scared about the terrifying creature in the dark, about the violinist. And I was. But I couldn't tell her the other part. That I was still processing everything Ma had told me. About what had happened to Grandpa during the war.

That being said, Grandpa seemed pretty fine. Completely unaffected by the ink. I guess after everything he'd been through, a strange night like the one we had was really not that big of a deal. He was back to his old self and only disappointed I'd thrown out the drawings and the ink. He wanted me to practice more. But I told him I couldn't. Not now.

Maybe not ever, a part of me said.

I sat on the bed first thing the morning of the party, holding the suit bag in my arms. I'd never felt this heavy before. So weighted down. By . . . what, I didn't know. I just had a feeling that that night was not going to go well. I wanted to have faith in Mister Drew, but the more I learned, the harder it was, and it made me feel foolish. But then I thought about everyone else at the studio who seemed to trust him, to believe in him. I didn't know what to think.

"Sad?" Grandpa asked, sitting next to me.

I didn't even know he was here. "Tired."

He nodded. "Yes," he said. I could tell he was looking at me but I didn't want to look back. He took my hand in his and said, "Buddy. Your heart is good. Your soul is good. This is good."

I finally looked at him, at those eyes that had once frightened me and now seemed warm and thoughtful. I wished I could speak to him properly. I felt like I didn't have the time to learn. But I heard him. I wanted to tell him I wasn't sure. I wasn't sure of anything anymore. That the world confused me and scared me. But I didn't know how to express that to him.

"Grandpa, I'm sorry," I said instead.

He looked at me a little confused. "Sorry?" He shook his head. "No, no need sorry."

"No, I am. I was angry you were here, I was angry about the art, I didn't understand."

Grandpa turned and gazed at the painting at the foot of the bed. I had no idea if I was making any sense to him.

"Anger is okay," he said.

Was it? I wasn't sure it was. Didn't feel okay, that was for sure.

"Anger can inspire person. Can make change. Can make art." He reached out and touched the painting, just the tips of his fingers, but I was shocked. Who just touched a painting? "Passion."

I nodded. I wasn't sure where he was going with this but I needed to listen. I needed what he was saying.

"Too much anger . . ." He pushed gently at the canvas, still just with his fingertips. The paint cracked and the canvas pushed backward, like a hidden door. There was a hole in the painting. I stared. How did he know that was there? Wait. Unless . . .

"Did you . . . is this your painting? Did you paint this?" I asked.

Grandpa nodded. He stared at the hole hard. He made a fist and placed it slowly inside. It fit perfectly. "Hate," he said turning to me.

I don't know how I understood him finally, after all this time. But I did. It was his painting, he had created it. Something had made him very angry. He had tried to destroy it. Grandpa smiled again at me and turned back to the painting, carefully pulling out his hand. He delicately took the edge of the broken canvas between his two fingers and pulled the loose piece slowly back into place.

"Anger inspire. Hate destroy. Love fix." He smiled wide then. "Fancy lesson," he said with almost a laugh.

I couldn't help but laugh too, seeing him like this, self-aware. I wondered what his thoughts were like; were they like mine? All over the place and confused? Commenting on everything? Had they maybe been like that and now they were calm?

He took my hand and patted it. "You okay."

That, I didn't think was true. But maybe I would be. Maybe I would be okay.

Grandpa gave me one more smile and pat on the hand before he let it go. He stood up, gave me one last look, and with a satisfied nod, left the room.

Saying good-bye is hard. Especially when you don't know when you'll see someone again. If you ever will. Saying good-bye to Pa felt impossible, like I was squeezing the words out of my chest. Holding on to his hand because letting go was too hard.

But now I know something worse.

Not getting to say good-bye at all.

I brought my tux to work to change

because I didn't want a repeat of when Mister Drew drove me home. I also couldn't imagine sitting on the subway in that suit, being stared at. And walking was out of the question. I'd show up at some classy joint soaking wet from sweat.

So I brought the bag with me, which meant, of course, everyone who saw me instantly knew I'd been invited.

Ms. Lambert hadn't said anything. She just looked at the bag and shook her head and got back to work. But both Richie and Jacob had fun messing with me. I don't know, maybe they were actually jealous and hiding it, but they seemed pretty decent about it all.

"Well, we were going to invite you to join our little party tonight, at Duke's across the street. But I guess not, Mr. Fancy," said Jacob.

"Does Dot know?" asked Richie, leaning against my desk.

"Dot?" I asked.

"Is she your date, is what he's asking," said Jacob, giving Richie a look.

"Oh, no, no. Just me. Alone. I . . . kind of wish I wasn't going." I didn't mean to be so honest, but it kind of came out like that.

"Are you kidding, young bachelor on the town? Surrounded by gorgeous dames, all dolled up? You have to go, for my sake," said Richie.

Well, I couldn't *not* go anyway. I felt like Mister Drew would take it personally. "Okay, okay," I said with a laugh. And then the guys laughed too, until Ms. Lambert yelled at us to get back to work.

And then things were pretty normal. It's funny how normal can be weird. Sometimes things shouldn't be normal. After everything I'd been through, being teased, doing work, going to a party, that felt really strange.

I didn't see Dot all day. Not once. I don't know why. I went to Story many times, but she wasn't there. I knew she was at work that day, other folks told me so. It was almost like she was avoiding me. Maybe she was. After all, I'd been avoiding her all week. It was only fair.

I wanted to wait until the team left before changing into my tux, but they had other plans in mind, and so I was forced to do a little fancy walk and show off my suit to them as they all whistled at me. I'll admit that wearing that suit did make me feel pretty good. There was something about clothes that fit you properly and looked good on you that actually affected your mood.

Finally we were off, and that's when I saw Dot. In the lobby. Waiting for the other guys to go to Duke's Pub with them.

"You're in a tux," she said, furrowing her eyebrows.

"Yeah, Buddy's going to Mister Drew's swanky shindig," said Jacob, slapping me on the back.

"Really?" She was looking at me hard.

"Yeah," I said. "I don't really want to go."

"Good," she said. "I think we should go back tonight, with the party and everyone else leaving early. We need to find that machine. What it does."

My face started to feel warm, and my gut clenched. But it wasn't fear. For once. I realize I was feeling angry. With her. "Why? Why do we have to do that?" I asked sharply.

She looked taken aback. "Because we need to figure out what is happening in the studio," she replied slowly.

"No, we don't. We don't," I snapped back. *Don't let the anger turn to hate, Buddy*, I told myself, hearing my grandfather's words in my ear. *Don't let it grow.* "And even if the mystery for some reason needs to be solved, we don't have to be the ones to do it."

"Buddy . . ." said Dot. She looked uncomfortable, and unsure. I didn't like seeing her unsure. "What about the violinist?"

My throat closed as I tried to swallow. I leaned in and

whispered, "That's exactly why we need to stop."

"That's exactly why we *can't*," she fiercely whispered back.

I shook my head. No. It wasn't worth risking my life over. I had a family to take care of. I needed to protect them. "Why do you need to do this? What's it to you?"

"I need to," she said, her voice shaking with emotion.

"But why?" Of all the things she couldn't be direct about.

"Because I can do this!" She was still whispering, but it felt like shouting. "Because it's something I can do. I can actually make a difference. I don't have to just sit there, and wait, and worry, and watch people die. I can stop it. And help. You have no idea what it's like to feel like there's nothing you can do."

I couldn't help it, I laughed. It was crazy, of all the things I knew, it was feeling helpless, out of control.

"Don't laugh at me," she said.

"I'm going to the party. I'm tired and I don't want to, but it's important for Mister Drew."

Dot laughed. "After everything Norman said to us, you think he cares about you, Buddy?"

That was going too far. "I do. I think he cares. I think he cares at least about me. He might not be perfect, but no one is. Not me. Not him. Not you."

Dot bit the inside of her cheeks. I took a step back as Jacob sidled up to us. "Alright, let's get this party started!" he said, clapping his hands together.

"I thought you weren't coming," I said, distracted by Dot's expression.

"Not the boring party you're going to, Buddy, the fun party. My party." He smacked me on the back.

Dot continued to stare at me. "Well. Have fun," she said. Then she turned sharply for the door and started to head out the building.

"Whoa, Dot, wait up!" called Jacob. "Sorry, Bud, gotta run. Come join us at Duke's if you're not all swanked out!" He dashed after her, followed quickly by Richie, who gave me a wink.

And then I was alone in the lobby. Feeling both really frustrated and really stupid.

Of course that level of stupid was nothing compared to how I felt arriving at the hotel for the party. First of all I'd paid for a cab, and after tipping the driver and stepping out onto the street I just felt so dumb for wasting my money like that. Just because I didn't want to wrinkle my tux. And anyway, looking sharp really didn't seem to matter because, next to all the perfectly dressed couples gliding into the gleaming lobby, I suddenly felt like clothes did *not* make the man. Well, maybe they did, if that man was the doorman. Which is what I looked more like. Or a waiter. Basically anything other than a guest. It wasn't just the quality of my tux, which I realized was not quite as nice as the gentleman's standing next to me waiting for the elevators was. It was the way he carried himself. The way he and his wife glanced at me. The way she pulled her fur stole a little tighter around her torso.

They could probably smell my neighborhood on me. Even if they couldn't see it. They knew.

The doors to the elevator opened and an attendant in a bright red uniform and cap held them for us as we stepped on.

"Joey Drew Studios party?" he asked.

I nodded. The woman with the fur said "Yes" in this way that gave the word two more syllables.

The doors closed.

We stood for a moment in silence, rising up through the building.

"Well, this will be interesting," said the man with a sigh.

"Oh, hush," said his wife.

He rolled his eyes and looked at me, like he wanted me to roll my eyes in solidarity with him. "You know Joey?" he asked.

I didn't want to speak, I didn't want them to hear my accent. So I just nodded again, and made a kind of yes sound in the back of my throat.

"Don't know what he thinks he's trying to prove. Can he even afford this?"

"Dear, hush," said the wife with a little more emphasis.

The husband looked at me and sighed. I was able to roll my eyes back this time, which he seemed to appreciate.

The doors opened.

"Rooftop," announced the elevator operator with a smile. We made our way into a small plush foyer, all pink carpet and pink shiny wallpaper. A chaise lounge leaned against the opposite wall, and a woman in a purple dress sat on it checking her lipstick in her compact.

I followed behind the man and his wife to a set of double doors where two men dressed almost exactly like me opened them to a large, loud party on the roof in full swing. Literally. The dance floor was packed with couples swing dancing, and a live band played for them at the far end. I wondered for a moment if any of the musicians worked for Mister Drew.

I remembered the violinist.

Then I tried instantly to forget her and just take in everything I was seeing.

This is another time I wish I could draw the scene. It was impressive, but what does that mean when I say that? I can say that we were on the rooftop patio with the lights of New York City sprawled out before us. It felt like being in the sky surrounded by stars. There were bright lights shining on the dance floor, on the mirrored bar, on the crowd, dressed in every color of the rainbow. Huge planters overflowing with yellow hyacinths framed the edge on all four sides. I only knew the kind of flower because for a while there we were getting a lot of them. After Pa died. The only way to not want to throw them out the window was learning a bit about them.

There was laughter and conversation and the clinking of champagne glasses.

I stood there, paralyzed in awe, overwhelmed. And in that moment I realized how different the lives of others really were. Not that I hadn't always known that. But this was like a kick to the gut. A kick to the gut after you've already been punched and are on the ground all curled up. I shook my head and blinked hard, and then decided getting a drink might just help.

So I turned and found myself staring eye-to-eye with Bendy.

I stared at the large smile, the teeth, the solid black eyes. I stared at this face I knew so well in front of me. Living, right in front of me. I felt this wave of nausea pass over me as I stumbled, and staggered forward.

"Hey, watch it!" he said. Or I guess the muffled voice inside of Bendy said it. It was hard in the moment for me to understand what was going on, my heart was pumping so fast. But when he shoulder-checked me and walked away everything came into clear focus. I turned to quickly watch him wander through the crowd as folks noticed him and laughed with delight. A man in a giant Bendy costume.

That's when I saw a large Boris on the dance floor doing a kind of awkward Charleston. And Alice standing over by the band pretending to conduct. Each mascot was around six feet tall, maybe taller. They looked off. Not in the right proportions. The way they looked didn't match their images in my head. It didn't match the cartoons. They weren't meant to be oversized like this. Weren't meant to be life-sized.

"They don't work at all, do they?" said a familiar voice. I looked to my right and, sure enough, Mister Drew had come up beside me.

"No," I replied, hoping he wouldn't mind. Even though he'd just said what he had.

"Come check out this view with me, Buddy," he said, motioning with his arm.

I followed him through the crowd. He said hi to everyone, shook hands, patted backs, laughed at jokes he only heard the punch line to. It was almost as much of a dance as the people swirling about to the music. He led me to where a few couples were gathered along the edge of the rooftop, looking out toward the glowing Empire State Building. The view was, well, magnificent.

Not a word I think I'd ever used before that night.

"Amazing, isn't it?" said Mister Drew, leaning on the wrought iron railing. I had a flashback to standing beside him on the catwalk. To his prank. I stayed a couple feet behind him.

"Yes," I said.

"Every single one of those buildings out there, every single one was built by someone who had a dream. Who worked hard and never lost sight of that."

I nodded, though he couldn't see me. I didn't think he really needed me to react anyway. He was going to say what he wanted to say.

He turned around, though, and looked at me. "You don't agree?"

"No, I do," I said quickly. "I nodded. I'm sorry, I do agree." I felt really uncomfortable all of a sudden.

He squinted at me. "Because some people will tell you that you should give up. That it's a fool's errand."

"There are always people who do that," I said.

Mister Drew kept staring at me. Then suddenly he was really close. "Don't let anyone hold you back," he said in a loud whisper. I could smell alcohol on his breath.

"Well, Joey, this is some party, but I'm not sure I deserve all this." A bombastic voice broke his intense stare, and Mister Drew was suddenly giving a big, burly man a big, burly hug.

"Bertie, you old so-and-so!" he said with a chuckle. "So you made it to your own celebration at last."

They pulled apart as the bigger man laughed heartily. "Sure, sure. You say this now, but you'll be tossing me off the side of this building when you-know-what hits the fan and we have to move the deadline."

"Well, fair's fair," said Mister Drew and they both laughed again. "Buddy!" he said, turning to me and wrapping an arm over the man's shoulder. "This is Bertrum Piedmont. He's a genius."

"Well, I'm something alright," replied Bertrum, sticking out a beefy hand and shaking mine vigorously. "Nice to meet you, Buddy."

"Buddy's an apprentice at the studio. An artist," said Mister Drew.

"Well, we always need those," said Bertrum, and I wasn't sure if he meant it or not.

Mister Drew laughed and then smacked him on the back. "Come on, now that you're here it's time for the speech."

"Oh, great, you know I love those!" said Bertrum, and they laughed together and walked away toward the stage.

How could two people who seemed so happy and carefree make me feel so completely the opposite?

I wandered over to the dance floor but stayed on the opposite side of the stage near the doors to the foyer. I don't know why, but I felt like I needed a quick getaway. Just in case.

When the band finished their song, Mister Drew took to the stage and was ceded the microphone by the sparkly singer. He smiled and kissed both her cheeks before turning to the crowd.

"How's everyone doing tonight?" he called out. His voice boomed over the crowd, and I wondered for a moment if all of New York could hear him.

There was a healthy cheer from the audience, though it didn't quite match his level of enthusiasm.

"First of all, I want to thank everyone for coming out tonight. I want to thank the band, Janie and the Bandits. And most of all I want to thank our special guest here this evening, Bertie Piedmont."

There was another smattering of applause. If applause could sound confused, this did.

"Who is Bertie Piedmont, you might ask?" he said, clearly sensing the confusion. "He's many things. A genius, some might call him. A friend, is what I say. But most of all he is a man with vision."

There was that word again.

"It's been a project six years in the making, but thanks to Bertie, Bendy and his friends are about to go on a whole new adventure. Have no fear, their stories that you love aren't going anywhere. But now you'll all be able to be a part of them yourselves!"

I looked around. I saw people whispering and a few smirks. I didn't like this. Yes, the man could be larger than life. But this was his party. They were his guests. They should at least be a little respectful.

"Yes, ladies and gentlemen, may I introduce you to Bendyland!" With a flourish of his arm Mister Drew brought out a pretty brunette model in a short black dress, wearing a sparkling halo in her hair. She pushed a trolley on which was the model display Dot and I had seen on my very first day at the studio. It was painted now, not just black and white. And even though they had been laughing at him only a moment before, I could see the audience now straining to have a closer look.

"Imagine: rides, games, and getting your picture taken with the stars of the cartoons themselves!" he said, grinning broadly. "But that's not all! Expansion in all ways, I always say! As of tomorrow, Joey Drew Studios now owns the Court Theater. We'll be bringing all Bendy production back into Manhattan. Everything will be produced out of this one location: animation, toys, and anything related to the amusement park. This is a new era for Joey Drew Studios, and that's what we are celebrating tonight!"

The crowd applauded one more time and this time I did too. It was exciting, how could it not be?

"Yes, yes, it's quite something, isn't it? It's all about to change . . . everything . . ." Mister Drew looked a little distracted. Like he'd noticed something. "Uh . . . everything is going to change. But not tonight! Tonight we dance and . . . yeah, hit it!" He motioned with his finger for the band to start again, but he was already walking toward me before the music began.

No. No, not toward me. He was looking behind me.

I turned.

There standing framed in the doorway were a pair of figures. The woman, I realized, was Allison Pendle. The actress who voiced Alice Angel. She stood there in a dress that fit as if someone had poured silver over her body. It hugged all her curves and shone in the light on the rooftop. On her arm was a man who I barely recognized but looked familiar to me.

"You shouldn't be here," said Mister Drew as he approached me, making his way toward them.

"Tom, we should go," I heard Allison say, but the man just stood there, solid as stone.

Tom Connor. Of course. It was Tom Connor.

20

I was pushed aside as Mister
Drew approached them. He went right up to Tom and seemed
to be shaking with anger despite his outward appearance.

"I'm not leaving until I get what's mine," Tom said as
Mister Drew stared him down.

Mister Drew laughed like Tom had just told an excellent
joke, and looked around at the few people watching. They
quickly moved away. Mister Drew turned back to Tom and in a
low voice said, "You're fired, Tom. I told you not to come anywhere near my studio. Let's step into the hall, shall we?"

"We aren't in your studio right now, are we?" replied Tom.
There was no way Mister Drew could physically intimidate
this man. Tom wasn't burly and bearlike like Bertrum
Piedmont. He was more wall-like. Still Mister Drew grabbed
him by the elbow and through clenched teeth said:

"The hallway. Now."

"Come on, Tom, no need to make a scene," said Allison
with a warm voice, gently placing a hand on his shoulder.

Tom allowed them to escort him to the pink lobby. I followed. I had to know what was going on. I didn't even think about it, or realize how strange it was that I was coming along.

Mister Drew signaled for the large doors to be closed, and just after the waiters did so, he whipped around, his smile having vanished, and said, "You need to leave immediately before I get security to throw you out!"

"I want my patent back," Tom said right into Mister Drew's face. They were practically nose-to-nose. Or more like, nose-to-chin.

"It's mine, legally and ethically. Now, get out." He turned to Allison. "And, Allison, I'm ashamed of you. You're fired."

Allison just smiled her dazzling smile that made me melt a little, even though the scene was making me incredibly tense. "We'll talk about that in the morning, Joey. Come on, dear." She gave Tom a little push on his shoulder, and evidently she could move mountains because once again he gave in and took a step back.

"It's my machine, Drew, it's mine."

"You ruined everything and I'm going to have to fix it. It's my machine and your mess. Now get out."

I heard it all. Everything Mister Drew said. But I didn't really manage to absorb it at the time because all I was focused on was the word "machine." I watched as Tom and Allison slowly headed toward the elevators. Mister Drew turned and swung open one of the doors himself, not even really noticing I was right there. He stormed back into the party. And the door closed behind him.

I turned, walking quickly away from the doors, from the party. Following Tom and Allison. And then I was grabbing the man by his shoulder. Trying to stop him. Needing to stop him.

Stop him I did.

He spun on his heel in a fury and stared at me like I was insane.

"I heard you say something about the machine," I said as he twisted out of my grip.

"Get your hands off me, son." He was looking at me with daggers in his eyes.

"Tom, it's okay. He's the gofer at the studio. Buddy," said Allison.

I stared at her for a moment. How on earth did she remember me? I was stunned that someone like her would even notice I took up space on the planet.

"I don't care. No one grabs me like that," said Tom.

"I'm sorry, I'm so sorry, but you said something about the machine, and I need to know." I stopped. I could tell they were both taken aback by me. By what I'd said. I wasn't sure if I should go on.

"How do you know about the machine?" asked Tom, moving a step toward me. He might have looked elegant, but I noticed how well he filled out his sleeves, how his arms strained against the fabric. I definitely didn't want to get into a fight with this man.

I couldn't think of anything that made sense. I couldn't tell him about Norman, or hiding in the closet. So I let fly the only word I could think of: "Sammy."

Tom sighed loudly, and Allison gave his arm a squeeze. "Should have figured," he said. But he didn't say anything more.

I don't know where I found the courage, but I guess I channeled some of Dot's directness in that moment. I was so tired of people not quite saying things. Of only getting part of the story. "What is the machine? What's it for? And why did Mister Drew fire you?" I wanted to ask more questions than that. I wanted to ask if he thought Mister Drew was evil or good. I wanted to ask about the ink and Sammy. About the creature, the violinist. But I also knew that too many questions confused people.

I know now when I ask myself too much I start to shut down. He starts to whine. We don't like it.

Tom took in a deep breath and glanced around the plush foyer. "Fine. The machine was meant to create . . ." He paused. "Characters."

"Like the mascots inside?" I asked. This didn't sound that odd. They already made toys, why not have a machine that made large Bendy costumes?

Tom shook his head. For the first time I realized he wasn't just holding back out of stubbornness. He was . . . scared.

"I shouldn't be telling you this . . ." he said, shaking his head.

"Look, I know about the . . . ink," I said. "And I know . . . about . . ." I stopped.

Tom looked at me carefully. It was hard maintaining eye contact with him. I just wanted to look away. At anything else. Finally he said, "You know about *it*."

"I'm not sure," I replied. Because I didn't know what I knew.

Tom took in a deep breath. "Okay. Okay," he said, making a decision. "Okay. It wasn't mascots. Nothing like that. It was . . . a way to take the cartoons and make them real. Not people in mascot costumes, but actual, real versions of the characters." He looked at me in this way that said, "You get it?" I didn't think I did.

Allison interrupted. "Think of it like a printing press, but for . . . people."

"People?" I asked.

"Not people, Allison. Please," said Tom, shaking his head. "I don't want you involved in this."

"I am, Tom. You can't make me not care because I care about you. What you helped create was astonishing."

"What I helped create was monstrous and you know it," he snapped back at her. Then he shook his head. "I'm sorry, I'm sorry."

"It's okay. But we should go. I'm certain he's called security."

Tom nodded. "It wasn't my fault," he said. Then he looked at me with that intense look again. "It wasn't my fault."

The word "it" stood out to me. He was saying he wasn't to

blame, but also, I thought maybe he was saying that "it," the "it," also wasn't his fault. I didn't know for sure. But my gut clenched. *Dot*, I thought to myself. She was alone with "it."

"What wasn't?" I asked carefully.

"He fired me because it wasn't my fault," continued Tom, not really listening to me anymore. "He fired me to blame anyone but himself." He looked over his shoulder at me. "But he still kept the machine. Even though. And that's Gent's invention, I helped invent it, and he took away my rights, my design, everything."

"How could he make you do that?" I asked.

He turned slowly and shook his head. "Not all of us are well connected, son. Not all of us have chances. Especially to get a job as an engineer when I ain't had no proper education and training. No one of any status had given me that kind of respect since I was working on planes during the war. I trusted him. He paid me extra. He had a legal contract with Gent. Treated me like a real businessman. But I didn't read the fine print."

I didn't know what to say to all that. I just stood there.

"We all trusted him," said Allison. "I don't know anyone who really understood what they were signing. I think Mister Drew likes finding people who are talented but also need the job. Who *really* need the job."

My gut now felt funny. Not clenched anymore, not butterflies, just a weird kind of ache.

"Let's not forget Susie," she added.

Tom sighed.

"Who's Susie?" I asked. Hadn't Norman also mentioned something about her?

Allison looked at me sadly and shook her head. "That's not the point, Buddy. The point is everyone here agrees that Mister Drew owns whatever we make. Drawings. Stories. Songs. And"—she looked at Tom—"inventions. It started with Henry, and it continues with the rest of us. It's the sacrifice we made."

I was processing everything they were telling me. It was all coming crashing down, all the walls I'd put up in defense of Mister Drew. I just couldn't hold them up anymore, and I was getting buried under them.

"Now we need to go, and you take care of yourself. And take care of that writer girl. She's swell," she said with a small, sad smile.

"She's the one who takes care of me usually . . ." I said.

The feeling in my gut grew stronger.

"Get out while you can, son," said Tom as the elevator opened and they stepped in.

The doors closed and I was alone. The sounds of the party wafted through the doors, but now they no longer tempted me. They just made my uneasy feeling worse. *I shouldn't be here*, I thought. *I shouldn't. I should be with Dot. And Jacob. I don't belong here. I belong with the people who I care about. Who care about me.*

Duke's Bar was as packed as it always was when I pushed my way through to the bar. For the first time folks in there took notice of me. Some laughed, some nodded like we had some kind of shared secret about my tuxedo, and some others glared at me. I missed being an invisible nobody.

"Hey, kid," said the bartender, a happy guy with a receding hairline he refused to acknowledge. "A Coke like usual?"

I shook my head. "I'm looking for Dot," I said.

The bartender smiled. "Of course you are. Well, I haven't seen them in about an hour."

"Oh," I said, feeling deflated. I leaned my body against the bar, feeling heavy now.

"Yeah, think they went back to the office." The bartender moved on down to the next customer who was flagging him.

The office? "Wait!" I called out. "You mean all of them? Dot, Jacob, and Richie?"

The bartender was pulling a pint and nodded in my direction, the wall of sound between us too thick for him to say something I'd hear.

I turned on my heel and pushed my way outside and across the street. Of course I was panicking again. And of course somehow Dot had convinced the guys to go with her back to the studio. I wondered if she'd explained everything. I wonder if they understood what was waiting for them.

She had to have. She wasn't a liar, and she wasn't going to put someone in danger if they didn't know about it. Still. Then. Why on earth did they go with her? They couldn't have known what hid in the dark shadows, or that the shadows themselves were alive.

The lights in the studio were all on, though for some reason it didn't look any less ominous than it had that night Dot and I snuck inside. Especially because I got it, they were on so that if the monster was coming there'd be a sign.

The thought didn't hold me back or make me slow down. It was amazing how entering a monster's den felt so right to me all of a sudden, but going to a fancy hotel party had felt like doom.

The front door was open. Maybe Dot had left it that way on purpose, just in case I showed up. Because she knew I would show up. I raced across the foyer to the elevator, glancing up at the posters as I went by. I remembered the life-sized versions of the characters at the party in their awkward weirdness. And then what Tom had said. About the purpose of the machine. And about "it."

I started to sprint and skidded into the elevator grate, bashing it hard. I sighed as I yanked it open and stepped inside. I needed to take it easy, not be as panicked. But it was hard not to be. They were down here, somewhere, tracking that beast on their own.

I arrived on the Music level and stepped cautiously into the hall. The lights were on full blast and that gave me the confidence to make my way carefully toward the Music Department. I didn't know for certain they were there, but I was pretty sure. After all, it's where everything seemed to happen.

I dreaded the dimming lights, sometimes my imagination got carried away—thinking I'd seen a flicker out of the corner of my eye but when I turned, lights still buzzing strong. The shadows weren't coming for me. They weren't here. Yet. As long as the lights stayed bright I was pretty golden, I reminded myself. But I'd forgotten about the ink on the walls. If I'd thought that catching glimpses of glistening ink in the beam of a flashlight was creepier than seeing it lit regular, well, turned out I was very wrong. As I turned the corner and came upon the ink, there was something extra unsettling seeing it so . . . there. Not trying to hide. Not trying to be anything. Just proudly splattered everywhere.

And something new too. Something that hadn't been there before, when Dot and I had crossed the police barricade. Something written in the ink, drawn on by a finger, I guessed:

"He Will Set Us Free."

I stopped and stared at it. Like the notebook. Like the ink that had slipped out of the music notes, half on the page, half on the stand.

"He Will Set Us Free."

I had a sudden thought. A strange deep and disturbing thought.

What if Sammy wasn't missing. What if . . .

What if he was hiding?

"Hey, there, Art Department," said a voice behind me.

I turned instantly, only to be face-to-face with Bendy.

Again.

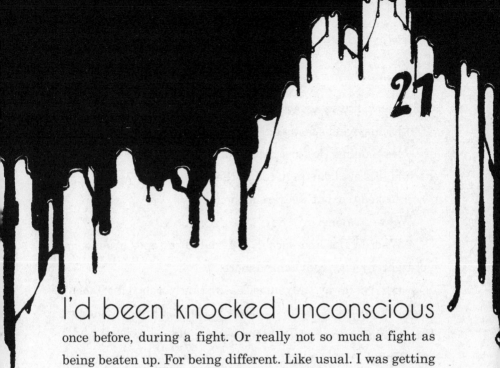

21

I'd been knocked unconscious

once before, during a fight. Or really not so much a fight as being beaten up. For being different. Like usual. I was getting better at defending myself. Getting better at running away. But this time the bullies had surprised me. Leapt out at me as I was turning the corner to my street.

They hadn't meant to knock me out. And I'm pretty sure it scared the bullies. Scared not of consequences. But of their own power. They left me alone for a while after that.

But I didn't remember much of what it felt like. The getting knocked out part. The waking up part. And opening my eyes up in the Music Room, on the stage, tied to a chair, I was pretty sure I didn't remember the headache that was searing past my eyeballs right then.

"Hey, Buddy, are you okay?"

I blinked a few times trying to get reoriented and turned in my chair to see Richie staring at me, tied up just like me. He smiled in relief. I don't think he'd ever smiled at me sincerely before now. It was always a bit . . . sarcastic.

"Richie, what's going on?" I asked in a panic.

"It's Sammy. He's lost his mind. Or whatever was left of it," he said, his eyes darting around the dark room.

I looked too, but we were alone.

We were alone.

"Where's Dot and Jacob?" I asked. The ropes around me got tighter as my body tensed more.

"Dot got away." My muscles instantly relaxed. "I don't know where she is. Jacob . . . he took. He took him . . . Buddy, I think he plans on . . ." Richie stopped talking like he'd heard something.

I heard it too. The sound of the door opening.

We turned and looked at the same time.

"Is that Sammy?" I whispered.

Richie nodded a kind of crazy fast nod but didn't say anything. His eyes were wide, his whole body shaking.

"Well, look what the beast dragged in," said Sammy in that superior-sounding voice. It was him. It was him behind the mask.

It was so strange and wrong. He was wearing a cardboard cutout kind of mask, the sort of thing you'd get from the back of a cereal box for Halloween. Like a mask of a kitty or something.

But this was no kitty.

It was Bendy. Bendy's face. With that grin. That wide, toothy grin. For the second time that night I was staring at that face and I was starting to realize just how not-cute it was.

But the mask wasn't the only disturbing thing about him. Sammy was dressed in his trousers and suspenders like always, but he wasn't wearing a shirt. Instead his torso, hands, neck, and—I assumed—face behind the mask were covered in shiny black ink. It was hard to tell if it was wet or dry, as it glinted in the lamplight. But it looked like somehow it was a part of him. Had been a part of him for a while.

"Sammy, what are you doing?" I asked as he slowly walked over to his music stand and looked at us.

It sounded like he was smiling behind the mask. Like he was happy. "Only I know what he wants."

This was crazy.

"What happened to you?"

"Ha!" laughed Sammy in a bark. "What happened to me? You know what happened to me! You were there! You saw it!"

I was? I did?

"That day the ink found me. It wanted me. He wanted me. At first I was scared. At first I could feel it inside, the drops I'd swallowed by accident. By luck. I could feel them moving around inside me. I shouldn't have been scared. I was foolish." He was picking up speed, his words tumbling out almost faster than he could speak them. "Then the cravings started. I needed more ink. There was no choice. I had to. And the more I consumed the more I understood. The more I felt him. Heard him. I need to please him."

Sammy started pacing the room now, and if I could just

keep him talking . . . I started pulling at my hands in the ropes. Trying to wrestle my way free.

"Look at the two of you in your sad little lives. Living day to day. For what? To please Joey Drew?" He laughed again, this time longer and heavier. He breathed in deeply. "Why please a man when you can please a god?"

I pulled harder and harder at the ropes.

"Where's Jacob?" I demanded.

"Where it all began. A small gesture at the start. And then, well . . . then . . ."

"Where is that?"

Sammy stopped walking. He stood in the center of the room, far enough away that he was almost entirely in shadow. The Bendy eyes stared at me, stared into my soul. Even though it was just cardboard and ink.

Ink.

Damned ink.

"Shhhhhh. No more questions, little sheep." He giggled after he said that. "Sheep, sheep, sheep, it's time for sleep," he said in a singsong voice.

Crash.

And then Sammy was flat on the floor, under a large projector, unconscious and mercifully quiet.

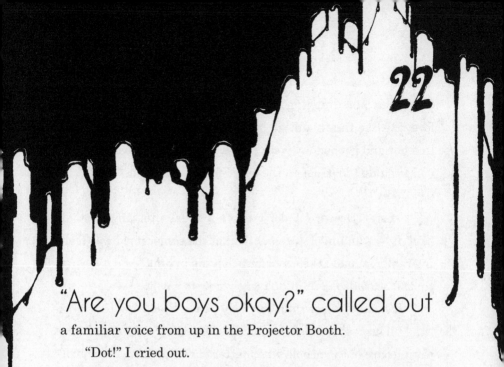

"Are you boys okay?" called out

a familiar voice from up in the Projector Booth.

"Dot!" I cried out.

"He does go on, doesn't he?" she asked, shaking her head as she leaned over the railing.

"Yeah," I replied, stunned, but a little giddy to see her.

"I'll be right down." She vanished into the dark again.

I looked at Richie with a grin, but he was white as a sheet, like he'd seen a ghost. "What the hell was that?" he squeaked.

Just as I opened my mouth, Dot opened the door and ran into the room.

"I'm sorry it took so long, I needed him to be in just the right spot. I'm not strong, but I am strategic. I had one push in me," she said, coming up behind Richie and untying his hands. Then she made her way over to mine.

"What happened?" I asked.

"When he attacked, I'm not even sure he really noticed me, just the boys. I was able to escape and I hid for a long time, but then I saw him dragging Jacob, and I knew I couldn't just hide forever." She finally untied my hands. I brought them around in front and rubbed my wrists for a moment. "You came."

I couldn't look her in the eye, I felt so ashamed. "Yeah."

"Why?"

"Mister Drew . . . I don't think I trust him anymore," I said. It was an understatement but at the same time I was feeling really stupid. Like a fool for believing in him. "And it wasn't that. It was also . . ." I didn't know how to say it.

"It's okay—" Dot said. But I shook my head.

"I'll just say it quick. Direct. Like you do," I said. "I thought taking care of the people who mattered was making money for my ma and grandpa, was looking after them. And it is. But it's more than that. I can get another job, I'll always support them. But you needed my help tonight. You were in danger. I was at some stupid party. What I said to you before, what I did, was wrong, and I'm sorry."

Finally I looked her in the eye.

"It's okay," she said. "I understand. You have no idea how much I understand." She had an expression that I couldn't read, it wasn't anything I'd seen before. Sad, but kind. And tired.

"Guys," said Richie. I'd forgotten he was there.

"We have to save Jacob," said Dot, her voice all business again. I nodded and bent over quickly to free my feet while she helped Richie, who was still sitting there stunned.

"Do you know where he took him?" I asked, standing up.

"I don't. I think it's wherever the machine is. But I feel like I've searched every corner of the studio over the last few weeks. I've been everywhere, Buddy. It's like it's invisible or something." Richie was free and stretched out his whole body as he stood.

It hit me then. The speech. At the party.

"The theater," I said. "It's got to be the theater."

"What theater?" asked Richie.

"Next door. Mister Drew bought it. The play closed ages ago. Maybe . . . I don't think it's a maybe. That's where it is."

Dot nodded, agreeing with me instantly. She turned back to Richie. "Okay, Richie, you have to go to the party and tell someone what's happening here. Get Mister Drew," she said.

My stomach turned at that. It felt wrong. "Are you sure?" I asked. I thought about Tom, maybe he could help. But then I realized I had no way of knowing where he was or how to contact him.

"I don't know what else to do."

I nodded. We didn't have time to just stand there and talk about all our choices. "Yeah, he won't approve of what Sammy's doing, so whatever else he thinks, he'd want to stop it," I said.

"Exactly. We can't call the cops," she said. "This is all just too strange, and who knows who they'd blame?"

At this point, all of us could be arrested, for trespassing, for just . . . being in the wrong place at the wrong time. "Okay. Richie, go get Mister Drew. He's at the party."

"Yeah," said Richie. He was shaking.

"You can do it," I said, placing a hand on his shoulder the way Dot always placed one on mine. It seemed to have the same effect on him.

"I can do it," he said with more confidence.

"Good." Dot turned to me. "And you and I, well, I guess we're going to the theater."

"We're up high, so be careful," I warned her. She nodded and we entered the dark catwalk. Immediately Dot turned on her flashlight, and I felt a wave of relief knowing we had some light to keep us safe. Or to at least warn us if we weren't. We stood there taking stock of our surroundings. The theater was a lot more intimidating in the dark. I wasn't able to see as clearly. The shadows of the ropes ahead were toying with my imagination, sometimes almost appearing alive, like a forest of snakes. Then Dot shined the light through the grated walkway down to the stage far below. The crisscross of shadows as they grew and disappeared with the light reminded me of the grasping shadows in the Music Room. And then the light caught something. A quick glimpse and it was gone.

"Dot, go back," I whispered. She brought the light back and that's when we saw it. Something. Something dangling just below us on one of the bars used to hold up backdrops.

"What is that?" I whispered.

Without answering she moved toward the mass in the center of the space and I followed close behind. The something just below us swung slowly in response to our shaking the catwalk.

Like a slight breeze was blowing. We were above it now, and Dot got onto her stomach. Again I followed her actions and we lay on the catwalk, staring through the grating.

The light bounced off the mass suspended in the middle of a series of ropes coming from all different directions, like a fly in a spider's web. It shone in the light, that sickening, inky-wet shine.

"Is that a person?" I asked, suddenly feeling sick to my stomach.

"I don't know." Dot didn't sound scared or sick.

"Is it Jacob?"

"I don't know. It doesn't matter. Whatever or whoever it is, we have to get it down. There has got to be a way to lower it. After all, there was a way to get it up there."

We stood and quickly made our way to the far side of the catwalk to a narrow ladder attached to the theater's outside wall that would take us down to the stage level. Dot went first, turning off the light as she did. I followed her. Climbing down in the dark like that, just taking each rung of the ladder as it came, felt like time had stood still. I could hear every creak in the place. I held my breath to listen for more than that. For a lot more.

"I'm at the floor," Dot whispered up to me, and then I was too. We stood there for a moment. I could hear her steady breathing that somehow didn't feel calm. It sounded more like she was trying to keep it under control, and failing.

She turned on the light once more and swung it upward. She gasped.

I understood why. There wasn't just one mass suspended up there. There were at least three. Dark inky figures each within a web silhouetted against the theater curtains.

"Three," I said out loud.

"There!" Dot pointed. She shone the flashlight on one of the figures. It was struggling against the ropes. Not with a lot of effort, but it was moving.

"We need to get them all down," I said, but Dot was already racing toward the pulleys that ran along the wall. I was glad she was with me, but also terrified that any moment it might be us up there. That we'd be snatched up from behind and suddenly in a web of our own, covered like them. Ink on our faces, mouths, dripping down the back of our throats.

"Buddy, help me!"

I tried to shake away the fear but it held fast as I quickly joined her and we counted the ropes until we found the ones that seemed to match with the bar. Dot carefully undid the knot holding the rope in place, and together we began to lower the bar. The webs began to descend. The winches the ropes were fed through squeaked as we did, and even though it wasn't loud, it was enough for my heart rate to pick up even more. I glanced down at the flashlight glowing on the floor. A steady beam. Good.

A few more moments and the masses were on the ground. I ran over right away, and as I did the lights buzzed on overhead. I turned and stared as Dot ran to catch up. "We can't see anything, and I figured the light would actually make us safer."

It was true. But there was something terrifying about being so exposed now, standing on the stage in the lights. I quickly looked around, just to see. In case the creature was somewhere. In case the ink was slowly crawling to us, like I'd seen it crawl up my grandfather. There was no one. The seats in the audience were a black hole of nothing. But there was something. There, right in the middle of the stage, in the middle of everything, was the machine.

I held my breath as I stared at it. It was large and square, with a huge curving tube out of which thick goopy ink dripped. It looked like you could easily climb up inside of it if you wanted to. It also looked rough, like it was homemade, not finely crafted. The bolts were big and clumsy, and the sides were welded to each other, buckling and bubbling at the seams.

"Buddy, it's Jacob!" Dot had completely ignored the machine and raced over to the masses.

I quickly joined her and saw what it was. She was right. It was Jacob. Covered head to toe in thick globs of ink. It reminded me a bit of when I'd first met Sammy. That first day. The day the ink took him.

"We have to clean him off," I said, quickly removing my jacket and wiping his face. His features materialized from under the goo and Jacob took a sudden sharp inhalation of breath.

"Run, you have to run," he gasped.

Dot shook her head. "It's okay, the lights are bright. We're okay." She pulled off her sweater now and we continued to wipe the ink off him. "I'll do this, you undo all the ropes," she told me.

I stared at the web. They were tied all over his body, slick with ink. It seemed impossible. "I need something to cut with."

"There's an axe in the firemen's box," said Dot.

"In a minute—I'm going to check on the others."

I was up quickly on my feet and I ran to the other bodies. I began to clean off the ink. A face appeared. It was Dave. From my department.

"It's Dave," I said. Old, always quiet, just doing his job Dave.

Dot looked up in shock.

I didn't even know he'd been missing. Of course not. The man went home early every night. He barely seemed to be around sometimes, always on break or something. I shook him by the shoulders. "Dave," I said. "Come on, wake up!" His head flopped to one side, lifeless. How long had he been up there? How long had he been suffocating in that ink? Struggling to escape? The horror was too much to imagine. "I'm so sorry, Dave," I said. I had to turn to the other body, but I was deeply scared. Scared that there was an order to the madness. The way the bodies had been put up on the bar. I tried to wipe the ink away as fast as I could, but I knew, deep down, it wouldn't make a difference.

A face appeared.

Norman.

Oh no.

Oh, Norman.

Of course no one would notice he was missing. Of everyone in the building. He watched everyone, but no one really saw him. Not much anyway.

I stood slowly and looked at the two bodies side by side. I felt a huge sadness well up inside of me. I didn't have time to mourn, and I didn't know either of these men well. But dead. Really, truly dead. Whatever this machine had done, however it had happened, people were *dying*. I thought about the violinist. I thought about her on the ground. I hadn't thought she might actually be dead now.

Mister Drew couldn't know about this. He couldn't. This was too much and he never wanted this. He'd destroy the machine. Now that he knew.

Wouldn't he?

"No, Jacob, please, just stay calm," I heard Dot say. It brought me back into the moment and I went over to her.

"You have to listen to me," he said, trying to push himself up but failing, slipping on the ink beneath him, falling hard onto his elbows. He grunted in pain and lay back.

"What is it?" I asked Dot.

"He's traumatized, obviously. From the creature. We need to get him out of here. We all need to get out of here."

I nodded and turned once more to get the axe. But just as I did Jacob called my name: "Buddy, leave me."

I looked up for a moment at the stage floor, at the light. It was still bright. I was still safe.

"Not before we untie you." I ran now to the wings,

searching frantically for the axe. Finally I found it locked in its glass box. I ran back to Dot, grabbed her flashlight without even thinking about it, and charged back. With one big swing I smashed the glass. I flinched as the pieces flew in the air. I felt a sharp pain on my cheek where one sliced me. I reached through the broken pieces and grabbed the axe, tearing up my dress shirt as I did. I really didn't care, though, about any of it. I just ran back to Jacob.

"Lie back." Dot pushed on his shoulders a little. He was still struggling.

"No!" His eyes looked almost red with fury. "You don't understand. It's *toying* with us!" He struggled hard, and I quickly came up and swung down the axe on the first rope. I hit it and felt very satisfied watching it split in two. I kept going, and going. It was hard, as Jacob wouldn't stop pulling and thrashing around, but I was focused and when I finally came to the last rope I said, "There!" with satisfaction.

Jacob flung himself up with the same amount of energy as if he was tied down. He crashed into Dot and she fell backward hard against the stage.

"Dot!" I called out.

Jacob was pushing himself upward, struggling in the pools of ink around him, totally out of his mind. His body language looked a lot like Sammy's. It could've *been* Sammy.

The ink. The ink had him. But he was also fighting it. I watched as he flinched and flung his arms out wide, as if trying to wave the ink away. He twisted and then screamed an otherworldly, inhuman kind of scream. He reached one arm out as if clawing for Dot, and the other hand grabbed it and pulled it back. I stood ready to toss the axe aside and tackle him.

"Stay away, Buddy! I don't want to hurt you!" he cried out again. He thrashed around, flinging his own body in all directions. And then we made eye contact for a moment. For a brief moment. And I saw Jacob in there. I saw him. And he had this strange look in his eyes, like he was sad, but happy, determined. And then he turned his head toward the ceiling and roared loudly and threw himself hard down onto the stage.

And he stopped moving.

I raced to his side, placed an ear to chest. His torso moved just a bit, and I could hear his heartbeat.

Dot was next to me immediately. "He's still alive," I said.

"He did that for us. He knocked himself out to protect us."

I nodded, still in shock.

"Come on," I said. "Let's get him out of here."

That's when the lights went out.

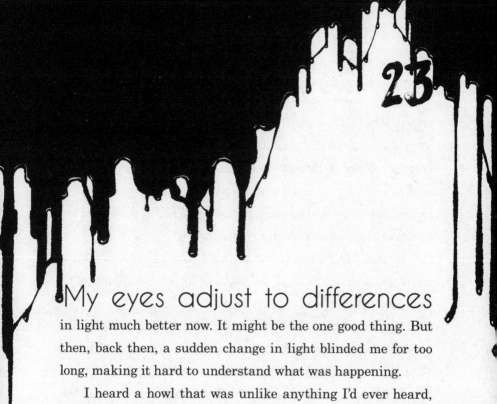

23

My eyes adjust to differences

in light much better now. It might be the one good thing. But then, back then, a sudden change in light blinded me for too long, making it hard to understand what was happening.

I heard a howl that was unlike anything I'd ever heard, guttural but also a high-pitched scream. No animal at the zoo, no train screaming through a subway tunnel, nothing was like it. And then a loud crash on the stage. Something grabbed at me, and at first I pulled away hard, but then I realized it was Dot taking my hand, making sure she knew where I was. I squeezed her hand in mine.

I tugged at her to follow me, and as my eyes adjusted to the dim light, we started crawling toward the machine to hide behind it. We managed to get up against it on the side opposite from the creature, which was making heavy footsteps across the stage.

"Ink," Dot whispered, and pointed. I followed the direction and saw four large buckets filled with it. We moved as far away from it as we could.

My eyes were finally used to the light. I saw now that it wasn't completely dark. The work lights were still on, but they were dim now in the inky shadows that seemed to follow the creature. They got brighter and dimmer as the shadows swam around, and I realized I needed to know what this creature looked like. If I could see now, then I could see it. And I needed to know what we were facing. Finally.

I carefully leaned around the corner of the machine, peering out just enough to see, most of my view still cut off by the side.

The creature stood still in the middle of the stage. Like he was sniffing us out, like that first time near the Infirmary. I wasn't really thinking too hard about that because what I saw in front of me froze me so completely. Not just my body but also my mind. My heart. My everything.

Standing there was the creature from Sammy's notebook. It wasn't just some made-up doodle, it was real. And it was . . .

Bendy.

At least some strange version of the cartoon character. The head was the most like him. Shaped in the same way, round with the two points for horns. He had that same smile too. Big and white, with lines separating each tooth, only these teeth were real. They glistened with saliva. The rest? Well, the rest of his face was covered in ink, ink dripping from his head over where his eyes should be. Did that mean he was blind? I didn't think there needed to be logic with such a creature.

His body was long and lean, and he too was dripping ink. No, not just lean, but almost like a dripping skeleton. I could see the indentation beneath his rib cage. But he was still partly cartoon character, which was probably the most terrifying part about him. He still had that white bow tie and one white glove like the ones all the characters had.

He stood there. A growl deep inside him like a revving engine. He knew we were somewhere. I watched as he made his way across the stage. As he made his way across to the bodies on the stage.

Jacob.

But he went to Dave instead. He sniffed at the figure carefully. Suddenly he snarled, grabbed at it, and pulled, yanking Dave's arm right out of the socket and throwing it across the stage.

I felt Dot grab my shoulder and squeeze. I nodded, but I didn't know what else to do. The beast now seemed to be growing in size. His arms and legs lengthening, his head spreading, his teeth getting sharper. He lumbered over toward Jacob now. No, no, no, no. This couldn't happen.

"Hey!" I said, standing up and stepping out onto the stage. The lights went almost black as the creature turned to me.

"Hey!" Dot cried out then. I turned to see she had jumped out from the other side. I stared at her. "It can't hunt both of us," she whispered to me.

She was right, of course. Like always. The beast looked at her, then back at me, with the eyes he didn't have. Or did have.

I think over this moment every day. I try to remember it in all its details. But it's hard. There was so much in this moment. So much that was happening. Not just with the creature and Dot and Jacob, but inside me. My fear, my need to end this all, my guilt. My guilt that I'd let this creature out in the first place.

I remember things, though not everything.

I remember that he decided to charge Dot, not me. I remember him racing toward her as she ran away, and I remember racing toward him. I tripped over a pipe that must have been part of the machine and for a moment felt hopeless as I watched him hunt Dot. But then the rage I felt watching him stalking after Dot made me strong again and I hefted the axe. I had a weapon.

I lunged at him. Leapt up and swung, striking him hard in the back. He didn't flinch. He didn't even stop moving forward. I fell backward like I'd hit a wall. No, I wasn't going to feel hopeless again, even if it felt impossible to win this. There had to be another way, I'd find another way.

He had Dot blocked in now, in the far corner of the stage, back in the deeper shadows of the wings. I stood up with the axe. He was too far away to swing at, so I threw it instead. I knew it wouldn't hurt him, but maybe, just maybe . . . it hit the back of his head and the monster turned sharply to howl at me. In that moment Dot dove between his legs and away from the corner. I was impressed for that one moment until the beast realized what had happened and lunged. Dot raced toward me and I ran, reaching out for her.

I grabbed her hand just as the creature caught her foot.

"Dot!" I yelled. I felt for her other hand and she snagged mine, her fingers slipping in my grip. I couldn't hold on. I was scared that if I did, the creature and I would rip her apart. She flew out of my hands and into the air as the monster whipped her across the stage.

She landed with a heavy thud.

"Dot!"

"Buddy," I heard her say softly. I tried to rush over, leaping over the pipes and around the buckets of thick black goo. The creature crashed between us and pushed me hard in the chest. I skidded backward, my head clanging on the side of the machine. "You have to get out of here," she called out, her voice hoarse and thin. "Take Jacob and get out of here."

"No," I replied. "This is my fault. I let it escape. We're going to fix this together."

"It's not—you didn't create him. You didn't—"

The creature roared between us. Spit flew out of his mouth and landed in thick globs in front of me. Suddenly I could see Dot in the air, her scream echoing through the theater. The creature had picked her up with one of his claw-like hands and squeezed tightly.

It's playing with us, Jacob had said.

He was like a cat torturing a mouse. Not squeezing hard

enough to kill her, but just enough to hurt her.

"Stop!" I yelled. I ran at the beast and grabbed his leg. I tried to trip him up, but he was solid on the ground, almost like he was rooted there. He raised his leg then, and with a wild kick I was thrown again.

I fell once more with a hard crash. I winced in pain. Everything hurt—my shoulder, my back, my head. I stared ahead of me on the floor, at the ink everywhere. At the . . . axe.

The pain somehow vanished as I grabbed the weapon. I charged the beast again and sliced hard at his leg. He staggered and roared. And I saw I'd created a deep, black wound oozing ink. Still he didn't let go of Dot but I felt better now. I chopped at the leg again and he swung at me with his free hand. I jumped away to catch my breath.

Then to my horror, I watched as the wound on the creature's leg with a sickening sucking sound began to heal, the ink reshaping and re-forming. He couldn't be hacked up. He couldn't be knocked out.

I stared at Dot. She seemed so far away.

No, this wasn't it. It wasn't impossible. Even when things seemed that way.

I looked at the machine in anger. I hated it so much. I hated that it existed and I hated the vats of ink surrounding it.

I never thought I'd ever hate ink this much.

Puddles of it everywhere, covering my clothes. Where did I begin and the ink end?

Dot screamed again.

"Dot!" I called out. "I'm going to drown it!"

I didn't know if she heard me but I remembered then; I remembered the trapdoor the actor had fallen through in the play I'd watched from above with Mister Drew. And I thought about all the ink that had come out of the pipe in the sheet music closet. And maybe . . . maybe if I could get the beast trapped under the stage, maybe if I could fill that sub-room with ink . . .

I staggered across the space as close as I could get to the monster without him lunging at me.

"You need to cut yourself free!" I called out to Dot. She wasn't moving much. My stomach felt hollow. No, she can't be dead. Please don't be dead.

Her head moved just a bit. There was a pause and then she turned it a little more. She could hear me.

"I need to get you the axe. I need to . . . throw it to you." Stupid plan. Stupid, stupid plan.

"Okay," she said. She was trying to call back but her voice was thin and breathless.

I couldn't. I couldn't just throw her an axe. That would kill her.

"I can catch," she said. "Just throw . . . slow." She sort of made a laugh sound.

It didn't make me feel better. It made me feel petrified. She was still Dot. She was still fighting. I couldn't let her down.

The beast roared and whipped around and staggered toward me. Good, in just a few feet he'd be over the door.

"Come on!" I yelled at him, and stepped back some more. I glanced down and saw where the stage had a square marked out. The edges of the door. The creature just stood still. Didn't move. Just held Dot up a little higher as if he was showing her to me. I was so angry, I was so full of rage, I just yelled. I opened my mouth and yelled at him from deep in my gut, from the back of my throat. From every part of me.

And the creature roared back and stepped forward and he was there, and Dot had pulled her hand free and this felt so impossible but it was all I had.

"Ready?" I called out.

"Why not," she shouted hoarsely back.

"One, two, three . . ."

I threw it and flinched at the thought of her catching it on the sharp end. But she caught it, just below the head, and she almost dropped it right away but she managed to catch the bottom part as it turned over in her hand. She grinned. I felt relief and then it was gone as I turned and raced toward the wings, trying to find the lever for the door.

It felt more and more like a terrible plan. But I didn't have another one. Finally I found the lever, dark red but in the shadows, almost black.

"I found it!" I called out. I hoped she could hear me, understand me. She probably didn't but at least I knew she could do this.

"Now!" I cried out. Dot swung the axe hard on the monster's wrist, once, twice, three times, while I pulled the lever.

The floor fell out from under the creature as I flew by, and he whipped his head back in shock as Dot fell to the stage, still wrapped in the creature's hand, but the hand no longer attached to the creature.

He fell into the darkness as Dot raced back to the machine. She hacked at the pipe feeding into the side, until the pipe burst. Ink flooded out and raced toward the hole. My shoulders ached, my breath was shallow, my feet slipped in the wet around me. I looked up and saw the creature reaching out of the trapdoor with his one good hand, grasping at the edge as the ink swallowed him. He was fighting hard against it.

"Buddy!" said Dot. She was suddenly beside me, helping me redirect the flow of the ink into the hole. Seeing her right there made me feel strong again.

That was it, it was all we could do. And we stared. And we watched. Watched as the beast's arm seemed to melt into the ink. His face appeared at the surface again for a moment, and he let out a roar that then was swallowed by a gurgle. His mouth got wide and then flat and then wasn't a mouth anymore.

It was mixing with the ink.

It was ink.

The lights brightened and seemed almost too much after having been so used to the darkness. Dot and I stared for a moment in quiet.

Then I could tell she was looking at me. So I looked at her.

"You did it," she said with a huge smile.

"Well, we did it . . ." I replied, and then suddenly she was hugging me. Out of the blue. I just sort of stood there and then realized I should probably hug her back. Which I did. For the first time in a long time my fears took a step to the side. And just let me relax into the moment.

"Do you think it's gone?" asked Dot when she finally pulled away.

I had no idea. I didn't trust that it was. I couldn't believe it was all over. "I don't think we have time to find out. Let's grab Jacob and get out of here," I said.

"Yes." She immediately went over to Jacob, who I noticed was moving a little.

I turned back to the hole. The ink was still there, like a lake under the stage. I wondered if there was any way to get rid of it. If it would just stay there. Forever. Haunting the studio.

Waiting.

Patient.

Hungry.

I took a deep breath. I was scaring myself again. It was time to leave. It was time to finally confront Mister Drew.

A hand burst out of the ink and grabbed my leg.

"Buddy!"

It happened so fast I don't actually know how. I just know I was suddenly through the trapdoor, neck deep in thick ink as Dot grabbed my hands just in time. He had me fast by the leg, in a viselike grip. There was no breaking free.

This time she was pulling me, trying to save me. I held her hands tightly, but there was no way she could win. The creature was too strong. And the ink all around me was pulling too. Almost like a suction both squeezing and drawing me in. She had to let go or I'd just drag her under. We'd drag her under.

"Let me go," I said, the ink splashing in my mouth when I opened it. I coughed and sputtered. It tasted bitter and salty. It burned the back of my throat.

"Buddy, I can't," she said, adjusting her grip on my wrist, her fingers slipping and then catching mine at the last moment.

My body ached, a wrenching stinging feeling shot up my spine. I felt something sharp in my thigh, like I'd been stabbed with a knife. The creature's claws. I couldn't scream out, not without inhaling more ink. I kicked and scraped my foot along his arm in the black depths. Then a white-hot pain. Something so different. So overwhelming that everything just stopped. The monster had sunk his sharp teeth into my torso, biting through my flesh, my muscles, my tendons. I gasped silently and ink filled my mouth again. Everything started to get dizzy and I didn't understand what was going on. Dot's look of horror swam through my vision.

Save yourself. I thought it and needed her to read my mind. The way she always somehow was able to read my mind. *It's okay. It's okay. Just save yourself. Save Jacob.*

It's okay.

I stared at her, gulping more and more ink, coughing and

unable to breathe as it filled my lungs. There was no air. There was nothing. Just ink.

Then a moment in her eyes. A moment I recognized.

She understood. She shook her head and I squeezed her hand. It was the last real choice I made.

It's okay.

You have to go now.

You have to save yourself. Save Jacob.

You have to save everyone.

And you let go of my hand. I was so grateful. The darkness came up fast around me and I saw you only for a moment longer, and I felt proud and so lucky to have met you. To have had that chance. And then you were gone. Or I was gone. And I sank into the ink, and it filled my ears and the creature pulled me down and the pain was so bad that I almost couldn't feel it anymore. I couldn't feel anything.

The five senses:

Touch: nothing.

Taste: nothing.

Sound: nothing.

Smell: nothing.

Sight: blackness.

And then:

Nothing.

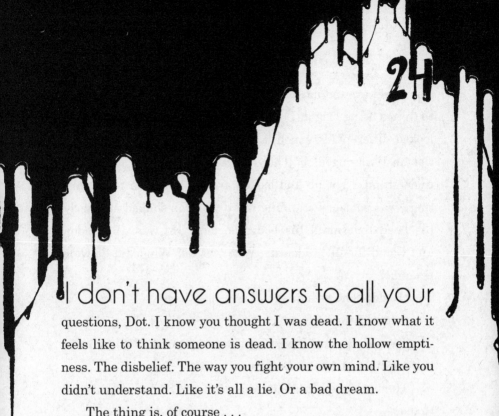

24

I don't have answers to all your questions, Dot. I know you thought I was dead. I know what it feels like to think someone is dead. I know the hollow emptiness. The disbelief. The way you fight your own mind. Like you didn't understand. Like it's all a lie. Or a bad dream.

The thing is, of course . . .

Dreams come to life.

I'm not dead.

But I'm also not alive.

And you can't save me.

But you can save everyone else.

I don't know the moment when I woke up. It came in stages, which isn't normal. Normally you are asleep and then you are awake. But I've learned that when you have two minds living together, when you have two sets of memories, sometimes one mind wakes up sooner than the other.

The first time I woke up I was confused about where I was.

The world around me was dark and shadowy, and I was used to things being bright. I touched the floor and saw my hand. It looked different. I turned it. It seemed rounder. It wasn't as flat as I was used to. There were more sides to it. I didn't understand. I sat up and looked around now in a panic, and there was someone standing there. He was shaped strangely, his head too small, his body too long. He was all shadow and was difficult to identify. Who was he? What did he want from me?

"Buddy?" he asked.

Who was Buddy?

The second time I woke up it was my mind. Not his. I was staring right at Mister Drew.

That confused me. Why was he here? He was still in his tuxedo.

It was then that I realized I was sitting upright and I didn't remember how I'd done that. Where was I? I closed my eyes for a moment and then remembered. The theater. The creature.

Dot.

Drowning.

Death.

The monster. I quickly turned to look, but he was gone. We were alone. I released a long sigh and it felt really good. I'd never realized how good breathing felt before.

I looked at Mister Drew again and he was smiling at me. I realized then that I wasn't under the stage, I was on top of it.

Right in the middle. The audience seats sprawled out into a dark void behind him. I turned to look the other way. Above me loomed the machine. Huge from this angle. It dripped a steady drip. The sound was hypnotic and also a little painful.

All this time Mister Drew had said nothing. Had just watched me. It was strange and unsettling. I looked back at him.

"Am I dead?" I asked. It was a foolish question, and I realized after I asked it that I knew the answer. Obviously I wasn't. I knew where I was, I knew who I was. Unless this is what death looked like.

Mister Drew walked slowly over to me then.

"Buddy?" he said.

"Yes?" I replied.

"Is that you, Buddy?" He was standing right over me now. His skin drooped. He looked almost inhuman at this angle.

"Yes, it's me," I said back. Of course it was me.

He grabbed under my chin and held my head still. I tried to shake him off, but his grip was like a vise. He brought up his other hand and held me tighter. He came even closer and looked at me hard in the eyes. His scent was powerful. I'd never really noticed that before. But now for some reason I could smell him clearly. It wasn't just cigar smoke and pomade. I could smell his dinner, the hors d'oeuvres from the party. I could smell whiskey and champagne. I could smell the city air and the heat of the day.

His sweat.

His madness.

"I can see you in there," he whispered.

"What are you talking about? Let go of me!" I shouted it right in his face. I didn't care anymore about impressing him or offending him. I didn't care what he thought of me. His machine had done this to all of us. Had killed them. Had killed me.

And now . . . now slowly it dawned on me. Had the machine brought me back to life?

"Of course you can't answer me," he said, suddenly realizing something. His eyes sparkled and he bit his lip. "Of course you can't. Oh, this is just incredible, Buddy."

Can't answer him? What on earth?

I reached up and pushed him away, hard. Harder than I'd ever pushed anyone before, and he fell back against the wooden stage with a loud crash. I felt strangely powerful. I also wasn't in any pain anymore. I stood up. I marched over to him. It was my turn to stand over him.

He cowered. He actually cowered in fright. I felt really good about that.

"What did you do to me?" I asked.

"Now, Buddy," he said, holding up a hand, "don't be angry. Just remember I saved your life."

"What did you do?" I took a step closer, placed my hands on my hips. I enjoyed that my shadow loomed over him like this, filling his small world with darkness.

"You're angry, you're frustrated. You can't express yourself, I understand, but don't you see that I fixed you? And now you're, you're—perfect!"

"What do you mean?" That word took the air out of my lungs, pulled back on my confidence.

"See, not so bad, is it?" said Mister Drew with a small smile.

"What are you talking about?" I said. I felt like I was talking to a wall now. Why couldn't he give me a straight answer? "Tell me what you did. Tell me what is wrong with me." I sighed with frustration, and turned to look first over at the machine and then back down at him again. "Tell me . . ." At that moment, I finally noticed my shadow. "Tell me . . ." I was suddenly distracted.

Tell me . . .

I stumbled backward. My shadow was long and thin as it always was. It bled over Mister Drew, now standing up, no longer cowering in fear. Watching me closely. He was curious, not afraid. He seemed to be understanding something I wasn't. Something I was about to figure out.

I touched the top of my head. What was that in the shadow? Two tall curved points that seemed to be growing out of either side of my skull. They were soft to the touch. And when my fingers felt them I felt my fingers. These points were a part of me. As much as my arms or my legs.

I dropped my hands and looked at them.

I took another step backward.

"Behind you, Buddy," Mister Drew said.

I turned slowly. I didn't want to do what he said, but at the same time I knew I had to.

On the ground was a figure covered in ink. Lying sprawled. Lifeless. Dripping. I walked up to it carefully.

"Who is that?" I asked, but it came out as more of a moan. No words. Just the feeling behind the words.

I didn't want to know the answer.

Because I already knew the answer.

I bent to look closer.

The body on the ground was mine.

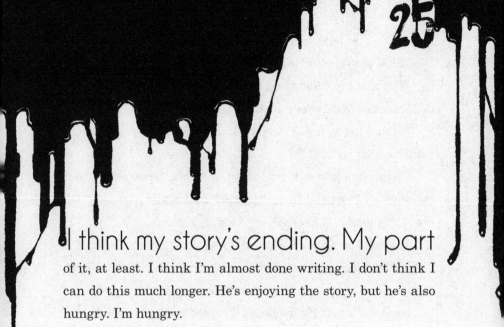

I think my story's ending. My part

of it, at least. I think I'm almost done writing. I don't think I can do this much longer. He's enjoying the story, but he's also hungry. I'm hungry.

Dot, if you find this, share it.

I hope you can tell them if this story is true.

I know it's not all true.

But I think most of what I wrote is real.

My mind and his mind.

Our mind.

I wasn't alone, Mister Drew was standing beside me. Looking down at the body. At my body. My dead body.

No one gets to see themselves dead. No one has to experience that. How would my mind possibly have a way to understand it?

I'm dead. That's my dead body.

"You see, I saved you," said Mister Drew.

"I don't understand," I replied.

"Shh, stop trying. It's only going to frustrate you."

"I'm already frustrated. I need to understand this. You need to explain it to me," I said, turning on him.

"Please listen to me. Stop trying to talk, Buddy. You're just going to hurt yourself."

"What are you talking about? I'm not frustrated about talking . . ." I stopped then. I stopped and really listened. "I'm not . . ." A grunt. "Mister Drew." Another grunt.

I opened my mouth. I tried to say my name: "Buddy." A kind of barking sound almost. I froze. I couldn't breathe. I collapsed onto my knees and grabbed at my throat. I stared up at Mister Drew, and for a moment I thought maybe he looked concerned. But he didn't, not really. He just seemed pleased with himself.

I turned back to the body, my body. I wasn't sure what to do anymore. I wasn't sure what I was thinking anymore. Part of me was feeling oddly fascinated by everything, like I was seeing the world for the first time. Part of me was terrified, desperate.

I crawled, pulling myself along the floor to the body. My body.

I looked at my hands, not on my old body but on my new one. My gloved hands.

I didn't own gloves. I'd never owned gloves. Not even in winter. Just shoved my hands into my pockets.

I didn't understand at all. And yet I did. I knew exactly

what had happened now, but it was so unbelievable.

Just because something is unbelievable doesn't make it not true.

Remember that, Dot. Oh, please, above all things, remember that.

I touched my face. Not the face that I was looking out of, but the cold dead one belonging to the body on the floor.

Have you ever seen a dead body before? It's not just scary in the way ghost stories are scary. It's scary because that's the person right there in front of you, but you know it's not really them.

Something is missing.

"That's your body, Buddy. But it isn't you," said Mister Drew, crouching beside me. He said it as if he could read my mind.

I looked at him angrily. I knew now I couldn't speak. I didn't even bother trying. I pointed instead, at the body's face, torso, legs . . .

"Those are just parts. The real you. The real you is here." Mister Drew reached up and touched my chest, placing his palm firmly on my ribs. "Your soul."

I pulled back.

No.

"Listen to me, listen to me, Buddy," he said, placing a hand on my shoulder. I wanted to shake it off, but I couldn't. I just didn't have the strength. "I'll explain it quickly. I made my machine to create real versions of my characters." "My" and "my," he said. But they weren't his. The machine was Tom's and the characters were Henry's. "I used my special ink. It was supposed to work. But the creature that came out, that ink demon. That was not the plan. I realized that the man I'd hired to help had led me astray. It was his fault for not understanding the machine." A lie. "Something was missing. It almost worked. So what was it? Well, it was the thing that makes us all alive."

The soul, I thought right away.

"Can you guess?" he asked.

I knew the answer. It wasn't that hard.

"The soul. But how do I get a soul? Sammy lured those people down here . . . I thought I could use them, but the ink had infected them for days. There was no soul left in there. I needed someone real. Someone good. I never thought I'd be so lucky as to have you, Buddy. But this was meant to be. This was the plan all along. That's why you were sent to me. When I came here, when I saw you—in the clutches of that beast—I understood your purpose."

No. That's not my purpose. I felt the anger rise in me, and I pushed his hand off my shoulder finally. I stayed where I was, white-hot rage now energizing me, making me almost afraid to stand up. Of what I might do.

"I saved your soul, Buddy. And you saved me. You're going to save Bendy."

I didn't do that. My purpose was saving Dot and the others. That was my purpose. He couldn't and wouldn't take that away from me. My purpose now was and always would be to protect the world from this beast. This machine.

"This is going to be so wonderful. You'll see, you'll see," said Mister Drew. "Now come with me. I've set up a nice little room for you. A nice place. You'll like it. There's food."

He was talking to me like I was stupid. Like I was *him*, the happy wolf who shares my mind. I know he was excited about it then. I could feel him pulling me, wanting me to go to Mister Drew. But at this moment, back then, I was much stronger than he was. Mister Drew didn't understand that.

That was my advantage.

I turned to him. We stood face-to-face. He smiled. "Come with me." He extended his arm toward me and I grabbed it. I held it hard, and he cried in pain. I wasn't going to kill him. I can't kill. That's not who I am. I threw him to the floor.

And I stood over him.

And breathed for a moment.

I ran then. I ran away. Into the darkness of the theater, down trapdoors and through vents. I just ran. I disappeared into the building. Into its secrets that even Joey Drew himself didn't know. I hid.

I hid and he didn't find me.

He couldn't find me.

And I got to know the world underground. I got to know the theater and the studio. I watched, hidden, as they were merged together. I watched Mister Drew fire people and hire new ones, and I watched as he tried to make the machine work.

I learned that pictures came to life. Like I always feared.

Like I always knew.

And so I decided to write this down.

And I think, I think I'm done.

I think I have to be done, because, Dot, I'm so tired. And he's getting stronger. Now I'm not really Buddy anymore.

I am also Boris. Descending deeper into this world of aging, yellowing madness.

And we have to keep running because . . .

The Ink Monster.

Because it's still alive.

And it's still hungry.

Stop him. You have to . . .

Stop . . . him . . .

Save them.

Save . . .

ADRIENNE KRESS is a Toronto-born actor and writer. Her books include the award-winning and internationally published novels *Alex and the Ironic Gentleman,* *Timothy and the Dragon's Gate,* and *Hatter Madigan: Ghost in the H.A.T.B.O.X.* (with bestselling author Frank Beddor), as well as Steampunk novel *The Friday Society* and the gothic *Outcast.* She is also the author of the quirky three-book series The Explorers.

Dreams Come to Life is Adrienne's first foray into writing horror, but as an actor she has had the pleasure of being creepy in such horror films as *Devil's Mile* and *Wolves.* And she took great pleasure in getting to haunt teenagers in SyFy's *Neverknock.*

Find her at AdrienneKress.com.

Twitter/Instagram: @AdrienneKress